Chasing Horizons

ALLISON A. ANDREWS

ABOUT THE AUTHOR

Allison A. Andrews is a romance author, wife, and mum based in Brisbane, Australia.
A lifelong book lover with a vivid imagination, she turned her passion for storytelling into swoon-worthy novels filled with men who don't need to be taught how to be human, strong women, and unforgettable stories.

www.aawpublishing.com

ALSO BY ALLISON A. ANDREWS & ANTOINETTE W. MAY

Order of the Dragon Trilogy (Paranormal Romance)

#1 Illusions

#2 Blood Memories

#3 Phoenix Rising

Circle of Friends Series (Contemporary Romance)

The Winning Ticket

Chasing Horizons

Dance With Me

Pieces of Us

Calgary Mounties

(Contemporary Hockey Romance)

On Thin Ice

Melt The Ice

Coming Home For Christmas Anthology

From Snow to Surf (Circle of Friends and Calgary Mounties

Crossover)

Dark Desires (Contemporary Spicy Romance)

(Writing as Antoinette W. May)

Reckless (Intro Novella)

Ravage

Ruin

CONTENTS

WANT A SNEAK PEEK OF DANCE WITH ME?

Song List

So Good - Halsey

Echo - Jason Walker

Coal - Dylan Gossett

Greedy - Tate McRae

Forget Me - Lewis Capaldi

Get Happy - Matt Maeson

Don't Give Up On Me - Andy Grammer

Last Night - Morgan Wallen

Trust Me Mate - Dean Lewis

I Can Feel It - Kane Brown

New York - The Kills

Heaven - Ziggy Alberts

Fight Song - Rachel Platten

Something In The Orange - Zach Bryan

If You Want Love - NF

Where You Belong - Matt Hansen

Heartbroken - Diplo, Jessie Murph, Polo G

Life Goes On - Ed Sheeran, Luke Combs

Lose Control - Teddy Swims

Something To Hide - Gradson

Numb Little Bug - Em Beihold

For everyone who has felt like they are too much.
I see you, and you are the perfect amount of enough.

1

FINALLY IN PARIS

KYLIE

"I CAN'T BELIEVE we're finally in Paris!" Tara grips my arm, a wide grin on her face while we stare up at the Eiffel Tower.

I laugh, reaching up to pull my long brown hair into a ponytail. "We've been here for four days already, lady! Are you planning on exclaiming this every time we see it?" I gesture towards the tall structure across the road.

Beside us, children are happily riding the most gorgeous merry-go-round I've ever seen.

"Yep. It will never get old."

"I'm sure if you lived here, it would eventually," I say with a smirk.

Tara sighs. "You're no fun."

"We both know that's a lie. I'm the funnest person you know."

"True. That's why you're my favourite." She slides her arm through mine, and we begin to stroll closer to the tower.

We've been saving this for the first day of our official tour to bond with the other people in the group. So now we're trailing along behind our tour guide and a few others who also decided to start their Parisian adventure by climbing its iconic landmark.

Well, climbing isn't quite accurate - more like riding several elevators to arrive at the top and stare out through the chain-link fence.

All of Paris stretches out as far as the eye can see, and it's breathtaking. I snap a few photos on my phone before stopping to stare out at the view.

Regardless of how I'd teased Tara earlier, it really is a pinch-me moment. We've been planning this holiday for over a year now. Our best friend, Brianna, was originally planning to join us, but she'd had to stay in Australia for work, so it's just the two of us now. It's Tara's first time travelling overseas, and she's been blown away by everything we've seen so far.

"It's just beautiful. Nothing at home even comes close to this," I say, turning to my right before realising at the last moment that Tara has moved and a very tall, very attractive blond guy has taken her place.

"Whoops, sorry! I thought you were my friend," I say with a smile.

"I mean, I could be your friend," he says with a cheeky grin, and I detect an accent.

Given where we are, that isn't surprising, but I'm pretty sure I saw him this morning at the hotel when we all met up for the start of the tour.

"You're on the tour too, right?"

"Yep. I'm Lincoln. Or Linc for short. You're Kylie, right?"

"Right. Good memory." We'd all done the meet and greet at breakfast, but I was impressed he remembered, as there had been about forty other people there.

"I meet a lot of people with my job, so I seem to have developed a skill with remembering faces and names." There's that cheeky grin again. "You're Australian?"

"Right... And you're... I want to say you're from somewhere in

North America..." I say, knowing that if I said the wrong country, it could lead to hurt feelings.

Lincoln throws his head back and laughs. "Very diplomatic. Yep, Canadian. I'm travelling with my buddy who's here somewhere." He looks around, trying to find his friend.

He gives up and looks back at me with a shrug.

"Cool. I've got family in Canada. My dad's from there."

"Nice! I'm from a small town a few hours from Vancouver. Same as my buddy Seth, the one I can't find right now."

I smile, nodding. "I've been to Vancouver once, but my family is in Alberta, so that's where I've been the most," I say with a shrug.

Lincoln nods. "I travel for work and get to see a lot. Don't know how I'd be if I had to stay in one place for an extended amount of time."

"I'd love to travel for work," I say absently while I look around for Tara, and I can see Lincoln scanning the crowd again himself.

I finally catch sight of her long, deep red hair. "Ah, that's where she got to. Is that your friend she's talking to?" I point towards the tall brown-haired guy, standing with his back to me, nodding at something Tara said.

Lincoln follows my gaze and nods his head.

"Yep, that's Seth. Good, they found each other. Saves us time." He moves towards them, and I follow behind, taking advantage of his ability to part the crowd with his height and broad shoulders.

"Hey, there you are!" Tara smiles at me.

"What are you talking about? You're the one who disappeared," I say with a laugh while I shake my head.

"Sorry, it was so crowded over that side, I thought you were behind me and then I got to talking to Seth here. He's Canadian." She waves her hand towards Lincoln's friend.

I turn to smile at him, and I finally get my first look at his face. And my mouth immediately goes dry. He is possibly the most beautiful man I've ever seen. I'm no stranger to attractive men, but this guy could be a model. Or a movie star. At least six-foot-four with broad shoulders and tanned skin, his piercing blue eyes shine with amusement while I try to find my voice and stop looking like an idiot.

"Hi," I manage to squeak out.

How on earth has Tara been talking to him without turning into a puddle at his feet?

My friend is clearly finding this all very amusing, because she covers a laugh with a cough. I was never one to drool over guys in the past, so seeing me now turn speechless must be quite the spectacle for her.

"Hi. Seth," he says, sticking his hand out.

I shake it, and he squeezes it lightly while continuing to hold my gaze.

"Kylie, Tara's friend. It's nice to meet you."

"It's nice to meet you too, Tara's friend Kylie."

Lincoln snorts beside me and introduces himself to Tara.

"So, what were you ladies planning to do until dinner tonight?" he asks, and Tara and I shrug.

"We've been in Paris for a few days already, but we haven't been to Notre Dame or checked out Montmartre yet," I reply. "What about you guys?"

"Yeah, we got here two days ago. We haven't done those places yet, either. Would you mind if we tagged along?"

Lincoln is clearly the chattier of the two guys, and I notice Seth shoot him a wary look while I turn to Tara.

She nods. "Sure, why not? Are we done with the Eiffel Tower?"

We all nod, heading off to explore Paris together.

Two hours later, we find a cafe in Montmartre to have some lunch and rest our legs. I always forget just how much walking happens when I am in a new city.

"So, where in Australia are you ladies from?" Lincoln asks.

Seth hasn't really spoken much, looking content to let his friend do most of the talking, though I have noticed him watching me, looking away each time I've tried to catch his eye. He produced a baseball cap from his back pocket earlier, and the way that he's casually wearing it backwards while sprawled out in the cafe chair has my heart fluttering in a strange way.

I force myself to focus on Lincoln. "We live in Brisbane. I'm from Sydney originally, though."

"Oh yeah, I know Brisbane. We were there a few years ago for work, remember Seth?" Lincoln looks over at his friend.

"Yeah, I remember," Seth replies before taking a mouthful of coffee, giving his friend another indecipherable look.

Weird.

"What do you guys do for work?" Tara asks.

The guys look at each other for a moment, some sort of silent communication occurring.

"We both work for the same company. We work for a professional sports team, so we travel a fair bit," Lincoln answers for them both.

"Oh, that sounds really cool. It's way more interesting than my job. I work in insurance," Tara says, grimacing.

She and Lincoln begin to chat easily amongst themselves.

I peek over at Seth every now and again. He is watching his friend with a small smile and catches me looking at him.

My cheeks redden. "So you guys work together? That's cool you can travel at the same time," I say, taking a sip of my drink to hide my face.

Seth shrugs, reaching up and scratching the back of his neck. "Yeah. It's the off-season, so easier to get time off. But we've known each other since we were kids, and he convinced me to go on this trip with him. Work's been a bit... rough."

I can tell he isn't going to elaborate further, so I nod like I have any idea how a job working for a sports team could be rough.

"Have you guys been to Europe before?"

"Yeah, but never for fun. Linc talked me into it a few weeks ago, so here we are."

"Wow, a few weeks ago? Tara and I have been planning this trip for an entire year," I say, marvelling at how someone could just leave it until the last minute to plan a trip like this.

"Sure. It's not like we needed to do much. We just get on a bus and go to all the places they pick for us, right? What's to plan?" Seth asks with a shrug.

"I guess. But when you are travelling from as far away as Australia, planning is kind of required."

"Very true."

We fall into silence while our friends continue chatting. I shift, feeling a little awkward. While I've never been good at dealing with silence, Seth doesn't seem like the chattiest guy. I pull out my phone and start scrolling through social media while we wait for our food, glancing up every now and again to find him either staring at his drink, or, surprisingly, at me.

But he looks away each time, and I can't tell if it's because he's interested in me or if he's trying to work out how they can ditch us.

2

RATHER DO THE DANCING THAN WATCH TOPLESS WOMEN SWING BOOBIE TASSELS AROUND

I'VE BEEN WATCHING Linc work his magic on the two Australian women all day, envying his ability to talk to anyone.

He'd been talking to Tara, the redhead, the most, but Kylie, the gorgeous, curvy brunette, seemed to be equally as chatty.

I feel bad that I haven't been able to engage in conversation with them as much, but I've never been the best at talking to people I don't know. Throw in my job, and I tend to just stick with those I know well.

"Seth, seriously, get out of your head, man." Linc claps a hand down on my shoulder, startling me out of my reverie.

I've been hanging out in the hotel's seating area, waiting for him to finish getting ready in our room. It was too small for the two of us to get ready at the same time. The French definitely didn't have two hockey players in mind when they designed their hotel rooms.

"I'm fine. I was just waiting for you. Brendan told us all to be in the lobby in about ten minutes," I say, getting to my feet and ignoring the twinge in my knee, an old injury that sometimes acts up when I sit for too long.

It's like my body decided that thirty was the age to start falling apart.

"You are a shit liar, my friend. You gotta get over it." Linc falls into step beside me while we head into the lobby area.

"Easier said than done. No one is blaming you for ruining the team's chances at winning the Cup for the first time in twenty-five years."

Game seven of the Stanley Cup finals and it's on our home ice- there's three minutes left on the clock and we're tied with New Jersey, three all.

Can't let this go into overtime. I want to win this game, for the team and for the fans. We deserve this!

Seeing an opening, I manage to steal the puck from their centre, an old college buddy, and break away, flying towards our net.

Their goalie tenses, readying himself. I can feel someone close behind me, but I find my last burst of energy, moving faster and lifting my stick, ready to take the shot.

Suddenly, I'm flat on my stomach, and I have no idea how I got here. The screams of the crowd echo through the arena, and everything is a blur.

Even though it's been almost a month now, the memory of stumbling just when I tried to take the final shot, causing New Jersey to steal the puck and score the winning goal right before the buzzer went off, has been playing in a near-constant loop in my head.

"This is exactly why we are here. You've been punishing yourself for a month now. It wasn't your fault. It's not like you're the first player taken out by choppy ice at the end of a game. There'll be plenty of other chances. You are only thirty."

Linc has been saying the same thing for weeks, and it's not that I don't get where he's coming from, but it's easy to say that when you don't have all the sports commentators and fans criticising you every time you turn on the TV. I can't even look at my official social media accounts and handed them over to one of the marketing girls back home to deal with until people find something else to complain about. It's doubtful that it will happen until the new season starts in a few weeks, though.

"It's not that simple, and you know it."

"Right, we're not talking about this anymore. We are going to spend the next three weeks talking about anything but hockey, got it? And, by some stroke of dumb luck, none of these people seem to have recognised either of us, so that's even better. You can create a whole new you for a few weeks and put last season out of your mind."

"Again, easier said than done. I'm still me, man. You know I'm shit at talking to people."

"No, Seth Davidson is shit at talking to people. But Seth James... Well, he could be the charismatic, friendly guy that I've known for the better part of two decades."

I've been using the second half of my hyphenated surname for my entire professional career. Basically, Linc is now telling me to drop the name that every hockey fan in North America knows and to become a version of myself who isn't wrapped up in the game.

"I'll think about it."

"Just have a few drinks tonight, let your hair down and have some fun. Be my wingman for a change!"

I shake my head with a laugh. "I have never asked you to be my wingman."

"You haven't needed to. Women basically throw themselves at you."

"Only because of our job," I say, giving him a pointed look.

"I don't know, man, Kylie looked pretty interested." He nods towards where Tara and Kylie have just walked through the door, and I raise an eyebrow.

I have to admit how cute they both look. My gaze follows the more obviously outgoing of the two women, Kylie, while she moves through the small group to chat with a few of the other women on the tour. I also notice the looks she is getting from some of the guys. From the time I spent with her this afternoon, I can tell she has a bubbly personality and is almost like a female version of Linc. I assume that comparison is why I'm so drawn to her and kept finding myself watching her while we'd wandered around Paris.

"I don't think so, Linc. I think she got bored at lunch. And she spent the rest of the afternoon talking to you and Tara."

"Well, yeah, because you kept giving her one-word answers when she tried to talk to you. I can't be the only person you talk to over the next few weeks. I plan on getting laid at least a few times, and I think it's about time you do, too. You've essentially become a monk. So, as the person who spends almost all of his time with you, I am telling you to let loose while we're on this trip. Talk to the pretty girls. Have a few drinks. Enjoy seeing the sights and just be a normal guy," Linc says, the look on his face telling me he won't hear any more excuses.

"Aye, aye, captain."

"Good, and while we're at it, I want you to actually speak up when you want to do something. Don't just be along for the ride, for a change."

Jesus, he's challenging all my natural instincts right now.

Before I can respond, Tara sidles up to Linc and squeezes his arm. "Are you ready for a night of dancing girls, Lincoln?" she asks with a cheeky grin, and he rolls his eyes.

"I've never really been one to watch half-naked women dancing around with an audience," he replies, and I laugh, quickly covering it with a cough when he glares at me.

I guess the strip clubs he frequented earlier in our careers don't count. Then again, he's bi, so I guess maybe he preferred watching the half-naked men instead.

"Not my idea of a good time, either. But it's the Moulin Rouge. We can't come to Paris and not at least check it out."

"Well, we could always just not go inside and find something else to do..." Linc replies, looking over at me with a questioning look, and I shrug.

"What else would we do?" Kylie asks, coming to stand beside me.

I try not to make it obvious when I inhale, breathing in her perfume. It's some sort of faint fruity scent, and it's intoxicating.

"I mean, there are other things to do in Paris at night. Why don't we just see the inside and then let Brendan know we're going to go find a club or something? I'd rather do the dancing than watch topless women swing boobie tassels around anyway."

I snort at Linc's very accurate description of what I'd seen on the tour website when they advertised a visit to the Moulin Rouge.

"That sounds great. I'm in," Tara says with a grin.

"Me too," Kylie says.

The three of them turn to look at me, and I raise my hands up.

"Hey, I'm just along for the ride. If you guys are up for a night out, I'm in."

Linc shakes his head when I use his words to describe myself, but grins all the same, and I can tell he's proud of me for agreeing to a plan that will force me to mingle with the girls and not hide amongst a crowd. "I'll go tell Brendan."

Two hours later, Kylie grabs my hand and drags me out onto the dance floor of a club I will never remember the name of. I've had a few drinks, enough to feel a slight buzz without crossing over into drunk territory, and I feel more confident around her than I was earlier.

"You're not much of a dancer, are you?" she asks, giggling while I shuffle my feet awkwardly.

"Not much, no," I reply, narrowly avoiding being trampled on by Linc, who is bouncing around with Tara beside us.

Linc is not much of a dancer either, he just hides it better.

"It's okay. I am." She winds her arms around my neck, and I automatically grasp her hips. "Just follow my lead."

I do my best, but in the end, she just sways around in front of me, moving gracefully, while I hold her close.

"Are you looking forward to tomorrow?" she asks, her mouth close to my ear so that I can hear her over the loud music.

"Yeah, it should be fun. Although, it's not like I don't see more than enough snow back home."

Our next stop is a small village in Switzerland for two nights, with a trip in a gondola up the mountain to check out the snow.

"Tara can't wait. She's never seen snow before."

"Wow, really?" I look down at her with raised eyebrows.

"Yeah. It's quite common where we're from, actually. It definitely doesn't get that cold in Brisbane."

"But you've seen snow, right?"

"Of course. I'm actually half-Canadian. It's basically in my blood."

I tense up a bit.

"You okay?" she asks, her eyebrows raised a little.

"Yeah, sorry." I tighten my grip on her hips. "I didn't realise you'd been to Canada."

She studies me for a moment before answering. "Only a few times as a child. I've spent more time surfing than skiing over the years."

Her not mentioning ice skating or hockey relieves me a little. And also has me wondering about my intense paranoia that she's going to work out who I am.

Linc's right. I need to get a grip and just enjoy spending time with people who know nothing about me, starting with the beautiful woman standing here weaving her fingers through the hair at the nape of my neck.

I pull her in closer, and her eyes widen for a moment, then a smile plays across her lips and her chest presses against mine. I've finally found a rhythm, and she allows me to move us together in time with the music. Her lips are close to my ear again, and I suppress a shiver at the feel of her breath against my neck. Confidence surges through me and she gasps when I dip her backwards.

She laughs, her eyes twinkling. "You're a fast learner."

I grin back, feeling more at ease with her with every passing moment. "You have no idea."

3
NEED A HAND?

KYLIE

I PEEL my eyes open after being rudely awakened by the alarm on my phone, smacking my hand around on the bedside table while trying to find the source of the noise.

"Time to get up, sleeping beauty. I've been up for an hour and am all packed," Tara says, grinning at me from her perch on the edge of her bed.

"Ugh, since when are you the morning person and I want to stay in bed? And you were the one drinking last night, too!"

Not that she drank much. She's never been much of a drinker, sticking to one or two cocktails at most. We had stumbled back to the hotel with the guys around two in the morning, and I knew I'd struggle to get up in only a few hours. Now that the reality is here, I'm even less impressed with last night's version of myself and her poor decision-making skills.

"True. I guess I'm just excited to see snow soon."

I drag myself out of bed, and once I'm showered, I forego makeup and rake my hair into a messy bun on top of my head. Feeling semi-awake, I throw my belongings haphazardly into my suitcase, ignoring Tara's comment about how it's going to be impossible for me to find anything without some organisation. Organisation and I have never been close.

"As much as I love how we get to see so much of this continent this way, I can tell already that I am going to hate the sight of this damn thing in the next few weeks," I say, sitting on top of my suitcase to attempt to zip it closed.

Tara stands at the open door, waiting for me, but she turns when I look up to ask her for help, distracted by something in the hall. Lincoln and Seth appear behind her, each rolling a medium sized suitcase behind them. How do guys manage to travel so light? Mine could fit a small army inside of it and it's still not big enough.

"Need a hand?" Seth asks, seeing me still sitting on top of my overstuffed suitcase.

"Yes, please." I give him a cheerful grin, and he smirks a little while he squeezes past Tara and enters the small hotel room.

He's so tall and broad that he looks out of place in this tiny space.

Crouching in front of me, he pulls on the zip that I've been struggling to move more than a few centimetres. The strength in his fingers makes it look so easy, and I watch him zip it closed, bringing both zips together between my legs before looking up at me with a smile. There's something about the look in his eyes, though, that gives me pause, and I find myself holding my breath for a few seconds, lost in those beautiful blue eyes.

"All done," he says, and I detect a slight wobble in his voice.

He hesitates momentarily before rising again, putting his hand out to help me up. I place my hand in his and allow him to pull me up, pretending not to notice when his grip tightens a little before he lets me go. Although he'd taken a while to come out of his shell yesterday, after dancing with him for hours last night, I feel like we're on our way to becoming friends now, and I am glad we've found some others to team up with on the tour. I'd noticed a few other women on the tour checking the two Canadians out, and

I'm not ashamed to admit I enjoyed the jealous looks thrown our way last night, now that it seems as though they've decided to hang out with us.

"All ready to go?" Lincoln asks, and Tara and I nod. "Well then, after you, ladies." He waves us ahead, and Tara and I join them in the hall, leading the way to the elevators.

"How are you guys so cheerful? I'm barely functioning right now," I grumble, and Lincoln shrugs.

"We went for a run earlier. It's all the endorphins."

Tara shudders. "Ugh, exercise while on holiday? No thanks."

I consider the two men for a moment. "Next time you go, can I join you as well? I haven't felt safe running in strange neighbourhoods, but I have missed it since we've been here."

"For sure! We go every day," Lincoln replies while Seth nods.

Once an empty elevator arrives, we all squeeze in together. With very little room to move, I find myself with my back pressed up against Seth's chest, the pair of us sandwiched in between our suitcases. Tara and Lincoln manage to find room without touching, and the doors close behind us.

"They really didn't take Canadian lumberjacks into account when they designed these Parisian hotels," Tara says.

I feel Seth shaking with silent laughter behind me while Lincoln snorts. "No, they really didn't. But those two seem comfortable over there." He nods towards Seth and me.

I roll my eyes and shake my head, catching sight of Seth's face in the mirrored wall while he glares at his friend. But he makes no move to put space between us - in fact, he seems to have moved closer. And I don't mind a bit.

Once we get on the bus, I slide into a seat towards the back, and Tara sits down beside me. Lincoln and Seth sit down across the aisle, squeezing their tall, broad frames into the small space. Tara and Lincoln immediately start chatting, but I'm still sleepy, so I pop my earbuds in, ball my jumper up to use as a pillow and lean my head against the glass.

I don't recall drifting off, but when I wake up, I find Seth sitting beside me, reading a book. Outside, the Parisian streets have been replaced by rolling green pastures and stone houses.

"Hey," I say, sitting up straighter and pulling my earbuds out.

Across the aisle, Tara has taken Seth's seat next to the window, beside Lincoln. The two of them are still chatting away animatedly.

"Hey," Seth replies, holding his finger between the pages of his book so he doesn't lose his place.

I notice that both guys have their legs stretched out into the aisle. "Get a bit too squished over there?" I ask.

"Yeah. There were no spare seats, otherwise we'd try to have one each. Tara suggested this would be better, at least. Is that okay?"

"Of course it is ." I smile at him.

He nods towards the earbud in my hand. "What are you listening to?"

I hand him the earbud. "The classics."

He raises an eyebrow and takes it from me, holding it to his ear. He listens for a few seconds and then glances at me. "You didn't strike me as a Green Day fan. What else have you got on there?"

I grin and pull out my phone, handing it to him so he can scroll through my playlists. "Have at it, buddy."

He smiles at me, and we spend the next few hours scrolling through both our playlists, comparing favourite songs. As it turns out, he's a fan of 90's music as well. He still isn't overly chatty, but it's nice to find common ground with him. And I can talk more than enough for both of us.

Eight long hours later, we arrive in Engelberg, a tiny village in Switzerland. I climb stiffly down out of the bus behind Seth and Lincoln, closely followed by Tara. I watch while the guys stretch, trying not to appear affected when Seth's shirt rides up when he lifts his arms, exposing a tanned, toned abdomen.

The air is crisp, and I look up at the mountain before us to distract myself, smiling when I spy a hint of white just below where it disappears into the clouds.

"Tara, look." I point towards the snow.

My best friend squeals, causing the guys to look at her with raised eyebrows.

It's been years since I've been even close to snow. I have fond memories of running around my grandparents' yard in Calgary in the winter, hurling snowballs at my older brother Will, and making snow angels with our younger twin sisters, Emma and Dayna. But we haven't been back since I was a teenager, and I look forward to introducing Tara to the joys of snow tomorrow morning when we catch the gondola up to the top of the mountain.

"It still blows my mind that you've never seen snow," Lincoln says, shaking his head with a grin.

"Well, believe it, buddy. The day it snows in Brisbane, hell will have frozen over," Tara chirps back, and we all laugh while helping the bus driver pull suitcases out from under the bus.

Once they give us our room information, we head inside the small hotel, and the guys once again let us go ahead.

"Such lovely manners. Are all Canadian men so nice?" One of the other Australian girls on the trip, Georgia, I think, levels them with a flirtatious smile, her eyes drifting over them both when we file past her towards the stairs.

"Only the good ones," Lincoln replies, and I turn back to see him giving her an easy smile and a wink while Seth shifts his weight a little beside me.

I've noticed he isn't comfortable around new people, preferring to leave Lincoln to deal with them while he remains silently watchful. After just one day, I feel honoured to have made a little dent in the armour he has up around him.

Almost as though he felt my eyes on him, Seth looks over at me and gives me a small smile before nodding at me, a sign I take to mean to keep going, so I turn and keep heading up the stairs, a similar smile of my own playing across my lips.

After a meal that was clearly aimed at tourists which had far too much melted cheese for my liking, we take ourselves for a walk through the small town. A few others on our tour join us, and our little group of four has become a party of ten while we stroll through the darkened streets. The others chat amongst themselves, but for the most part, it's still Tara and me with the guys.

"So, when was the last time you were in Canada?" Lincoln asks me, draping his arm over my shoulders while we walk.

He links his other arm through Tara's, while Seth walks quietly on my other side, his hands in his pockets.

Lincoln is possibly the most easygoing guy I've ever met, all smiles and jokes. The guys we hang out with back home are similar, but something about Lincoln draws you in. I can see why Seth hangs back and lets his more outgoing friend handle most of the socialising. Seth reminds me a little of Brianna, although even quieter and more withdrawn in large social settings. Since we've been with the larger group, Seth has kept his head down and barely said anything.

"My parents took us back when I was fourteen, just before we moved to Brisbane. We went for Christmas, so I had the full white Christmas experience for the first time, and it was amazing. We'd been back for winter before, but never Christmas. My little sisters still believed in Santa at the time, so my grandparents went all out to make it as magical as possible. I think it's one of my best childhood memories, actually."

"You said it was your Dad who is Canadian, right? Where's he from?"

"Calgary. We've got family all over, but he grew up in Calgary, and that's where my grandparents live," I reply, and Lincoln cocks his head to the side.

"Calgary, huh? Is he a Mounties fan?" he asks, glancing over at Seth, who has stiffened slightly.

I recognise the name, remembering my grandfather talking about his favourite team. "That's the ice hockey team, right?" I ask, and Lincoln nods. "Would you believe my father has no interest in hockey? Besides the few games our friend Chris has forced us to watch in his attempts to get us interested, I have never watched a game all the way through and don't understand the rules."

I notice Seth's shoulders drop back down and wonder briefly what that's all about.

"A Canadian who has no interest in hockey? It's a good thing he left because otherwise, we'd have to revoke his citizenship," Lincoln says with a laugh.

I shake my head. "You joke, but honestly, he is the most unCanadian-Canadian you will ever meet. The first thing he did when he got to Australia was take surfing lessons, and he had us in Little Nippers the second we could walk."

Seth looks over with a confused expression. "What on earth is a Little Nipper?" he asks, finally breaking his silence for the first time since we left the hotel.

Clearly, curiosity got the better of him.

"It's part of the Surf Life Savers. At the beach, it's the kids who learn to become lifesavers–or lifeguards, as you would call them," Tara pipes up from Lincoln's other side.

I nod while still looking at Seth, whose eyes are running over me, a small smile playing over his lips.

"So you're a lifeguard?" he asks.

It's hard not to preen a little under his attentive gaze, but I push aside the desire. I am determined to avoid falling into any old patterns while on this trip, and hooking up with an incredibly hot guy on the second night of the tour would definitely fall into old patterns. I've avoided drinking so far, and with a bit of luck, I'll have proven to myself by the end of this trip that I'm capable of keeping my impulses in check for a change.

"Not anymore. When we moved to Brisbane, it was too far to go to a surf beach each weekend, so I kind of stopped that hobby. I still surf when I can, though, when my brother is going. It's kind of our bonding thing now." I try not to look at Tara at the mention of Will, but out of the corner of my eye, I notice her stiffen a little next to Lincoln.

"You alright, Tara?" Lincoln must have noticed Tara's reaction.

"Completely fine," my friend responds with the most fake smile imaginable.

Lincoln is obviously smart enough not to push it, so he changes the subject, and our group continues down the cobbled street. But I notice Seth watching us again and can tell he picked up on the weirdness. It's the first time since we left Australia that I've spoken about my brother in front of Tara, and I've been constantly walking on eggshells around her for months. I'm beginning to wonder if things are ever going to be entirely normal between us all ever again.

4

BEAUTIFUL, ISN'T IT?

SETH

WATCHING an adult experience snow for the first time is something I never thought I'd see. My entire life revolves around ice. Coming from Canada, and with most of my travel occurring during the North American winter months, I've seen more than my fair share of snow.

But seeing Tara's absolute delight the minute we get to the top of the mountain gives me a whole new appreciation for its beauty. It helps that I don't have to scrape any of this snow off a driveway or my car.

"Oh my god, it's so cold!" Tara squeals when she reaches to touch the snow on the railing beside her.

Linc snorts and shakes his head. "This is summer weather. And, of course it's cold, it's frozen water, you weirdo."

I smirk when they start bickering, but I content myself to look around at the view. Although I've lived in the mountains most of my life, something about these ones takes my breath away, and I'm so lost in the majesty of my surroundings that I don't immediately notice when Kylie appears at my side.

"Beautiful, isn't it?" she asks, her voice wistful while we both look out at what seems like endless mountains around us.

I look over at her and notice, not for the first time, just how beautiful she is. She's left her long brown hair loose, and it flows down her back in waves beneath the cutest little white toque. When she turns to look at me, her green eyes full of life, I'm once again in awe at how open she seems. She doesn't appear to have any reservations and is an open book. While we've only known each other for two days, I already feel like I've known her for years.

I doubt she could say the same about me, though, as I've remained my usual, socially awkward self for the most part. I feel like I've spoken to her more than any other woman I've spent time with in the last few years, though, and I wonder what it is about her that makes me want to open up more.

I realise that I've been staring at her for far too long, and she's looking at me with her head to the side, a bemused smile dancing across her lips.

"Sorry, lost in thought for a moment there. Yes, it's gorgeous," I blurt out.

Kylie's eyes twinkle. "You're not great at small talk, are you?"

"Not especially, no. It's not that I don't like people. I've just never been great at socialising," I say, my usual self-consciousness kicking in.

"I get that. You seem okay with Lincoln, though?" She nods her head over towards Linc, who is gathering snow in his gloved hands behind Tara's back while she continues to play with the snow on the railing.

"I've known Linc since I was eight. We grew up together, went to the same college in the US, and after a few years, ended up working for the same company. He's basically a brother at this point."

"Our group of friends is close like that. I don't really see anyone I knew from Sydney anymore, but the friends I made in school when we moved to Brisbane have been like family for the last eleven years. Well, they were," she says, her words trailing off.

Her smile drops a little, and she turns and looks out at the view again.

Before I can stop myself, I ask, "Do you want to talk about it?"

She looks at me with raised eyebrows, and I'm pretty sure she's as surprised as I am by my question.

"Do you really want to know, or are you just being nice?" she asks.

I shake my head. "I rarely say things I don't mean, if you haven't already worked that out. I might not talk much, but I'm a pretty good listener."

She regards me for a few seconds before nodding, then turns back to look at the view while she speaks. "My older brother, Will, is one of my best friends. And he was madly in love with Tara's older sister, Annelisa. Well, I'm pretty sure he still is, to be honest. I usually avoid mentioning him too much in front of Tara since Annelisa up and left him out of nowhere just over a year ago. Will kind of pushed Tara away cause he couldn't cope, which hurt Tara badly. Will was like a big brother to her as well, something that I've tried to remind him of so many times, but he keeps saying he doesn't want to hound Tara about Annelisa, and he couldn't stop himself if they hung out now. But Annelisa's leaving has kind of split the group apart. Everyone is still talking, but there's a weirdness to it now. Tara knows where Annelisa is, but she cut off contact with everyone else, so it's put Tara in a really shitty situation." She turns to look back at me and smiles a little. "Bet you're wishing you hadn't asked now, huh?"

"Not at all. That sounds like a lot. It's hard when stuff happens, and you can't really control how others react to it," I say, knowing that feeling all too well.

"Yeah. Have you had something similar?"

"Well, not quite like that, but I had some shit happen at work about a month ago and have been dealing with the weight of a lot of people's expectations ever since. Kind of why we're here now - Linc convinced me to get away for a while til people find something else to divert their attention to." It's the closest I've come to talking about work with anyone other than Linc on this trip, and even this feels like too much.

"I've honestly never had a job that I cared that much about to cause me that sort of stress. I'm sorry you went through that." She places a hand on my arm, and the familiarity of her touch startles me for a moment before I realise I like it.

"It is what it is. Just gotta hope things are better once we're back," I say with a shrug, wondering how we can turn the conversation away from me again.

But Linc unintentionally comes to my rescue when he smacks an unsuspecting Tara in the back with a giant snowball. She screams, and Kylie doubles over, laughing beside me, while her best friend turns on Linc with murder in her eyes. He darts off with a laugh, and she takes off after him. Kylie is gasping for air from laughing so hard, and I look down at the snow at my feet, a sudden urge to be included in the fun washes over me. Without a second thought, I scoop up a handful of snow and fling it toward her.

She gasps and stares at me for a moment. "Oh, it's on now, buddy," she says, reaching down to grab her own handful before I can react.

She raises my shirt and smears the snow all over my abdomen. While I'm more than accustomed to the cold, the sudden touch of snow on my bare skin is a shock and I jump back with a yelp while the icy substance slides down my stomach. She laughs again, sprinting off with surprising speed. I stand in shock for a moment before rushing after her, grasping her around the waist, and softly tackling her to the snow-covered ground, keenly aware that she is not a padded-up defenceman ready for a fight. She gasps when her sweater and shirt ride up, and she arches her back when her skin makes contact with the snow.

A mental image of her lying beneath me wearing far less clothing flashes through my mind at that movement, and it takes all my self control to shake it off.

I look down at her. "Not so funny now, is it?"

She grins up at me. "Nope, still funny."

Too late, I realise she's grabbed another handful of snow and shoved it down the neck of my shirt.

"Ah, fuck!" I arch my own back and let her go, sitting up to try to shake the freezing ice out while she giggles uncontrollably.

I pretend to glare at her, but truthfully, this is the most fun I've had in a while, and watching her giggle away makes me smile.

"Incoming!" Linc yells, and I stupidly turn, catching a snowball in the face. "Seth, rookie move! You know you don't turn into the snowball!"

"My mistake, I'm clearly rusty at this," I yell back, jumping to my feet and reaching down to help Kylie up.

Once she is standing again, my hand lingers in hers, and she looks up at me with a little smile. I don't know what this is, but I wonder what she would do if I were to kiss her, and my eyes flick to her lips.

Realising the danger behind this thought, I let go of her hand and step back a little. I really like Kylie, and Tara as well, so the last thing we need is for me to complicate the new friendship by kissing her. That doesn't stop me from wanting to, though, and I can't help but watch her when she runs off to join her friend in pelting Linc with snowballs while he screams his surrender.

After dinner, which mercifully does not include melted cheese this time, I head out to the firepit with my book and a beer, ready for a bit of a break from the constant conversation required when surrounded by the tour group. It feels oddly familiar, like when I'm on the road with the team, and I need to recharge my social battery before I can 'people' again.

Linc and Tara have gone for another walk, having become fast friends. I thought Kylie had joined them, but I spy her now familiar form, pacing back and forth along the fence line while she holds her phone to her ear. Even though I had been craving solitude, part of me wants to go over and talk to her. I resist the urge though, not wanting to interrupt her rather animated conversation with whoever she is talking to.

A few others have already congregated around the fire, so I scan the area for somewhere out of the way and see two empty chairs that are still close enough to have light but far enough away that, hopefully, none of them try to come and talk to me. I've noticed one or two of the other Australian girls have been trying to get my attention, but I've reached my limit on new people to get to know, so I've been avoiding their attempts with a polite smile and letting Linc run interference.

I'm several chapters into my book when a shadow falls across the page, and I look up to see Kylie standing in front of me, her phone in her hand.

"Hey. Have you seen our partners in crime?" she asks.

I blink up at her, attempting to bring myself back to reality and avoid being distracted by her smile yet again. "Uh... Yeah. Sorry. They went for a walk."

She sighs and looks down at the book in my lap. "Sorry, I didn't mean to interrupt."

"No, it's fine." I close the book and put it on the ground beside me, gesturing at the other chair.

"You sure?" she asks, hesitating until I nod, then takes a seat.

I hold up my beer. "Do you want one? I can go grab one for you."

She shakes her head. "I don't drink."

I think back over the shared meals, and realise I've not seen her drink anything other than water and pop. I nod slowly, opening my mouth to ask if there's a particular reason, but think better of it and clamp my mouth shut. There's something about her that makes me want to know everything there is to know about who she is, but a question like that would be far too personal.

She cocks her head to the side and studies me closely, seeming to sense my curiosity. "I used to drink. A lot. To the point of blacking out. I didn't like who I was when I was making those choices... So I decided to just cut it out completely."

I nod again. "Well, no judgement from me. I can get you something else though, if you want?"

She waves her hand. "I'm good, but thank you for offering." She gives me another one of those heart stopping smiles, and I blink a little, mesmerised.

"Were you talking to someone from back home?" I ask after a moment, surprising myself again by asking her a question about her life.

"Yeah. Our other best friend, Bri. She had to bail because she and her boyfriend started renovating and work got busy, even though she was meant to come on this trip with us. I wish she were here, though - she would have loved all this." She looks out toward the mountain that we had been up earlier.

"Seems like you have quite a few people you are close to," I say, feeling a slight pang in my chest that I can't explain.

"Yeah. I'm a bit of a social butterfly. Always have been. But until last year, I didn't realise that I'd become reliant on being the life of the party. I'd leaned too heavily into that party girl persona, I guess. Sometimes... I worry that I'm too much for people." Her voice has dropped a little, and I notice the sadness in her expression while she looks away.

"Why?" I ask, astounded by how someone so inherently friendly could feel like she was too much.

"I often feel like I've dominated the conversation when I'm with people. It's fine with my friends, they all know what I'm like and I can be completely myself with them. But when it's new groups, like this tour, I leave interactions feeling like I've talked too much. Like people just want me to shut up. But..." She pauses, looking like she's searching for the right words. "It's like I get word vomit and need to get all the words out." She cringes and shakes her head at me. "Like right now, in my head, I'm yelling at myself to shut up, but I can't get my mouth to listen." She clamps her mouth shut, and puffs air out of her nose.

It's adorable, and I smile, placing a hand on her arm. "I don't think you talk too much, Kylie. If anything, I don't talk enough. Linc always tells me I need to socialise more, but I don't think I'm wired that way. I enjoy being around people who are so full of life though, even if I don't always seem that way."

She lets out a breath and grins at me. "Well, now you've gone and done it. You'll never be able to make me stop talking."

I smile back, finding her energy infectious. "I can't imagine ever wanting you to be quiet, Kylie."

"Good. Because honestly, I actually don't think I'm capable of being quiet, no matter how hard I try." She shrugs.

We fall into easy conversation once again, and by the time we notice everyone else has gone to bed, I realise how much she's made me feel at ease around her. And I haven't once thought about that last night on the ice.

5
WISH YOU COULD SEE
YOURSELF LIKE I SEE YOU

KYLIE

AFTER A WHIRLWIND two days in Florence where I've managed to eat more than my weight in gelato, we arrive in Rome, and I am stunned by the stifling heat. No one had warned me how much the temperatures would change on this trip, and now I'm grateful for the over-packing I did while I dig around in my suitcase to look for the summer dresses I hadn't needed til now. On the other side of the room, Tara is glaring at her clothes, grumbling to herself about poor packing choices.

"See, you were making fun of me for packing too much, but now it's an advantage for you," I say, tossing her one of the dresses that I've wrenched free from the depths of my suitcase.

She holds the dress up in front of her and then looks back at me. "There is no way this is going to fit me."

We are the same size, always have been, but for some reason, Tara insists on claiming she's bigger. She leans towards baggier clothes, which bugs me. I love my curves, something my mother worked hard on with both myself and my younger sisters after years of dealing with disordered eating before we were born, so watching my best friend hide hers and hate on herself has long frustrated me.

"Tara, put the damn dress on. You are hot, and I don't want to hear another word about it," I snap, sounding more annoyed than I mean to, and she blinks at me, her face dropping even further. "Sorry. I just hate it when you are so hard on yourself. I wish you could see yourself like I see you." Going to stand in front of her, I give her a hug before moving back to my side of the room and getting changed.

Tara looks at the dress she's still clutching in her hand, then nods at me before heading into the bathroom. While I've never had a problem stripping off in front of her, she prefers to do it in private, so I head down to the lobby to wait for her, ready to explore the city.

Lincoln and Seth are already there, and I walk towards them. Lincoln notices me first and says something to Seth, who turns to look at me, his eyebrows flying up while he runs his eyes over me. I've caught him looking at me so many times now that I know he finds me attractive, and I revel in the attention, even though I assume he will never be brave enough to say anything. There's no denying that there is chemistry between us, and I find myself wishing he would make a move, although I'd promised myself that I wouldn't hook up with anyone on this trip.

This feels different to any of the guys I've previously hung out with, though. I've never had an actual boyfriend, just a series of flings, some more serious than others. But none of them ever looked at me how Seth is looking at me now, and I've fantasised about what it would be like to have those big, powerful hands moving over my body while he kisses me. Despite how quiet and socially awkward he is, something tells me he knows his way around a woman's body.

Lincoln whistles at me, and I do a little twirl before curtseying, and Seth gives me one of his devastatingly beautiful smiles.

"Looking hot, Kyles," Lincoln says once I join them.

"Why thank you, good sir."

"No, seriously. Seth, doesn't she look stunning?" He nudges his friend, and Seth glares at him for a moment before nodding.

"You look great, Kylie."

I can tell that Lincoln's interference is bugging him, so I wave it away, not wanting him to feel uncomfortable, even though I am very aware of how he is looking at me right now. He might not be so great with words, but he more than makes up for it when he runs his gaze over me again, meeting my eyes and giving me a little wink. It's the boldest he's ever been with me, and I love it.

"Oh wow, Tara! You look hot, too! We'll be beating these Italian men off with a stick!" Lincoln declares.

I turn back to see my friend coming down the stairs, and I clap with a grin when I see she is indeed wearing the dress, which fits her perfectly, and the green goes well with her long red hair.

Once she joins us, she fidgets with one of the straps, and I swat her hand away. "Don't - you look perfect."

She gives me a grateful smile, letting her hand drop to her side, and I look back at the guys, finding Seth's eyes on me once again.

"So, where are we going?" Tara asks, looking at Lincoln, who has become the unofficial leader of our little group.

"Well, I heard there's a really nice restaurant around the corner. We're in Rome. I just want to gorge on pizza and pasta," Lincoln replies, rubbing a hand over his flat stomach.

"You did that in Florence," Seth says dryly, flashing me a grin when I snort.

It was true - I don't think I've ever seen anyone pack away so many slices of pizza in a two-day period, and it was impressive.

"I wouldn't mind a fancy dinner. We can check out the sights tomorrow?" Tara says, and Lincoln nods.

I screw my nose up a little, hesitant to say that I don't feel like a fancy dinner tonight. I really just want to walk through the city, but all the walking has exhausted Tara, and I don't want to push her when she's ready to drop.

"Actually, I'm kind of up for a walking dinner. I'm keen to check out the sights, " Seth pipes up, and I look over to see him watching me closely.

Tara and Lincoln exchange a look and then shrug.

"We can split up for the evening, I guess. Kylie, what do you want to do?" Lincoln asks, and suddenly, all eyes are on me.

I stand frozen for a moment, not loving having all the focus on me. Tara flicks her eyes towards Seth, who seems to be waiting for my answer. She wiggles her eyebrows, something she does often when she's trying to communicate silently about a boy. She excelled at it when she was trying to convince Brianna to date Jake, and now I understand why Bri was throwing couch cushions at her.

"Uh, I mean, I wouldn't mind seeing the city at night. If that's okay with you, Seth?" I'm pretty sure he was trying to get me to say I'd join him, but he's so hard to read that I'm hoping I'm not overstepping.

"Sure." He smiles, and my heart does some weird fluttery thing.

I'm beginning to wonder if I need to be concerned about how my body has started to react to this man.

Lincoln claps his hands together, and I jump a little as I'm brought back to reality. "Well, that's settled then. Tara, let's go have a date night and leave these two to go look at stuff. Don't do anything I wouldn't do, kids." He winks at Seth, who goes bright red, and links arms with Tara, leading her out the door.

Once they are outside, they turn back together and give us a cheeky wave. Tara's eyebrows wiggle again, and Lincoln looks at Seth while jerking his head in my direction.

"Fucking subtle," Seth mutters under his breath, and I giggle while we watch them saunter off down the street.

"About as subtle as a freight train," I say.

He huffs out a laugh. "Shall we?" He waves for me to go first, and I lead the way out the door before stopping and waiting for him on the footpath.

"Where should we go?" I ask.

He pulls out his phone and brings up a map. "We're pretty close to the Trevi Fountain and the Spanish Steps. We could start there and just walk?"

"Sounds great. Lead the way, tour guide," I say, falling into step beside him.

He's so tall that he has to shorten his steps to stay at my pace, but he doesn't seem to mind, and I find myself looking at him out of the corner of my eye every few seconds.

"Do you know much about Rome?" I ask, feeling the need to fill the silence that he seems much more comfortable in than I am.

"A bit. I did an elective in Ancient Rome in college for something different. I'd kind of always been interested in ancient history growing up, so it was good to learn more about it. This was actually the place I was most looking forward to seeing on the tour." His face lights up, and I can hear the excitement in his voice.

Before now, he's just let Lincoln, and now Tara and me, call the shots on what we were going to do each day, so watching him take the lead and actually do something he's choosing to is refreshing. This is the most animated I've seen him, and it's adorable.

"I basically only know what I learnt in high school and that Gladiator movie. But I love being in new cities and exploring," I say and am rewarded with another one of those heart-stopping smiles.

"I've noticed," he says, his voice low, sliding his hands into his pockets while he continues walking beside me.

He seems content to remain quiet again, but I can't handle it, and now that I've got him talking, there is so much more I want to learn about him. "So, what did you study at college?"

"Sports Medicine," he replies, and I raise my eyebrows.

"Wow. I mean, I guess that makes sense, given you work for a sports team. So, what are you, like the team doctor?"

I notice him stiffen slightly before giving me an almost panicked look. "Um, no, not quite. Sports Medicine is more like physical therapy."

"Okay, that makes sense."

Doesn't explain his bizarre reaction, though.

"What about you? Did you go to college?" he asks quickly, and I look at him for a moment before answering.

"Um, no, no college for me. It's not as big of a deal in Australia, I guess. I just went straight into office jobs once we graduated from high school. Nothing really stuck, though. Still don't know what I want to be when I grow up."

He looks over at me with a raised eyebrow. "Aren't you already a grown-up? You're twenty-six, right?"

"I rarely feel like a grown-up, Seth." I grin, and he laughs a little.

"True, you definitely seem to have embraced the fun in life. I kind of envy that."

"Stick with me, Seth, and I'll have you finding your inner child in no time."

"I'd really like that," he says, his voice so low that I almost wonder if I imagined it.

But there's no mistaking the smile on his face or the way he takes my hand, lacing his fingers through mine and squeezing gently.

Well, hell, there goes that heart flutter again.

I clear my throat while we continue walking side by side, trying to seem as though his words and actions aren't sending my lady parts into a complete spin. "So, while I've got you talking so much, tell me more about yourself."

"What do you want to know?"

"I don't know." I shrug. "Boring stuff, I guess. Any siblings? I feel like you know all about me, but you're still a bit of an enigma."

He laughs. "I don't think anyone has ever described me as an enigma before. No siblings, just me and my parents growing up."

"I can't imagine coming from a small family. What's that like? Are you close to your parents?"

"I was lucky enough to spend time with Linc and his siblings growing up, so I kind of got to experience both sides, I guess. But yeah, I'm close to my parents, especially my Dad." He squeezes my hand again. "What about you? I know you mentioned your brother. Is he your only sibling?"

I shake my head. "No, we've got two younger sisters as well. Twins. They are six years younger than me, so my relationship with them is different to the one I have with Will, but overall, we're all pretty close. And don't think I didn't notice what you did there."

He looks over at me with one eyebrow raised. "What'd I do?"

"You deflected and put the questions back on me."

He smiles a little. "Nothing gets by you, I guess. I don't mean to do it, I'm just... Not great at talking about myself. I've always been better at listening."

I nod. "Okay, I'll let you off easy this time, then."

"Oh, why thank you Miss Kylie."

I grin. "You're welcome, Mr Seth."

He's quiet for a moment, and I wonder briefly if he's reached his word quota for the day. But when he does finally speak, my heart flutters again.

"Did anyone ever tell you that you have the most beautiful smile?"

I blink, momentarily stunned. "No... No they haven't."

He squeezes my hand again. "Shame. Because you should be told that every day."

If I'm not careful, I could easily fall for this man.

6

KIND OF DESERVE A
PUNCH IN THE FACE

SETH

THERE'S JUST something about this vibrant Australian woman that draws me in. Her sunny personality and confidence are hard to resist, and combined with her gorgeous curves, long brown hair and beautiful green eyes, I've been finding it hard to think of anything other than kissing her whenever we're together.

Linc noticed almost immediately and has been encouraging me to make a move. Actually, his exact words were, "If you don't make a move on that woman, I am going to have to tell Claire that you need more sessions when we get home."

Threatening me with more therapy sessions appears to have been the kick up the ass that I needed. That and the little yellow sundress that she's wearing, her tanned skin on display while it skims along her perfect curves.

When I took Kylie's hand, it felt so right. Like our two hands fit together perfectly.

We walk through the city, neither of us acknowledging the hand holding, but there's electricity in the air that wasn't there before. I've caught her looking at me a few times while we've walked side by side towards the Trevi Fountain, and by the time we get there, I'm wondering if I should just ask her if I can kiss her.

Just as I'm working out what to say that won't sound weird or would totally kill the mood, Kylie lets out a gasp and drops my hand. She covers her mouth with both hands while she stares at something in front of us.

"You okay?" I ask, unsure if something is wrong or if she's just in awe of the fountain.

I look over to where she's staring and see what appears to be a professional photo shoot set up on the other side of the fountain. A male photographer is snapping photos of women in various stages of undress while they pose with the fountain behind them.

"Asshole!" she exclaims, and I'm thrown by the venom behind her words.

"What?" I'm trying to work out what I've done, but Kylie seems to have forgotten I'm even there.

She glances around, and I'm utterly lost as to what is going on while she stomps over to a little food cart that has been set up nearby. She briefly exchanges words with the vendor before purchasing a bottle of Coke and tearing the lid off.

"Kylie, what's going on?" I ask, following her when she stalks towards the other side of the fountain.

She finally seems to remember I'm still here, pausing so that I can catch up. "Do you remember I told you about my friend Brianna?"

"Yeah?" I'm sure the confusion is written all over my face while I try to work out how her friend in Australia could have anything to do with why she's acting so weird now in the middle of one of the busiest tourist attractions in Rome.

"Well, last year, her rich, older boyfriend dumped her. Didn't even talk to her about it, just locked her out of their apartment after putting all her stuff in her car and fucked off overseas with his assistant." She is shaking now, and I'm finding myself oddly turned on by the fire in her tone.

"Okay... That is a real dick move, but what has that got to do with whatever is going on now?"

"That is her ex." She points over towards the photo shoot, and I follow the direction of her finger. She is pointing at the photographer, who is calling out directions to the models in short dresses in front of the fountain.

"Oh." I scrutinise the guy, watching while he hands his camera to the woman beside him and moves closer to the models.

I cringe when he reaches out to cup the cheek of the young woman closest to him, locking eyes with her while he speaks to her. She can't be a day over seventeen, and he has to be in at least his mid-thirties. The way he gazes into her eyes, running a thumb over her lips, has an almost predatory quality.

"That guy was with your friend?" I ask, and Kylie nods, grimacing.

"Yep. And if you think he is a douche, you're on the right path. But he is actually a giant asshole." She moves closer to the photo shoot again.

I grab her hand to stop her. "What are you doing?"

She looks down at my hand, and I let go, not wanting to overstep, even though she appears to be on a warpath.

"I just want to say hi."

I stay where I am, watching as she makes a beeline for him.

"Hey, Richard." Although the area is crowded, I can hear her voice carry over all the other sounds around me.

He turns around, his eyebrows pinched together while he scans the crowd. His eyes narrow when he sees Kylie, though I can't tell if he recognises her or not.

"You probably don't remember me. I'm Kylie, a friend of Bri's." Her tone seems friendly, but Richard's face noticeably drops when she says her friend's name.

"Right..." he replies, stretching the word out while watching her warily.

I decide to move closer, not sure where this exchange is going.

Just as I reach her side, she lifts her arm and pours the entire bottle of Coke over his head. He gasps but doesn't move, and I'm pretty sure he's too stunned to process what is happening while the dark liquid flows down onto his white linen shirt.

Much like me.

After a few seconds, he finally comes to his senses and steps towards her, his eyes flashing with anger. "What the fuck?" he yells, raising his hand.

Oh, hell no.

I step between them and place a hand on his chest. "Nope, gonna stop you right there, buddy."

"Are you fucking serious? She just poured her drink all over me!" He turns his rage on me.

I shrug, not even slightly intimidated by him. "From what I hear, you kind of deserved a punch in the face, so I guess you should be grateful she just poured a drink on your head."

I'm at least a foot taller than him, and he glares up at me, blinking through the sticky liquid that drips from his eyebrows. For some reason, he reminds me of a small dog who believes he's larger than he actually is.

Kylie laughs behind me, and Richard opens and closes his mouth, his face growing redder. I'm surprised that steam hasn't started pouring out of his ears at this point.

Over his shoulder, I notice a security guard moving towards us. I turn back to Kylie, who is grinning at Richard, looking like an evil mastermind.

"Come on, Kylie. Let's go before we end up in an Italian police cell and Linc has to come bail us out."

"But you know how much he'd love that. It would make his night." She pouts at me but doesn't protest when I take her hand and lead her at a brisk pace through the crowd.

She overtakes me, breaking into a run and racing ahead. I follow her around the corner, finding her leaning against the wall, laughing so hard she is crying. Although I'm having trouble processing what just happened, seeing her so full of joy makes my heart race, and before I have a chance to think about it, I reach out to cup her cheek.

She stops laughing and looks at me, her eyes wide. Her breath hitches, and her gaze drops to my lips.

"You are quite possibly the craziest woman I have ever met. And I'd really like to kiss you now," I say, moving closer.

She nods slowly, lifting her gaze to mine again. "Okay," she says, sounding breathless.

With nothing holding me back now, I lower my lips to hers. Her arms come around my neck, and I feel her lift onto her tiptoes to get closer. Pulling her flush against my chest, she lets out a little moan before deepening the kiss, her hands tangling in my hair.

It's the perfect first kiss, the kind you want to bottle up and keep close forever. I have no idea how long we stay like that, but once we finally pull apart, we are both flushed and out of breath.

"I've been wanting to do that for days," I confess.

She smiles at me, her fingers still in my hair. "I've been wanting you to do that for days."

"Yeah?" I stroke her cheek with my thumb, and she nods.

"Yeah. I'm really glad my being insane finally gave you the courage to do it," she says with a little laugh.

"So you'd be cool if I did it again, then?"

She smiles and whispers, "I'd really, really like that."

I bend to kiss her again, my lips softly brushing hers.

"Hey!" We both twist our heads to see the security guard from earlier barrelling around the corner.

Kylie grabs my hand and starts running. "But maybe let's not get arrested first!"

We peel out of there and soon get lost in the streets of Rome, and I can't think of anyone else I'd rather be with in this moment.

7
WHAT COULD
POSSIBLY HAPPEN?

KYLIE

"So, you and Seth, huh?"

These are the first words I hear as soon as I wake up on our second day in Rome. Tara is looking at me from the bathroom door, already showered and dressed, while I blink at her sleepily from my bed.

"Uh..." I have no idea if Seth is cool with people knowing about us, and I'm also still trying to wake up.

I'm usually the morning person. How on earth is she constantly waking up before me on this trip?

"I heard the two of you in the hall last night. Sounded like one hell of a goodnight kiss."

The memory of Seth pressing me up against the door for a very, very intense goodnight kiss flashes through my mind. I pull the blanket up over my head for a minute before peeking back out and find Tara grinning at me while she sits on the edge of the bed.

I push the blanket back. "Uh, fine. Yes, we may have started kissing last night."

Although Tara is clapping her hands and smiling, the smile

doesn't quite make it to her eyes. I've seen this look on her face a few times in recent years whenever I've hooked up with someone. I know that she's found it hard seeing me with guys while she has remained mostly single since high school. I just wish she had more confidence in herself and was willing to put herself out there.

"Lincoln mentioned he was pretty sure Seth was into you. Apparently, Seth isn't so great about going after what he wants and needs a push every now and again. It's why he pushed it last night."

"Oh yeah, we definitely got that. Neither of you were exactly subtle with your little engineered date last night." I sit up and look at her with an arched eyebrow.

She shrugs. "I don't think either of us were going for subtle. I wasn't sure how you'd be about it though, cause I know you'd said you weren't interested in a holiday fling. But I really like Seth. I think he's good for you."

It's my turn to shrug now. "We've just kissed a few times. I am still planning to keep my vow of celibacy, though. I mean, he's hot, and I enjoy spending time with him, but it can't really go anywhere after this trip."

Tara cocks her head a little while she regards me closely. "Oh, you really like him."

"Shut up." I can feel myself turn red.

She laughs. "You really, really like him."

"Ugh!" I fling myself back onto the pillow and pull the blanket over my head again, attempting to block out the sound of my best friend laughing.

She reaches over and pulls the blanket away from my face. "I think you should just enjoy your time with him and see what happens."

I shake my head. "What could happen? Aside from me letting myself fall for him and then we never see each other again after the trip ends?"

Tara smiles softly. "No one is saying you have to marry him,

Kylie. But he seems like a really nice guy. Lincoln says he's had a rough time of it the past few months, which sounds like someone else I know." She gives me a pointed look, and I roll my eyes. "I think you two could be good for each other. Have a little fun and then decide what you both want to do at the end of the trip."

I consider what she's saying, tossing it around in my mind while I get ready for another day of sightseeing. Seth and I had only seen a few places last night, spending most of our time talking and kissing rather than actively searching for any of the landmarks that Rome is well known for. He'd mentioned that Rome was his most anticipated stop of the trip, so I decide to make sure he gets to see as many places as possible and not distract him too much with my lips.

But I forget all about that as soon as I see him and Lincoln waiting for us in the hotel lobby. He's dressed casually in jeans and a t-shirt, but the man would look good in anything - or nothing - and my libido does all sorts of stupid things to my insides as soon as I lay eyes on him. He runs his eyes over me, starting from my white sneaker-clad feet and drifting up to take in my little yellow sundress, the same one I'd worn the night before. I have put even more effort into my appearance this morning, taking extra care with my makeup and leaving my hair out. It has the desired effect when he finally meets my gaze and my insides melt on the spot from the heat behind it.

Without thinking, as soon as I reach him, I rise onto my tiptoes and press a kiss to his lips. He freezes for a fraction of a second before wrapping his arms around me, kissing me back, his lips parting to deepen the kiss while I run my fingers through his hair.

"Uh, morning, Kylie." Lincoln lets out a little cough while Tara giggles from behind me.

"Morning, Lincoln," I reply, my lips still pressed to Seth's.

"Offftt, saying another man's name while your lips are pressed to his. That's harsh, Kylie."

Seth pulls back slightly and smirks at his friend. "I'm fine. I'm confident enough in my manhood not to be concerned about the fact that she said hi to you while wrapped around me." He gives me a wink, and I laugh, loving seeing this more confident version of Seth.

He reaches down and takes my hand in his, lacing our fingers together once again.

"So, where are we going?" Tara asks.

Lincoln raises an eyebrow at Seth. "This is your wheelhouse, brother. Where do you want to go?"

"Well, we saw the Trevi Fountain briefly last night before Kylie decided to pour a drink on someone's head, and then the Spanish Steps. Didn't really get to any other places, so maybe the Colosseum to start with?"

"I'm sorry, Kylie did what now?" Tara asks, her eyebrows raised high.

"Oh yeah. I forgot about that. I ran into Dick last night. Felt the need to pour Coke on his head," I say with a shrug and a grin.

Tara shakes her head. "Only you would think to do something like that. But I would have paid good money to see it. Are you going to tell Bri?"

"Probably not. She's happy now with Jake, and there wouldn't be any point. But it felt really good."

The guys listen to us chat about my vigilante moment with Brianna's dickhead ex while we head outside and begin making our way through the city towards the Colosseum. I find it difficult to concentrate with Seth running his thumb over the back of my hand lightly, our fingers still entwined.

We spend the rest of the day like this, and it just feels effortless with Seth. While he's still fairly quiet, he seems to have come out of his shell further, and he's more relaxed. Perhaps it's because he's been looking forward to this part of the trip, but a small part of me is hoping it's because of me.

• • •

I step out of the shower, relieved to have had a chance to wash all the sweat off after the day walking around in the heat. Even though I'm used to Australian summers, the heat in Rome is stifling, and our Canadian friends had begun to struggle by the time five o'clock rolled around. The tour had left both nights in Rome open for us to do our own thing for dinner, and Seth had shyly asked if he could take me out tonight after we'd both cleaned up.

Tara holds up a short black dress that I haven't had a chance to wear yet. "You should wear this one. You looked so hot in it at Morgan's hens party."

The dress sits at my mid-thighs and clings to every one of my curves, revealing most of my cleavage.

"I'm not sure this is the right setting for that dress. I was thinking of wearing just my jeans and a singlet. I'll save that dress for clubbing in Berlin. Seth will probably have gotten over me by then, so I'll need it to hook in a hot German guy."

I'd meant it to be a joke, but there is more than a little truth behind it. While yes, I've dated a lot, it's rarely gone past four or five dates. I'm a lot to take, I know that. When I was diagnosed with ADHD a few years ago, it helped me accept I would never be the quiet, demure, lady-like girl, like Bri and Tara, but now and then, I get struck with moments of self-doubt that anyone will ever be able to put up with me long term.

Tara pauses and purses her lips while raising an eyebrow. "I hate it when you say stuff like that."

"It's true. I'm a lot to take, I know that," I say.

She shakes her head. "No, you aren't a lot to take. The guys you have dated before were just fuck boys who wouldn't know how to put a woman first if their lives depended on it."

"And you think Seth is different?" I ask quietly.

Tara regards me closely for a moment before answering. "I think he's good for you. And I think you're good for him."

I start getting dressed, digging out my favourite pink singlet top from what's left of my clean clothes.

"What are you going to do tonight?" I ask Tara, who has moved to lie down on her bed with a book.

"I am going to have a much needed quiet night in. Lincoln was making noise about finding a club, but I'm leaving him to do that with some of the other girls."

"Are you sure you don't mind me going out?" I ask, torn between wanting to spend time with Seth and worrying about abandoning my best friend.

"Of course not. You know I need to have breaks from people every now and then, or I turn into a pumpkin. Go have fun. Live my holiday romance fantasy. Just make sure you fill me in on all the details."

We both look towards the door when we hear a knock, and I feel like my feet are glued to the floor. Butterflies suddenly appear in my stomach, and I turn to stare at Tara, my eyes wide. Last night had been great, but I hadn't been thinking of it as a date, not expecting to be kissed. And today, we'd had constant supervision. But now this all feels real, and I'm terrified.

Tara shakes her head and gets off her bed, crossing the room to open the door. Seth stands on the other side, looking hot as hell in jeans and a button-down shirt with the sleeves rolled up. He's also wearing his cap backwards again, and I am ready to melt into a puddle right there in the middle of our hotel room. Every time I see him, he gets hotter, something I truly hadn't thought possible.

"Hey," he says, his eyes roaming over me for a moment.

When his gaze meets mine, the heat from earlier returns, and I'm relieved to see that I seem to have the same effect on him that he has on me.

"Hi." I give him a small smile.

Tara sighs. "Okay, love birds, it's not like you haven't just spent all day together." She rolls her eyes.

Seth blushes a little. It's freaking adorable.

"Yeah, yeah." I poke my tongue out at her and grab my handbag off the bed. "Have a good night, T."

"You too." She blows me a kiss when I pass by and then closes the door behind me, leaving Seth and me alone in the hallway.

He slides his hands into his pockets, shuffling his feet a little, and I smile.

"Shall we go?" I ask, feeling the need to fill the awkward silence.

He clears his throat, his confidence from earlier today seeming to have disappeared a little. "Yeah. I made a reservation for us. We'll need to cab it there, though."

"Okay," I say, nodding.

He turns to walk towards the elevator, and I hesitate for a moment, wondering why things suddenly feel so weird. After a few steps, he turns to look back at me. He raises an eyebrow, then slowly reaches out a hand. I move to take it, and once he links our fingers together again, it's like I can breathe finally. He pulls me in closer and presses a soft, chaste kiss to my forehead. I've never had someone kiss me like that before, as though I was something precious and loved, and I melt into his arms for a moment, savouring the feel of his hard body against mine.

"Hi," he says, like we didn't just greet each other moments ago.

"Hi," I whisper, loving the feel of his hand rubbing up and down my back.

I step back after a few more heartbeats and allow him to lead me towards the elevator, the apprehension I felt earlier giving way to excitement at getting to spend the evening with his undivided attention.

8

I WAS JUST GOING
FOR IMPRESSIVE

SETH

I'D LOOKED up the best places to eat in Rome, wanting to find the perfect place to take Kylie. I have no idea why, but I feel a strong need to impress her, something I've never experienced with a woman before.

The cab drops us off out the front, and I can tell right away that I'd made the right choice when Kylie comments on how cute the place is, with its red and white checked tablecloths and intimate atmosphere.

A waiter greets us at the door, and I try out some of my basic Italian to let them know we have a reservation.

"*Salve, ho una prenotazione sotto* Seth James."

The waiter nods with a smile, grabs some menus, and leads us towards a table near the window, a sign with my name on it in the centre.

Once we're seated and he leaves to give us a few minutes, Kylie looks at me with a raised eyebrow. "I didn't know you could speak Italian?"

"Only very, very basic Italian. One of my buddies at work,

Dean, spent some time in Rome, and when I told him we were coming here, he taught Linc and me some of the phrases we might need. Linc has forgotten every word, of course, but I have a good memory for this sort of stuff," I say with a shrug, grinning at her.

"Well, I have no idea what you said, but it sounded sexy as hell."

"Wow, sexy, huh? I was just going for impressive." I reach forward to take one of the glasses of water that the waiter left for us.

She grins at me. "Seth, I highly doubt that is the first time someone has told you that you are sexy. There is no way you have made it this far in life without realising how hot you are."

I stupidly choose this moment to swallow, and now I'm choking while the water goes down the wrong hole. Once I've coughed my way out of sudden death, I take another mouthful while she laughs.

"Look, it may have been mentioned occasionally, but I don't really run around asking for attention." I choose not to mention the endorsement contracts I've had where my looks have definitely been why I got paid. It just comes with the professional athlete gig, and I hated every second of those photo shoots. "Besides, you're one to talk. You can't honestly tell me you aren't aware of how attractive you are?"

She squirms a little in her seat, but her little smile reveals how she feels about the compliment. "Honestly, my mother raised me to love myself. A few of our friends back home are absolutely stunning, like model-level stunning, but I've never been one to compare myself to others. I'm fit. I run, surf when I can, and am always up for a hike and stuff, but I also like food. I will never be a supermodel, but that wasn't my dream, anyway."

I've spent more than my fair share of time around supermodels; some are even married to my teammates. But I think this is the first time I have ever heard someone say they love themselves. And I can tell she means it. Her confidence is one of the things that drew me to her in the first place, and having her own her identity in front of me like this makes her even more attractive. If we weren't in the middle of a restaurant right now, I'd be kissing her.

Instead, I settle for reaching across the table and taking her hand. "You are honestly the most intriguing woman I have ever met."

She smiles at me again, and I can't ignore the little flutter happening in my chest right now. When Linc forced me on this trip, the last thing I'd expected was to meet a woman so captivating. It's such a shame she's from the other side of the world.

The waiter returns and takes our orders, pausing when Kylie reads from the menu to study her.

"You both have different accents. Where are you from?" he asks in a heavy Italian accent.

"He's Canadian, and I'm Australian," Kylie answers for us both, and his eyes light up.

"*Ah, bellissima canguro*! I have a sister in Australia, and I would love to visit very much."

"It is a beautiful country. You should definitely visit your sister sometime," Kylie replies with a smile.

"What was that you just said? *Bellissima canguro*? What does that mean?" I ask, curious about the look on his face while he continues to stare at Kylie.

"Oh." He blushes a little, confirming my suspicions that he was flirting with her. "It means beautiful kangaroo." He grins at Kylie.

She laughs. "I don't think I've ever been called that before. Thank you."

He stares at her for a few more beats, and I clear my throat, causing him to jump. He bustles off, and Kylie laughs again.

"That was strange," she says, and I raise an eyebrow.

"Yeah? Don't get called beautiful kangaroo all that much?" I ask, and she shakes her head.

"Ah, no, that was definitely a first. These Italian men really do like to flirt."

"That surprises me," I say, and she cocks her head to the side, running her eyes over me.

"What surprises you?"

"That you don't have men falling at your feet wherever you go."

She blinks at me for a moment. "Wow... That was smooth. You are full of surprises, Mr."

"So are you, *bellissima canguro.*"

She tips her head back and laughs, and I could happily spend forever making her laugh like that.

Once we finish dinner, we decide to explore the new neighbourhood rather than take a cab straight back to the hotel. We're in a quieter area now, away from all the well-known land-marks, and it's nice not to be surrounded by other tourists for a change.

Grabbing some gelato, we find a bench to sit on in a local park and people-watch while we continue talking.

"So, what's your plan for after the tour? Are you guys heading straight home or doing more travelling?" Kylie asks, taking a scoop of her mango gelato.

I watch, captivated, while she delicately puts the spoon in her mouth, marvelling that something so innocent could be so damn sexy.

"I think we're staying in London for a few days and then heading home. I left the planning up to Linc. But we have to be back at work in a few weeks." I've been avoiding thinking about going back.

The trip has so far had the desired effect that Linc, my coach and my therapist had hoped for. I haven't been thinking quite so much about the pressure from the fans and the press about the end of last season. And I know a large part of that has been because of the very distracting woman sitting next to me.

"We're in London for four nights before we head home. I'd wanted to explore Scotland or Ireland, but Tara needs to get back to work. I quit my job before we came, so I guess I'll have to work out what I want to do once we get back." She says it casually, but when she stares down at her cup of gelato, I wonder if maybe she's not as carefree as she tries to appear.

"Do you have something you enjoy doing that you could find a job in?" I ask, and she shrugs.

"Nothing that I feel particularly passionate about. I can help Will out a little with his accounts stuff for a while cause he's just started his own electrician business. But I don't see myself staying in that line of work for long. I get bored in an office, but things like retail and working in the food industry also don't appeal either." She takes another mouthful of gelato before looking over at me. "What about you? Did you always know you wanted to be a physiotherapist?"

I freeze for a moment. So far, I've managed not to outright lie to anyone about what I do for work, just letting everyone think I work behind-the-scenes without going into any detail. But I'm not ready to tell Kylie that I'm the captain of my team and one of the highest-paid players in the NHL. The anonymity that I've had on this trip has been refreshing, and although I'm sure she won't care, I just can't do it.

"I've been active my whole life, so I knew I wanted to continue working with athletes as a career. Studying sports medicine was an obvious choice for me." There. Not quite a lie.

I still feel guilty, though. But not guilty enough to lay all my truths bare.

Kylie sighs. "I envy that. Must be nice to have something you enjoy so much."

Do I still enjoy playing hockey? Until this last season, I would have confidently said yes when asked that question. Now... I'm not so sure. My life has always revolved around the game, almost a little too much, but after the stress of the past few months and dealing with the expectations from the team and the fans, I'm just happy to have time away.

I shrug while the thoughts roll around in my head, deciding to change the subject to something less fraught. "So, you mentioned you surf?"

"Yeah, with my brother Will. We don't live super close to the beach like when we were kids, but we try to go at least once a month. I love it." Her smile transforms her entire face while she speaks animatedly with her hands. "There is just something so peaceful when I'm on the water. The rocking motions of the waves, the beauty of the beach first thing in the morning. And sometimes there are dolphins... It's just my happy place."

"I'm sure people have asked you this a thousand times, but don't you worry about sharks?" I ask, reaching into my limited knowledge about Australia.

She smirks. "You know, you're actually the only person on the tour who hasn't asked me about the scary Australian wildlife. Yeah, I've seen sharks, but I just let them do their thing. Most of our wildlife just want to be left alone. But you guys have got bears and mountain lions and shit!"

"I can promise you, I have yet to see a bear or mountain lion. So you're living far more on the edge than me."

She tilts her head to the side as she regards me. "I guess you're not big on taking risks, huh?"

I think for a moment before answering. My job itself is a risk every time I step onto the ice, but outside of hockey, I guess she's right. I've never taken many risks.

"Well, it's not like I jump out of planes or anything like that regularly. Or rub shoulders with sharks... But I've never really been in a position where I've had to."

"Do you think you would jump out of a plane if you were

given the option?" she asks, sounding far more interested than I was expecting.

"Um... I'm not sure," I reply, eyeing her with caution.

There's a gleam in her eye that I'm suddenly a little scared of. "Well, we could do it together in Austria. Tara won't do it, but I kind of want to. It could be fun to do together." She looks so excited, and my heart races a little.

I'd noticed there were options for several activities in Austria, but I hadn't thought about actually taking part in any of them. But now I have this beautiful, carefree woman asking me to step outside my comfort zone with her.

So, against everything I ever thought about myself, I'm stunned when the words "sure, why not" come out of my mouth.

What on earth am I getting myself into with this woman? I have no idea, but I'm a little excited to find out.

We catch a cab back to our hotel, and even though we have an early start tomorrow to drive to Venice, I'm still not ready to say goodbye to Kylie. We've chatted about everything and nothing for hours, and I can't recall the last time I talked this much.

Hand in hand, I walk her to her door, aware that Tara is likely waiting for her inside. That doesn't stop me from pressing her back against the door, bringing my lips to hers in what starts out as a chaste kiss. But when she fists my shirt and pulls me closer, deepening the kiss, I soon become lost in the sensation of her lips against mine, and her hand tightens on my shirt. I slide my hands down her sides and grip her hips, swiping my tongue across her lips softly, and she opens her mouth to me with a moan. She releases my shirt and slides her hand up, coiling her fingers in the hair at the back of my neck.

"Ack, get a room. No one wants to see that."

We break apart to see one of the other Australian girls glaring at us from the end of the hall when she steps out of the elevator. I can feel myself blush, but Kylie just laughs.

"Nice, Georgia. Jealousy looks great on you," Kylie replies with a grin, and Georgia stomps off towards her room.

Once Georgia is gone, Kylie turns to look back at me. "She has been eye-fucking you every chance she gets and has made it more than clear that she can't understand why you're interested in me."

This is all complete news to me, and I frown down at her. "That's ridiculous."

Kylie shrugs. "I don't care. Girls like that are just bitter. It's their problem, not mine."

"Well, good, because I am very, very interested in you. I actually didn't even know her name," I admit, and she laughs again while pulling me closer.

"Funny, I'm very, very interested in you, too." She presses her lips back to mine.

We pick right back up where we left off after our rude interruption, and within minutes, I'm breathless. She's pressed right up against my chest, and her hands slide up my back, making their way up under my shirt. I glide my palms along the top of her jeans, my fingers caressing the soft skin peeking out from where her top has ridden up, and she gasps against my mouth, shivering a little.

"We probably need to either go somewhere a bit more private or call it a night. Because this is fast moving away from a PG rating," I say, and she groans a little before pulling away.

"As much as I really want to take the first option, I promised myself that I wouldn't jump straight into bed with anyone on this trip," she says, looking up at me.

She seems nervous, so I nod and kiss her forehead. She closes her eyes, lets out a little sigh, and leans into me a little more.

"Good night, *bellissima canguro*," I whisper in her ear, and I feel her shake with silent laughter.

"I see I have a new nickname?" she asks, tipping her head back to look up at me.

"Ha ha, no. I just like calling you *bellissima*. Because you're the most beautiful woman I've ever seen."

She holds my gaze for the longest time, her eyes shining. "Good night, Seth," she whispers, stretching up onto her tip toes to kiss me softly on the cheek before pushing down on the door handle behind her and backing into the room.

She blows me a kiss, and I touch my fingers to my lips with a smile.

Once the door is closed, I stay where I am for a moment, just processing everything. This woman has consumed my brain for the past twenty-four hours, and I'm beginning to realise I'm fast becoming addicted to making her smile.

9
FREAKING OUT

KYLIE

I've decided that Venice is overrated and expensive.

While I could admit it was beautiful, after spending the entire day yesterday wandering through the floating city with Tara, Lincoln and Seth, I'd begun to wonder if I was over travelling or if the city just didn't do it for me.

But now that we've left and I'm once again watching the Italian countryside whiz by out the window of the bus, I know I'm done with travelling after all.

Something I've learned on this trip is that being super tall on a tour like this, where there are many hours spent in a cramped bus seat, can be very uncomfortable. Seth has managed to fold himself into the seat next to me, stretching his left leg out into the aisle again. I've turned myself so that my legs are draped over his so that he can have more leg room, but I can tell he's ready to be off the bus.

Not that he'd ever complain. Even though he has opened up with me, he is still fairly quiet with everyone else other than Tara and Lincoln. But I can see the pain cross his features occasionally while he rests his head against the top of the seat, so I have made it my mission to distract him from his discomfort.

"Are you looking forward to jumping out of a plane this afternoon?" I ask, and he rolls his head to the side to look at me with one eyebrow raised.

"Um... I don't know that I'm looking forward to it... More like looking forward to being back on the ground."

I look down at our entwined fingers and squeeze gently. "If you don't want to do it, please don't feel you have to. I don't want you to feel pressured into it."

He squeezes back. "Thank you. But when I decide I'm doing something, I always follow through. That being said, I will most likely be freaking out the whole time."

I grin. "Oh, I'll be freaking out too. But what better way to remind ourselves we're alive than jumping out of a perfectly good plane, right?"

Lincoln pops his head up over the seat in front of us, his smile wide. "I cannot wait for this. I've always wanted to skydive but never got around to it. I still can't believe you convinced Seth to do it, though." He looks pointedly at his friend, who shrugs.

"What can I say? I wasn't in my right mind. There was gelato and a beautiful woman involved."

I laugh. "You know, for someone who doesn't talk much, you can be pretty smooth."

"I taught him everything he knows," Lincoln says, and it's Seth's turn to laugh.

"Whatever. I've watched you flirt, and you are nowhere near as smooth as you think you are."

I lean back into my seat and watch them banter good-naturedly while Seth absently rubs his thumb back and forth on the back of my hand. It has amazed me how easily both men have slipped into mine and Tara's lives. We've known them just over a week, yet it feels like we've been friends for years. While we haven't really spent time with many others on the tour, it has apparently become expected that we will all be together. I guess it's normal on a trip like this for strong relationships to form in a short time, as we're all in each other's spaces, and it gives the illusion of closeness.

While Seth is still oblivious, I have noticed Georgia glaring at me a few times since she caught us making out in the hallway, something that has amused me to no end. But it's also made me wary about showing too much affection in front of the group, and we have had no other solo moments since that night. That hasn't stopped my libido from getting ahead of itself, though, and with the way Seth has been running his hand up and down my leg for the past hour, I've been forcing myself to think of anything else.

"Alright, guys, listen up!" We all look towards the front of the bus, where our tour leader, Brendan, is standing in the aisle, clipboard in hand. "Okay, so we're about ten minutes out, and those of you who have signed up for any activities need to be out the door first and straight to the different locations. Skydivers, you'll be stepping off this bus and onto the minibus that is waiting for you outside our accommodation." Seth's grip on my hand tightens. "Canyon jumpers, your tour starts in an hour, so you've got a bit of free time, and mountain bikers, you will start in the town, and I'll walk you over there once we get off the bus. Everyone else, you're free to explore the town for the afternoon."

Brendan sits back down, and Lincoln turns to Tara beside him. "So Tara, which is it for you, skydiving, canyon jumping or mountain biking?"

Tara snorts. "None of the above, thank you very much. I will be organising laundry and chilling out."

"Thank you for that, by the way. I promise I will try and keep my suitcase neater once we have clean clothes again," I say, and Tara shakes her head with a sigh.

She knows me well enough to know that, despite my best intentions, my mess will be spread far and wide within a day.

Lincoln screws his nose up. "That sounds far too boring. Can you at least go and explore the town? Do it for me, please?"

I'm distracted from their banter when Seth's leg begins bouncing beneath my thighs. I look over and notice he's paled a little. If this is what he's like now, I have no idea how he'll be in about forty minutes when we're thousands of feet in the air.

Seth has barely said a word since we left the bus, his grip on my hand growing tighter and tighter through the briefing at the tiny airport. He'd only really let my hand go for the time it took to put our jumpsuits on. Lincoln, on the other hand, has been excitedly bouncing around, and the contrast between their two personalities has never been more apparent to me.

Now we're up in the air with our tandem guides strapped to our backs, and my own nerves have finally kicked in. Seth is across from me, looking very awkward while essentially sitting in the lap of the man attached to him. His lips are drawn together in a straight line, and he's lost all the colour in his face while he stares out the window beside me. Not for the first time, I feel guilty for talking him into this when he is clearly terrified, but Lincoln keeps saying how proud he is that Seth is here, so I'm able to push past the guilt.

I kick his foot lightly with my own, and he slides his gaze from the window to mine.

"Are you okay?" I ask, and he nods briefly, attempting to smile at me.

Even terrified and grimacing, he is still the most handsome man I've ever laid eyes on, and I wish I could hug him right now.

"We're ready!" my guide, Greta, yells in my ear.

We'd decided I'd go first, seeing as it was my 'insane' idea - Tara's words, although I'm pretty sure Seth agreed with her.

One of the assistants slides the door open, and Seth's eyes widen before his gaze flicks back to mine.

"You got this, Kylie," Lincoln screams over the roar of the wind, and Greta and I shuffle forward.

I peer at the ground way, way, way down below while Greta braces her hands on either side of the door, and I feel my fear spike.

Why am I doing this? Am I crazy? Oh my god, I've talked this poor, beautiful man into this, and now I'm about to die.

"See you on the ground!" Seth yells, and I flick my gaze over to where he's watching me closely, a nervous smile flitting across his lips.

With that little boost, Greta pushes off, and we begin free-falling through the air.

10
DID I BREAK YOU?

SETH

When Kylie and Greta disappear through the open door, my heart feels like it's about to jump out of my throat. She'd managed to keep her composure right up until the seconds before Greta propelled them forward, her face dropping when she stared down at the ground, and I'd felt the need to boost her back up.

But now that she's gone, I'm pretty sure I'm about to wet myself. I have never been that concerned about heights in the past, but this is something else.

Why the hell did I let Kylie talk me into this?

"We're up!" my guide, an American called Stefan, yells in my ear, and I have to fight the urge to vomit while he shuffles us towards the open door.

Linc flashes me a thumbs up, looking far too calm for someone who is moments away from plunging towards certain death.

I feel like my legs are made of lead, and I'm trying with all my might not to show just how terrified I am. I have experienced adrenaline surges multiple times in my life, but nothing like this, and I'm pretty sure I'm going to crash big time once my feet are back on solid ground.

If I survive.

Stefan braces his hands on either side of the door, and everything inside of me screams to push him backwards. Before I can do anything further, he's propelled us forward, and we are free-falling towards the Austrian countryside beneath us.

"Are your eyes open?" Stefan's voice echoes in my ear, and I nod my head vigorously, hesitant to open my mouth in case I scream too loudly.

I'm tempted to close my eyes, but the longer we are falling, I forget what I'm doing and am looking around at the view. I can see Kylie's parachute far below, and I wonder how she's feeling right now.

After what could have been hours but is most likely seconds, Stefan warns me to prepare myself and pulls the cord. When the parachute unfurls, we are jolted upwards, and I'm relieved to finally be free of the dropping sensation in my stomach.

A sense of calm washes over me, and I start to understand why people become addicted to this feeling. The Austrian Alps are all around us, and I can see various little towns dotted around.

"You doing okay?" Stefan asks, and I give him the thumbs up, unsure how to put into words the emotions that are running through me right now.

Seeing the world from above like this is a stark reminder of how insignificant our individual lives are. For every little town I can see, that's thousands of people going about their everyday lives, each person dealing with their own issues. It gives me a perspective that I've never considered before, and the last of the stress that I'd been holding onto for the last few months begins to dissolve inside of me.

By the time we touch down in the large open field, I feel both energised and utterly drained. Once Stefan finally unhitches himself from my back, my hands are shaking with the adrenaline, and I need to sit down for a few minutes to regain my composure.

"Are you good?" he asks, and I nod, giving him another thumbs-up. "Good, because your girl is on her way."

I look up and see Kylie racing towards me through the long grass.

"Oh my god!" She launches herself at me, and I fall backwards with my arms wrapped around her waist. "That was fucking incredible! Wasn't it amazing? Are you okay? Did you enjoy it? Did I break you?"

"It was amazing," I reply, finally able to speak through her excited onslaught of questions, and laugh when she peppers my face with kisses.

"I am so glad you did this with me!"

"Me too. I'm not sure I'll be able to walk anytime soon, but that was the most surreal feeling."

We eventually get to our feet, but Kylie is still so hopped up on adrenaline that as soon as I'm upright, she launches herself at me again, and I catch her, laughing when she wraps her legs around my waist.

"Hi," she says before pressing her lips to mine, and I kiss her back hungrily, all the emotions racing through me while she grips me tightly with her thighs.

"Hi," I finally reply, feeling breathless once she pulls away to grin down at me.

"I'm pretty sure I'm going to be buzzing for days." She loosens her hold on me, and I grip her waist while she slides down and her feet hit the ground again.

"Oh my god, that was the most amazing thing I've ever done, and by the way, that PDA was intense." Linc appears at my side, a grin stretched wide across his face.

"Whatever, you love it," Kylie responds, wrapping her arms around my waist.

I slide my arms around her, holding her close for a moment, while my best friend watches us both with a sparkle in his eye.

"I do, actually. It's good to see you both happy."

We make our way towards the bus waiting to take us back to the accommodation, and I wonder when the high will wear off. The feeling reminds me of the intense adrenaline and excitement that surged through me when I skated onto the rink for the final game. I realise now that I'd become so wrapped up in everything that had happened since that I'd forgotten the joy in all the negativity that followed.

When we climb onto the bus, I vow to myself to keep striving for that feeling from now on and not to let the negativity get to me anymore. I have so much to be grateful for, and having this insane, beautiful and fun-loving woman crash into my life is number one on that list.

Early the next morning, Linc and I head downstairs and meet Kylie in the empty lobby. Except for the days in Rome, where the temperature was too hot, we've been up before the rest of the group, and the three of us have become running buddies every day. We've enjoyed running through new locations each time, and I've been impressed with how well Kylie has kept up with Linc and me.

We're all still on a high after yesterday's exploits, and Kylie hasn't stopped smiling. Neither have I, for that matter.

"We should try to convince Tara to join us one morning," Linc says while we warm up at a leisurely pace.

"Ha, that will never happen. Tara actively avoids exercise," Kylie responds, while I slow to match her strides.

"She just hasn't found an exercise that she likes. We'll have to work on that. Besides, this has been the best way to explore each new city. Watching the locals go about their business, the crisp feeling in the early morning air... What more could you ask for?"

"According to Tara, sleep. Sleep is what more you could ask

for." Kylie shrugs. "I only got into running a few months ago, but I've always been the morning person between the two of us. Probably from growing up surfing, but Tara prefers to read a book in bed if she has time. I've given up on trying to convince her that exercise can actually be fun. She says the only time she will run is if someone is chasing her."

"Come on you two, less chatting. Race you to the bridge," I interject, pointing to the bridge a few hundred metres ahead of us.

It's only a small one over a stream that's more of a trickle, but the setting is breathtaking. Another reminder of how beautiful these small European towns are.

Kylie grins at me. "Oh, you're on." She takes off, sprinting ahead of us.

"Seriously, Seth. Marry that girl," Linc says quietly before running after her.

I shake my head before lengthening my strides. I could easily outrun her, but I can see how proud she is to have taken the lead, and I love that she's so competitive. She makes it to the bridge first and does a little dance in the middle of the bridge, raising her hands in the air in victory.

I race towards her, catching her around the middle and swinging her around. She shrieks, clinging to my neck before laughing. It's the most beautiful sound I've ever heard. Her enthusiasm for life is infectious, and I realise that I could easily get addicted to the feeling of being with her. If only she didn't live half a world away.

11

YOU SCRUB UP PRETTY GOOD

KYLIE

THREE DAYS LATER, I'm still on a high from the skydive.

We only spent one night in Austria before hitting up Prague, and now we're in Berlin. The whole time, I've been on cloud nine. Between our daring act and the time spent with Seth, I can't remember when I last felt so content. Who knew just how much I would enjoy travelling?

Seth seems to have undergone some sort of change as well. I've noticed a lightness in his demeanour that wasn't there in the days before he threw himself from a plane. He's been quicker to laugh, and the banter between him and Lincoln has increased.

"I can't believe we get to go clubbing in Berlin. This is going to be huge." I'm rummaging through my suitcase, looking for the dress Tara had told me to wear in Rome, but I look up when she doesn't reply.

She's staring at her phone, chewing on her thumbnail, which she only does when she's anxious.

"You okay?" I give up on my search and move to her side.

She looks up at me quickly and drops her phone into her lap. I raise an eyebrow, unsure whether to be concerned about her weirdness.

"Yeah. I'm okay. I think I'm going to give clubbing a miss, though," she says, and I place my hands on my hips.

"Why?"

"I just don't feel like partying all that much. And I think I'm getting a cold."

I stare at her for a few seconds. "What's going on with you? You've been avoiding all the fun stuff for days."

"Just because I didn't want to jump out of a plane?" She gives me a defensive look, and I have no idea what is going on.

"No, I don't mean that. I knew that was never your thing. But you've been avoiding a lot of the fun group stuff. That's not like you. You've been looking forward to this trip, and now I'm worried you'll regret everything you have been avoiding."

She doesn't respond right away, and I don't know if we're in a fight or she's just being weird. We've been friends for ten years and had our share of disagreements, but she's usually pretty open with me about her feelings.

"I just haven't felt like going out. I was never a huge partier, you know that," she finally replies, and I watch her closely for a few moments.

"Okay... Why don't you just come to the first club at least? If you hate it, we can bring you back here and meet everyone else afterwards. I think, once we're out, you'll have a great time."

She sighs and drops her hands to her sides. "Fine."

"Yay!" I clap my hands together and return to searching for the dress, giving an excited cheer when I finally find it amongst the clothes buried in the bottom of my bag.

I'd lasted precisely one day before my suitcase was out of control again. I really do need to learn to be more organised, but it's never been my strongest quality. At least it's all mostly clean now, thanks to Tara arranging to do our laundry in Austria.

Tara slowly gets herself ready, and once we're both done, I

insist on snapping a selfie to share with Bri back home. I also send a copy to Will with yet another reminder to get over himself and start spending time with Tara again, but know he'll maintain his radio silence on the topic.

"Holy crap, you ladies look amazing!" Lincoln looks us both over appreciatively, and my gaze meets Seth's, who is staring at me with wide eyes.

I'm glad I left the dress for this occasion because it's the type of dress that needs a reason to be shown off. The way Seth is looking at me right now makes me feel like the most beautiful woman in the world. I stop before him, and he pulls me close, wrapping his arms around my waist.

"You look incredible," he says quietly, bending to kiss me softly.

"Aw, thank you. You scrub up pretty good, too," I reply, leaning back a little to appreciate how hot he looks.

He's rolled the sleeves up to his elbows on a button-down shirt again, and I wonder if he's aware that this amps his sexiness up even further. Judging by our past interactions, he is completely oblivious, but that doesn't stop the butterflies from going crazy in my stomach.

"You both look hot as hell," Lincoln pipes up beside me.

Seth shakes his head. "Thanks, Buddy."

Lincoln looks at us both, eyebrows raised. "Is that all?"

I grin at him, Seth's arms still wrapped around me. "You look very handsome, too, Lincoln."

He pops his hip out and places his hand on it, striking a pose. "Oh, why thank you."

"Alright, everyone, time to get on the bus!" Brendan claps his hands, and everyone standing around in the lobby makes their way outside.

· · ·

After a short bus ride through the busy Berlin streets, we pull up in front of the first club and pile out, milling around while we wait for further instructions. As much as I've enjoyed the trip, I'm looking forward to not having to follow people around constantly.

"So, we have a special VIP area roped off inside, and you each get two drinks - just present this card at the bar." Brendan hands each of us a card, and we head inside.

The techno music pumping loudly through the speakers is not my usual choice of music, and I'm pretty sure Tara is going to bail at the first opportunity. I'm grateful when Lincoln grabs her hand and immediately drags her out onto the dance floor. While their friendship seems to be purely platonic, they have become close, which is great to see. Her self-confidence has taken a huge hit over the years, and add in Will's ghosting her, and it's no wonder she's become so withdrawn lately. But Lincoln has definitely been helping her come out of her shell a little more.

"Dance?" Seth says loudly over the music, and I nod.

"Well, we can try. Not my favourite type to dance to," I reply while he leads me out to the dance floor.

"I'm sure we can make it work." He turns to face me, pulling me close to place his hands on my lower back, and I reach up to loop my hands loosely around his neck.

Somehow, I manage to find a rhythm, and Seth follows along, the same as the night in Paris. But there is so much more between us now, and it's not long before we're making out in the middle of the dance floor.

"I think I'm addicted to kissing you," I say, coming up for air and pressing my forehead against his.

"The feeling is definitely mutual." He gently rubs his nose against mine and kisses me softly.

I rise up onto my tiptoes and deepen the kiss again, pressing my chest against his. He moans, his grip on my waist tightening, our bodies touching in every place possible.

"Oi! Get a room!" Josh, another Australian on the trip, sidles up beside us and claps a hand on both our shoulders.

We pull apart, and I shoot Josh a disgusted look, but he just grins and wanders off to rejoin Georgia, who is glaring at me once again, and her little group of friends in the VIP area.

"Ugh, that woman is a pain in the ass," I say with a shake of my head, turning back to look at Seth.

"I don't understand what her problem is."

"Jealousy. I overheard her saying she couldn't understand why both you and Lincoln were so interested in people as boring as Tara and me. Which I think is hilarious, because I'm amazing." I grin, and Seth laughs. "She's just delusional though, because you've literally never even spoken to her. For all she knows, you're the boring one," I say, poking out my tongue.

"Must just be my good looks," he says with a wink, and I laugh, tipping my head back and feeling my hair brush against the skin that is exposed on my lower back.

He places a hand on my cheek, bringing my eyes back to his. "God, you're gorgeous."

"Right back at ya," I reply, biting my lip while my gaze drops to his mouth.

His eyes darken, and he surges forward, kissing me again. We pick right up where we left off, winding ourselves around each other, hands weaving their way through hair while we lose ourselves to the sensations running through our bodies.

After awhile, Seth pulls back, catching his breath while he strokes my cheek. "We should probably pump the brakes on this."

I eye him closely momentarily before nodding. "You're right, sorry."

"Hey, no." He bends his knees slightly to bring himself to my height and slides his hand along my jaw. "You have nothing to be sorry for. I completely respect your boundaries. I just don't want it to go further than what you're comfortable with."

How is this man even real?

I'm almost ready to give up on the whole tour celibacy thing and throw caution to the wind, but something is still holding me back.

I take his hand and lead him outside to get some distance from the deafening music. Once we're away from all other people, I turn to face him, keeping a hold on his hand.

"I really, really like you, Seth. And I would normally be jumping straight into bed with you. But I think it's because I like you so much that I'm holding back. We're from different sides of the world, and I'd hate to become even more attached to you than I already am when there's no future here."

He reaches to stroke my cheek again, a small smile on his face. "I respect that. I feel the same way. I don't want you to feel pressured in any way. I'm happy to stick with kissing. We've only got a few more days left on the tour, so let's just enjoy each other's company, okay?"

I squeeze his hand. "Thank you."

He pulls me into his arms and rests his cheek on the top of my head when I sink into the embrace. "Of course. I'm gonna miss you, though."

"I'm gonna miss you too, Seth."

12

IT WAS HALF A BROWNIE

When the bus arrives at our hotel in Amsterdam, it hits me that we only have two more nights left on the tour before it ends in London.

When Linc convinced me to come along, I never imagined that the time away would have such a positive impact on me. The break from routine at home has been just what I'd needed to find my old self again, and I know that it was all due to Kylie. This Australian woman who is so full of life has a hold over me, unlike any other woman I've met before. The idea of it all being over in a few short days unsettles me in a way I didn't expect. But I'm so grateful to have met her.

"We need to be back on the bus in an hour to head to the Red-Light District, so be quick, everyone." Brendan gives his orders, and we all file off the bus, grabbing our bags from underneath and heading inside to get checked in once again.

"I am going to be so happy to see the back of this suitcase, I swear," Kylie grumbles while she drags her overstuffed suitcase behind her.

I reach over and take the handle from her wordlessly, wheeling both our bags behind me while she gives me a grateful smile.

"So, are we really going to watch a sex show?" Tara asks, looking less than enthused at the prospect.

"It's not really my idea of a good time, to be honest," I reply, looking over at Linc, who shrugs.

"No? None of you are voyeurs? I'm shocked," Kylie says drily, and I look at her with a raised eyebrow.

"Why? Are you into that?"

"Fuck, no!" She shakes her head quickly, and I laugh.

"OK, so what's the plan then? Do we bail again?" Linc pipes up.

"Yeah, although we should at least see the Red-Light District, I guess," Tara says with a shrug.

"Of all the people I thought would want to check out women selling their wares in windows, you were at the very bottom of that list, Tara," Linc says.

Tara smacks his shoulder. "I'm not, asshole! But we're in Amsterdam, might as well check it out."

"Does that mean you're also keen to check out a cafe?" Kylie asks, and Tara pauses, considering her best friend for a moment.

"I mean... sure, why not?"

"Really?" Kylie stares at Tara with wide eyes.

"Might as well give it a go. It's not illegal here, after all."

The girls stare at each other in tense silence while Linc and I look from one to the other.

"Um... so are we going to get ourselves some hookers and blow?" Linc asks, breaking the tension when we all laugh.

"Let's just go for a walk and see where the night takes us, hey?" I ask, slinging my arm over Kylie's shoulder.

"Sounds like a great plan."

We get checked in and head up to our respective rooms.

"Should I have offered to share a room with Tara?" Linc asks once we're in our room.

I shake my head. "Nope. Kylie and I aren't going there."

"What do you mean you're not going there? I assumed you guys had already?" He pauses in the process of pulling his toiletries bag out of his suitcase and stares at me.

"No. We both decided we like each other too much for that."

"Okay, that's the dumbest thing I've ever heard." He shakes his head.

I shrug. "It wouldn't just be a hook-up, and we aren't able to have a future together."

"Yeah, but you guys are clearly into each other. From the sessions I've been forced to witness, I'm pretty sure the sex would be off the charts."

"Exactly. Why go there when we can't have anything more?"

He grabs his clothes and gives me a look on the way to the bathroom. "I still think this is dumb. You guys are thinking about this all too much."

Once he's in the bathroom, I flop back on my bed and stare at the ceiling.

He's likely right, but even without Kylie pumping the brakes on anything further happening, I know that it would be even harder to say goodbye to her if we spent a night together. The last thing I need is to fall any harder for her and have it as a distraction for when I go back to work in a few weeks. My head is finally in a good place, and I feel like I'm ready to get back on the ice. I need to focus on the team again and, once we're back, put this trip behind us.

Just wish it was that simple, because I know it's going to be incredibly hard to forget about the bubbly woman who lives half a world away.

It turns out that stoned Tara is hilarious.

Linc guides her along the cobbled street ahead of Kylie and me, laughing at her antics while she weaves all over the place. The pot had hit her in the taxi, so we asked the driver to drop us off a few streets away, hoping the walk might help.

"Has she ever had pot before?" I ask Kylie while we watch Tara giggle at nothing.

"Not that I'm aware of. It's still not legal in Australia outside of medical use, and Tara has never been one to break the law."

"It was half a brownie. I've never seen it hit someone like that before."

"I'm surprised you guys didn't have any. You know, being Canadian and all."

"What makes you think all Canadians are potheads?" I ask, pulling her close to my side.

"My father. Of all the Canadian things he rejected, he definitely embraced the pot. It drove Mum mad over the years, but he's a surfer as well, so it's just ingrained in him now." She shrugs, appearing unbothered.

"Have you ever tried it?"

"A few times when I was a teenager, but I didn't really like it. How about you?" She looks up at me, no judgement showing anywhere in her eyes.

"Same as you. And I can't do it with work, anyway."

"Oh yeah. I doubt anyone wants their physio to be stoned."

I know I need to tell her the truth about my job, but then, we're never going to see each other again, so what's the point at this stage?

I'm saved from yet another deflection when Tara stumbles and Linc catches her before she can hit the ground.

"We definitely need to get her home," Kylie says, moving towards her friend and taking her other arm.

I follow the three of them, my mind elsewhere, while we make our way back to the hotel.

The following morning, Kylie meets us alone in the lobby.

"No Tara?" Linc asks, and Kylie shakes her head while she slips her arms around my waist.

"No, she's a bit under the weather this morning. I told her I'd come back and check on her at lunch."

"I guess we better save the Anne Frank Museum until this afternoon. She was looking forward to that," Linc replies and Kylie nods.

"Sounds good. Anything you guys want to check out? I know nothing about Amsterdam."

"Neither do we. But if we check out those flyers over there, I'm sure we can work out some things to do." I point over to the front desk, where the usual tourist information stand is set up with a thousand flyers.

We wander over and begin checking out the different things to do and soon come up with a plan - a canal boat ride, the Heineken Museum, and, just for fun, the Museum of Sex.

Several hours later, after Kylie emerges from the Museum of Sex gift shop with a few bags and a grin on her face, we start the walk back to the hotel to get Tara.

"What are you smiling about?" I ask, noting the gleam in her eye.

"Oh, I just found some hilarious souvenirs in there that I can't wait to give Tara." She pulls out a t-shirt and holds it up against her body.

I squint a little as I try to read the different fonts. "I got gay married at the Museum of Sex, and all I got was this lousy T-shirt and a very messy divorce," I read out loud with a laugh. "Nice."

"Right? And I got her a packet of penis straws."

"Of course, cause that's something everyone needs," Linc replies, his expression serious.

"Correct. Now, hopefully, she is functioning enough to leave the hotel room."

Once we arrive back at the hotel, Linc and I wait down in the lobby again while she goes to collect Tara.

"Bud, are you sure you don't want the room for you and Kylie tonight?" Linc asks again once Kylie is out of earshot.

"I promise, I don't need the room. We talked about this already."

"I know, but I still think you guys need to give in to your lust and have a magical night together. It's the last night, after all."

"Do you need to get laid? Is that what this is about?" I ask, raising an eyebrow.

"I have indeed sowed my wild oats on this trip, so this is entirely about your needs, not mine."

"Sowed your wild oats? With who?" As far as I knew, he hadn't been with anyone on the trip.

"On my night out in Rome, I may have met a stunning Italian woman who helped me blow out the cobwebs, with the help of her very attractive boyfriend," he replies with a shrug, and I shake my head.

Only Linc could be so casual about a threesome with a hot Italian couple.

"Of course you did. Well, I'm very happy for you, but I don't need the room. Kylie and I are fine as we are."

Thankfully, I'm spared his reply by the return of Kylie, this time with Tara in tow.

"Hey Sunshine, looking a bit pale there," Linc says with a grin.

Tara shoots him a dark look. "Not a word."

Linc pretends to zip his lips, and Kylie giggles.

"Shall we go check out the Anne Frank Museum now?" I ask, jumping in before the conversation can escalate.

"We indeed shall, thank you, Seth." Tara nods in my direction.

I salute her. "Happy to help. Lead the way."

And I once again follow the three of them, trying not to think about Linc's pointed words.

. . .

That night, after the last group dinner, we head off in search of one last club. By tomorrow night, these two women will no longer be our partners in crime, and we are days away from returning to our normal lives.

I'm not sure I'm ready for reality.

"You okay?" Kylie asks, bumping my shoulder while I stare at the empty glass in my hand.

I put the glass down on the table and slide my arm around her shoulder, pulling her in close. "Yeah, just feeling nostalgic, I guess."

"Already? We still have all day tomorrow together, on a bus, then a boat, then another bus. Plenty of time to snuggle," she says with a smile, cuddling into my side and looking up at me while she places a hand over my heart.

"You're right." I lean down to kiss her tenderly. "Let's make sure we have plenty of snuggles."

13
NEVER A GOOD WAY
TO START A SENTENCE

KYLIE

LAST NIGHT, I'd said a tearful goodbye to Seth and Lincoln, unable to believe that our time together was over. When we'd embarked on this trip, I'd not expected to form such strong ties to anyone new, let alone fall in deep lust with someone. It absolutely is not love. It's not possible to fall in love with someone I've only known for three weeks and now will almost certainly never see again... Right?

"Ready to go?" Tara asks, coming out of the bathroom.

We'd only booked the hotel where the tour ended for one night, moving to a more affordable one where, at long last, we'll each have our own rooms. It's a welcome change after three weeks of sharing a room non-stop.

Of course, once again, I find myself perched atop my suitcase, struggling to zip it shut. "Yep, just gotta get this closed."

"Shame Seth isn't here to help you yet again," she replies, crouching down to help me.

Together, we manage to get it closed and I stand up, stretching my back.

"How are you handling it all this morning? You seemed pretty cut up last night." Tara bends to grab the handle of her own suitcase, and together, we head out into the hall.

"It sucks, but I guess it was never going to go anywhere. How could it, right?" I try to sound unbothered, but inside, my heart feels a little sore.

"Right... Still, though, he was good for you."

"Yeah," I reply quietly. "He was."

We arrive at our new hotel before check-in, so drop our bags off at reception and head back out onto the footpath.

"So, what's the plan?" I ask, and Tara looks down at her handbag, fidgeting a little. I get the distinct impression that she is avoiding looking at me. "Tara... What's going on?"

"Okay, so don't get mad." She finally looks up at me.

"Well, that's never a good way to start a sentence..."

"Annelisa is here."

I stare at her, trying to comprehend what she's saying. "Wait, Annelisa lives in London?"

She nods.

"Why didn't you tell me this before now?" I try to keep my voice neutral, but I am struggling to keep from getting angry.

"Because I knew you'd get mad at me."

"I'm only mad that you hid it from me. So you want to go and see her?"

She nods her head slowly, pushing her hair back behind her ear. "She wants me to meet her for lunch and spend the afternoon with her."

"Well, obviously, I won't be joining," I snap, unable to believe she'd kept this from me all this time.

"No, I figured you wouldn't. I'm sorry. I don't want to abandon you, but... I need to see my sister."

I stare at her for a few moments before deflating a little. "I get it... I know you've missed her. I just don't get why you didn't tell me this was your plan. I could have been working out what I wanted to do on my own."

"I'm sorry. I didn't want to put you in a position to have to keep anything from Will."

"There's no way I'm telling Will about this. That's the last thing he needs to know about."

She looks so sad, and I hate that our older siblings' drama has put us both in this position. I reach out and give her a hug.

"Go see your sister. I'll work out a way to keep myself occupied for the day."

She gives me a watery smile. "Thank you."

An hour later, I find myself standing in front of the British Museum, unsure if I want to go in or not. I feel like I've seen a thousand museums at this point, but I hadn't done much research on things to do in London, so had just gone to the place closest.

It's an impressive-looking building, all white with fancy columns out the front. People are flowing in and out, and the area is brimming with tourists.

"Kylie?"

I spin around, and my mouth falls open when I see Seth walking towards me.

"Hey! What are you doing here?" I ask, giving him a hug before stepping back.

"Going to the museum. What are you doing here? Where's Tara?"

"Um, it's a long story." I slide my hands into my back pockets and rock back on my heels.

Seth studies me, his head cocked to the side. "Is everything okay?"

"Yeah, it's fine. She went to meet her sister."

"Oh... The sister that abandoned your brother, I'm assuming?" He rubs the back of his neck.

"Yeah." I shrug, not really wanting to go into it any further and feeling awkward.

"Wanna come check out the museum with me, then?" he asks, nodding towards the door.

"You don't mind? We kind of already did the sad goodbye thing last night."

He smiles and shakes his head. "I'm not going to complain about getting to spend more time with you." He holds his hand out to me.

"Smooth. Very smooth." I take his hand and let him lead me inside. "So, where's Lincoln?"

"He is having a much-needed sleep-in. His words, not mine. Now that we finally have our own rooms again, he's taking full advantage of not having to be anywhere in particular today." He stops to buy our admission tickets for the special exhibit before I have a chance to pull out my wallet.

"You didn't have to do that," I say, but he waves me off. "Yeah, we moved hotels so that we could afford to have our own rooms, too. Tara loves me, but I think she was starting to get annoyed with my chaos encroaching on her space."

We spend several hours just wandering through the numerous exhibits, including the one we'd had to pay for - a travelling exhibit from Greece. Once we reach the gift shop, I feel a sense of loss creeping in.

"So, I guess this is goodbye again, huh?" I ask once we're outside on the steps.

I shove my hands in my back pockets while I try to squash down the sadness at saying goodbye once again. Being around Seth feels effortless, a fresh experience with a guy for me.

"Well... I mean, I don't have any other plans... We could spend the rest of the day together?" He shifts his weight from one foot to the other, hands in his pockets while he looks down, and I smile at his awkward delivery.

"That sounds great to me."

"Yeah?" He gives me a shy smile.

I step in closer. "Yeah, Seth. I would happily spend all the time with you I can."

He grins harder and pulls me towards him before tilting my chin up and kissing me softly. Although we've spent several hours together, it's the first time we've kissed, and it feels so right - like it's as easy as breathing.

After a moment, we step back, conscious of our surroundings. But my insides are screaming for more.

We spend the rest of the afternoon just wandering around London. Neither of us has ever been here before, but after three weeks of constant tourist attractions, it's nice just to explore with no particular destination in mind.

I messaged Tara earlier to let her know I'd found a way to keep myself occupied, so she didn't need to rush back, feeling no need to elaborate further. So much of my time with Seth has been shared with others that something about today feels like I need to keep it for myself, at least for now.

Eventually, we find ourselves sitting outside the Tower of London, watching people rush past. We start to play a game of guessing what each person is on their way to do. The tourists are obvious, as they are like us, in awe of the dominating structure that seems so out of place amongst the modern buildings surrounding it. The locals are easy to spot as well, taking no notice of the thousand-year-old tower casting a shadow over the river in the afternoon sun while they walk by, intent on making it to their destinations.

"That guy. He's on his way to the most important meeting of his life," Seth says, pointing to a guy in a suit who is rushing past with his phone pressed firmly to his ear while he shouts angrily at whoever is on the other end.

"Oh yes. Clearly, the weight of the entire world is on his shoulders." I nod along, and Seth laughs. I scan the crowd, looking for another person to play the game on. "Oh, her. She's smiling so hard. She's so happy to be here. It's the first time she's ever travelled, and everything is shiny and new." I nod towards a woman who looks to be around my age, staring up at the Tower with her phone in front of her while she snaps photos with a smile that lights up her entire face. "She kind of reminds me of Tara when we got to Paris."

"Not you?" Seth asks, raising an eyebrow.

"I have loved this trip, but it's not my first time travelling. I was incredibly lucky to have had the chance to travel growing up. Mostly Canada and the US, and some places in Asia. But this trip was Tara's first time out of Australia. She didn't even have a passport until we started planning for the tour. I guess that's why Annelisa chose to run away to somewhere out of the country." I can't hide the bitterness in my voice at the mention of the woman who had been like an older sister to me for years and had broken my brother's heart.

Seth is quiet for a moment, watching me with a tender look on his face. "Are you going to tell Will you know where she is?"

I shake my head. "No. There's no good reason to tell him. He's still barely holding it together. And after watching him push Tara away, I'd hate him to do that to me too if he found out I knew where she was."

"He's your brother. I doubt he'd do that." Seth curls his hand around mine, squeezing lightly.

"Logically, I know that. He's just hurting so much that I don't want to add to it." The closer I get to returning home, the more I've been thinking about Will.

It's hard not to, knowing that I'm in the same city as Annelisa now.

"I should have gone with Tara and demanded answers from her," I say, continuing my thoughts out loud.

"Well, selfishly, I'm glad you didn't. Besides, that would have just made things hard for Tara, and I know you wouldn't want that." He runs his thumb back and forth over the back of my hand.

We sit in silence for a few minutes, just watching the people walk by while lost in thought.

"So... should we do dinner?" Seth asks, breaking the silence.

"I would love that. I do need to check into my hotel first, though. We dropped off our bags, but our rooms weren't ready. And I'd really like a shower." Although an English summer's day is nothing compared to an Australian one, I've still managed to work up a sweat while walking around, and the last thing I feel like doing is going to a restaurant while in the same clothes I've been in all day.

"Sure. We can swing by yours first, and I'll work out a nice place to take us while you shower. Then we can head to mine so I can get washed up, too." He gets to his feet and reaches his hand out to me.

I squint up at him, the sun glaring in my eyes while I try to search his face. "Wouldn't it make more sense for us to just meet at the restaurant?"

He shrugs, keeping his hand out. "It probably would. But, I'm selfish, remember. I'm not ready to say goodbye again, even if it is for just a few hours."

I take his hand, and he pulls me to my feet and into his arms, kissing me before I have a chance to get my bearings. It doesn't take me long to catch up, though, and I slide my hands up his back beneath his shirt while I open my mouth to him, allowing him to deepen the kiss. He cups my face with his hands, holding my face still, and I let out a quiet moan, eliciting a small laugh from him when he pulls away.

"As much as I'd like to keep doing this, probably not the most appropriate place for this little public make-out session." He nods towards the family of fellow tourists walking past, the mother shooting us a scandalised look while she bustles her two small people past.

The father grins at Seth while he follows behind, and I step back with a sigh.

"Okay. Let's go then."

I lead the way into my hotel room, Seth following behind with my suitcase. The room is modest, but comfortable. The exciting part is that once I get settled, I can make as much mess as I want without having to worry about anyone else.

Once Seth puts my suitcase on the bed, he takes a seat on the small couch while I dig around for some fresh clothes and my toiletries. I feel a little weird and look over at where he's sprawled out, scrolling through his phone with a thoughtful look on his face while he works out where to go for dinner. It's the first time we've been alone like this, and the lack of chaperones is glaringly obvious when he looks up and finds me watching him. He raises an eyebrow, and I smile before turning back to my belongings. All afternoon, I've felt the heat between us growing, and now that there is no one to distract us, my resolve not to sleep with him is crumbling.

I roll my shoulders and avoid looking at him before heading into the bathroom. Stepping under the slow trickle of water isn't quite the relief that I'd hoped it would be. One thing I have not enjoyed on this trip is the crappy water pressure in most of the hotels we've stayed in, and disappointingly, this one appears to be one of the worst.

After the quickest shower I've ever had, I climb out and realise I stupidly didn't bring a towel in with me.

"Um, Seth. Are there towels out there?" I call through the door, water dripping from my body onto the floor.

"Yeah, hold on." I hear him move around the room before he knocks on the door.

I open the door a little and stick my head around to give him a kiss while taking the towel off him.

"Trying very hard not to think about the fact that you are not wearing any clothes while you do that." He gives me a pointed look, and I can't help but respond with a flirty smile.

"Maybe I left the towel on purpose," I reply, and I see him swallow hard just as I close the door.

After I finish dressing and put on some make up, I open the door to find he has returned to his seat, still scrolling through his phone. He looks up and runs his eyes over me, the heat behind his gaze undeniable as he takes in the blue summer dress that brushes my mid-thighs. It's one he's seen before, and I know for a fact that he'd liked it, as he'd had trouble keeping his hands off me the last time I wore it in Prague.

I move towards him, and he places the phone down on the side table as he sits forward, resting his elbows on his knees while watching me. I stop in front of him and run my fingers through his hair while he looks up at me, a wordless question in his eyes. Pushing him back gently, I drop one knee down beside him and straddle his lap.

"Hi," I say quietly while he inhales deeply, his eyes searching my face.

He clears his throat, shifting a little under me while placing his hands on my hips. "Hi."

"Did you find a restaurant yet?" I ask before leaning down to kiss his neck, and he groans a little.

"Possibly. But I'm slightly distracted now."

"What's distracting you?" I capture his earlobe between my teeth, and his grip on my hips tightens.

"Oh, I don't know... Maybe it's the incredibly beautiful woman in my lap..."

"That does sound distracting."

Moving fast, he reaches up and clasps the back of my head, pulling me down so that he can kiss me, and I moan when his tongue brushes against mine. My body takes over, and I grind down a little, the fly of his jeans brushing right against the sensitive spot at the apex of my thighs, and we both gasp together.

"Fuck," he whispers in my ear while I swirl my hips again, applying more pressure. "Keep doing that, and this is going to lead to something more."

"Maybe that's what I want," I reply, and he pulls back, looking me in the eye.

He strokes my cheek with his thumb while he considers my words.

"Maybe I want it too... But I don't want to rush anything. So let's stick with the original plan and see where the night takes us."

I search his face, thrown by the fact that he's put on the brakes when I feel his semi pressed against my inner thigh.

After a moment, I nod and get to my feet, realising there really is no glamorous way to get up from straddling someone. He stays put for a moment, and I'm pleased to see he is just as affected by what just happened as I am.

He eventually gets to his feet and pulls me in again to kiss me tenderly before grabbing my handbag and towing me out the door like he needs to get as far away as possible from this room to avoid temptation.

14

I THINK WE'VE WAITED
LONG ENOUGH

SETH

I HAVE no idea what possessed me to pump the brakes on things with Kylie in her hotel room, thrown by the incredible self-control it had taken to remove her from my lap when my body was screaming at me to take it further.

It feels like things are too important between us to let that be our first time together. I want to wine and dine her first. Today has felt like a second chance, our fortunate meeting away from any outside influences seeming like an opportunity that I don't want to waste.

Something has definitely shifted between us. The possibility of taking things further is buzzing through the space between us, and she keeps a tight grip on my hand while we ride the elevator up to my suite.

Until we'd walked into the lobby, I hadn't thought about how much more luxurious this hotel was than the modest one she was staying in. I wait to see if she says anything, but so far she's taken it in her stride.

Right up until the moment I open my door, when her eyes run

over the opulent furniture in the shared space between the two bedrooms. Linc had messaged earlier to say he was going out, catching up with a friend who lives here, so we have the place to ourselves. I anxiously watch while Kylie rotates slowly on the spot, absorbing everything, before giving me a questioning look.

"So... you're rich."

It's not a question, and I'm not sure how to respond, so I shrug while rubbing the back of my neck.

"I don't think I've ever seen a place this over the top before," she continues, moving towards the window to look at the streets of Mayfair below us.

I look around the room, trying to see it from her point of view.

"Linc picked the hotel," I reply.

He'd jokingly picked a hotel that really leans into the whole royalty theme. I'd not thought much of it last night when we arrived, but seeing it now through Kylie's eyes is making me see how extravagant it all is.

"Lincoln is just full of surprises," she says, her expression pointed while she looks back at me over her shoulder.

I duck my head, not sure how to reply. "You okay here while I get washed up?"

She's quiet for a moment, and I wonder if she's heard me, but she finally turns with a smile. "Yep. Go have a shower. I'll just be out here, not thinking about your naked body in there."

I cough a little, feeling myself blush while she laughs.

I head into my bedroom but leave the door open so that she can still talk to me while I grab some clothes.

I have no idea why she has this effect on me. The fact that I've never experienced nervousness with any previous women I've dated tells me what I already know - that Kylie is extraordinary.

I don't quite know how to feel about that, getting the sense that I've already entered the danger zone with my emotions... and I'm not sure I could turn back even if I wanted to.

. . .

When I finish in the shower, I throw on my fresh boxers and drag my jeans back on before noticing that I'd forgotten to grab a clean shirt. Stepping out of the bathroom, I stop short when Kylie clears her throat in the other room, and I look over to see her watching me with wide eyes from where she's sitting on the couch.

Hiding a smirk, I grab a button-up shirt from the closet where housekeeping has hung it after doing our laundry earlier today, putting it on as I walk out of the room. Kylie doesn't even try to hide the fact that she's checking me out while I button it up, her eyes honing in on my chest.

"I'm feeling objectified," I say, and she snorts, getting to her feet.

"I somewhat doubt it, given that you chose to walk out here in slow motion with those abs on display." She stops in front of me and pokes me in the stomach.

"I don't recall it being in slow motion," I reply, and she grins up at me.

"Oh, it was definitely in slow motion. With sexy music playing and everything."

"Yeah?" I kiss her forehead with a smile.

"Yeah, like that old guy who sings all the sexy songs in movies."

I shake my head and start rolling up my sleeves.

Her eyes follow the motion. "Seriously? Are you just purposely making this difficult for me, or are you completely unaware of your sex appeal right now?"

I raise an eyebrow, unable to keep from laughing when she pouts. "I'm sorry. I guess I wasn't aware of how easy it was to seduce you."

"Ah, so you admit it, you are seducing me!"

"That depends. Is it working?" I pull her closer, and she wraps her arms around my neck.

"Too well. I vote we just get super expensive room service and get naked now," she replies, rising to her tiptoes to kiss me.

I kiss her back, trying to hold myself back a little without losing myself completely and giving in to that suggestion. But my resolve crumbles when the kiss continues, and before I know it, I'm lifting her off the ground.

She gasps, wrapping her legs around my waist and grinning while I carry her back towards the bedroom. "Wow. I knew you were ripped, but I had no idea how strong you were. No one's ever carried me before."

"I guess they just weren't worthy of remembering then," I say, kicking the door closed behind me and lowering her onto the bed. "How hungry are you?"

"Depends on what type of hunger you're referring to." She looks up at me from beneath lowered eyelashes.

"Well, I was considering going out there and ordering dinner now, but if you keep looking at me like that, I'm not going to be able to leave."

She rises to her knees and loops a finger through one of my belt loops, pulling me forward. "Good. Because now that you've got me on this bed, the last thing I'm thinking about is food."

With those words, the last of my self-control snaps, and I surge forward, claiming her mouth with mine. She kisses me back, gripping my shirt tight in her fist as her tongue strokes mine.

"Just so that I'm one hundred percent certain, you're sure about this?" I step back to look her in the eye.

"Seth," she says, reaching up and pulling her hair free from her ponytail and shaking it out behind her. "I think we've waited long enough, so I can assure you..." She pulls her dress over her head in one swift movement and I swallow hard, my eyes roaming over her body. "I really, really want this." She pulls me back in, kissing me hard.

I honestly didn't think I could find this woman any more attractive, but her confidence and ability to voice exactly what she wants just draws me to her even more.

As we continue to kiss, she unbuttons my shirt, working her way down slowly until it hangs open. She kisses her way down my neck, before pressing her lips to the centre of my chest. I sigh, running my fingers through her hair when she looks up at me with wide eyes. I guide her face back to mine to kiss her hungrily again, reaching around to unclasp her bra. Sliding my hands down her sides, I grip the back of her thighs and lift her again before lowering her onto her back. I stare down at her for a moment, savouring every curve.

She rises onto her elbows, watching while I lower myself over her and swirl my tongue over her right nipple. She moans and arches her back, dropping her head back. I move my hand to her other breast, which is just the right size to fit perfectly in my hand, tweaking the tip between my fingers, eliciting another moan while I learn how to make her body sing. From her reactions, I can tell her nipples are highly sensitive, and I keep this in mind while I kiss my way further down her body.

Sliding my hands lower, I look up at her while I trail my fingers along the top of her underwear. "May I?" I ask, and she nods, seeming a little breathless.

I slip them down her legs, tossing them on the ground behind me while I brush my thumb over her clit lightly, and she gasps, bucking her hips a little. Grinning up at her, I slide my body off the bed and pull her down until her butt is on the edge. Her eyes widen again, watching while I lower my head and suck her clit between my lips, and her moans fill the room.

15
I KNOW YOU'VE GOT IT IN YOU

KYLIE

I'M PRETTY sure I'm having an out-of-body experience. I'd suspected that Seth would know his way around a woman's body, but I've never had a man go down on me the first time we slept together without any prompting from me. But Seth seems to revel in it, watching my face and changing pace depending on my responses.

"Oh, god," I moan when he inserts a finger and begins sliding it in and out while his tongue continues to swirl over my clit.

I grip the blanket in both my fists, rolling my hips in time with his movements, chasing the orgasm that is building.

Once it crashes over me, I cry out, my back arching clean off the bed.

As I come back down to earth, he moves back up my body to kiss me again, and I respond right away, opening my mouth to him while I tangle my fingers in his hair.

"Holy crap, Seth," I say against his lips.

He laughs, straightening up. "Glad you approve."

I sit up, my legs hanging off the side of the bed while I work on undoing his jeans.

"Hold that thought for one minute," he says, stepping back before disappearing from the room.

I stare after him, my brain not quite comprehending his absence. I hear the door across the hall open, and when he reappears, I smile when I see the square foiled packet in his hand. It seems that Lincoln has a supply on hand.

"Glad one of us considered that before it ended in disappointment."

He stops in front of me again, and I get back to working on the button on his jeans.

"Believe me... Disappointment is the last thing I think is going to happen," he says, letting his shirt slide off finally, and I pause in my work on his pants to stare at his abs.

"Wow... How are these real?" I trace my fingers over each muscle, leaving a trail of goosebumps on his tanned skin.

"A lot of work," he replies, looking a little embarrassed.

"Well, you have excelled." I lean forward to trail kisses down his chest, grinning against his skin when he runs his fingers through my hair.

"I'm glad you approve." His voice sounds strained.

I finally get his jeans undone and hold eye contact with him through lowered lashes while I push them down before sliding my hand over his shaft. His nostrils flare, and he takes a sudden breath when I lean forward and run my tongue over the tip. Holding him steady, I take him further into my mouth.

"Fuck," he whispers, continuing to work his fingers along my scalp. "I'm not gonna last if you keep that up, and I really, really, want to be inside you right now."

I pop off him and sit back on my heels, watching while he kicks his legs free from his jeans before climbing onto the bed and capturing my face in his hands. I rise to meet him and he crushes his lips to mine while I run my hands up his back and grip his shoulders, holding him as close as possible.

He guides me onto my back before grabbing a pillow and wedging it beneath my ass.

I raise an eyebrow, and he grins. "Trust me."

"Oh, I trust you," I reply, gasping when he brushes my clit again and thrusts a finger inside, adding a second while he leans down and sucks my nipple between his lips.

I writhe against his hand and feel him chuckle against my breast.

"I need you now," I say with a moan.

He looks up at me with the sweetest smile, and I stroke a hand over his cheek while he reaches over and grabs the condom packet. Once he rolls it on, he lifts my hips and guides himself inside me, so slow that I groan, trying to pull him in closer. He clasps my hand and laces our fingers together, raising it beside my head and holding it there while he thrusts, his movements slow and gentle, allowing me to get used to his size.

Our moans mingle together between kisses, and I feel him hit a spot deep inside that no one has ever hit before, causing my eyes to roll back in my head.

"I understand the pillow now," I pant, and he laughs, thrusting forward again, hitting the spot again. "Oh, my god!"

I've never been one to experience multiple orgasms, and rarely during sex itself. When I feel another orgasm building, I let out another moan.

As though he can tell I'm right on the edge, he slides his hand between us to rub my clit, and within seconds, the orgasm rips through me so intensely that I see stars.

He slows his pace, kissing me gently while I try to regain my breath.

"Think you can go for another one?" he asks.

I gape at him. "Are you kidding? Two was a miracle."

It's almost like I've set him a challenge. He pulls out and flips me over, raising my hips a little to slide back in, and I gasp yet again when he hits the spot from a whole new angle.

"Fuck! I didn't even know I had a g-spot!" I moan into the blanket, my fists gripping it tighter with each thrust.

He kisses my neck and assures me, "By the end of the night, I'll make sure you're well acquainted with it."

He raises both my hands up above my head on the mattress, our fingers laced together again while he holds me still and begins thrusting harder, and I cry out with each one, unable to keep quiet even if I wanted to. I've never been particularly vocal during sex, but sex with Seth is on a whole different level.

"Come on, baby, one more. I know you've got it in you." Leaving one hand holding mine in place, he reaches down and works my clit again.

With each motion, I can feel myself tightening. Unbelievably, my body listens to his command, and a third orgasm rips through me. I scream his name into the blanket.

A few thrusts later, Seth shudders, moaning in my ear while he comes.

I turn my head to the side, lifting it a little to look at him over my shoulder. "Well done, champ."

His body shakes while he chuckles before he raises his head and kisses my shoulder. "You too, champ."

He rolls off me and heads into the bathroom. I hear him open and close the bin before returning. I move off the bed, high-fiving him when we pass each other. Once I'm finished in the bathroom, I join him on the bed, curling my body against his while he wraps his arm around me, holding me close to his side.

"So... that was possibly the best sex I've ever had," I say, kissing his chest.

He squeezes me and kisses my forehead. "Likewise."

We lay still like that for a while, him running his hand up and down my side while I trail my fingers over his abs.

Eventually, I look up to find him watching me, and I scoot

myself up to kiss him. He cradles the back of my head, kissing me back with growing intensity, and I moan against his lips.

And just like that, we're on to round two.

Hours later, Seth has finally ordered room service, and I've got one of his t-shirts on while eating the fanciest meal I've ever had. He sits across from me in athletic shorts only, and it takes all my self-control not to climb him once again. But the chicken is so good that his lack of a shirt still isn't enough to distract me from dealing with my hunger finally.

We've been chatting about everything and nothing since our third tumble between the sheets.

"So, have you given any more thought about what you're going to do when you get home?" he asks, cutting into his steak.

I shrug before swallowing the mouthful of roast chicken I'd been savouring. "Honestly, no. I've had such a good time on this trip that the idea of returning to the real world actually makes me feel ill." I don't want to admit the prospect of not seeing him again is also contributing to that feeling.

He's quiet for a while, studying me while he chews.

Just as he opens his mouth to reply, the door to the suite opens and Lincoln breezes in. It dawns on me all at once that I'm naked except for Seth's shirt, but Lincoln doesn't even glance our way when he walks past on his way to his bedroom.

Seth observes his friend, his eyebrow raised.

"Hi Kylie," Lincoln calls back over his shoulder before closing the door behind him.

I stare at the door before looking back at Seth, who is shaking his head while chuckling.

"Did you tell him I was here?" I ask.

"Nope."

"I just assume you're everywhere now," Lincoln yells through the door, and I roll my eyes.

"Hello Lincoln, I missed you."

"I missed you, too! Now, put some pants on. And Seth - put a shirt on, you're both turning me on."

Seth snorts but makes no move to get up and find a shirt, and Lincoln remains in his room while we finish eating. Once we're done, Seth takes the tray and puts it back out in the hall. I get up and stand near the kitchen bench, not sure what to do now. We haven't discussed what we've been doing for the last few hours, and I now feel extremely awkward.

Seth comes and stands in front of me, brushing my hair back off my shoulder with one hand while sliding his other around my back and pulling me closer.

"So..." He kisses my forehead, and I lean into his embrace.

"So..." I mimic him.

He steps back to look down at me. "Stay?"

I search his face. "Don't you have to leave really early in the morning?"

"Yes. But that's hours away... And I'm not ready to say good-bye." He almost seems shy, traces of the Seth I first met shining through.

"Neither am I."

"So... stay?"

I close the gap between us and kiss him. "Okay."

"Woo hoo! Sleepover!" Lincoln yells from the bedroom and I laugh, pressing my forehead to Seth's chest while he shakes his head.

"Come on. I just need to throw everything into my suitcase and then bedtime." He takes my hand and leads me back into his bedroom, and I close the door behind me after yelling "Good-night!" to Lincoln.

Once Seth has packed his suitcase, he joins me on the bed, pulling me to his side.

"I wish we didn't live on opposite sides of the world," I half whisper, burying my face into his neck.

"I know. It sucks." He runs his hand up and down my back. "At least we got to have tonight."

"True. I guess we got one more day than we thought we would."

He presses a kiss on my forehead. "Come on, let's get some sleep."

He turns off the bedside light, and the room is engulfed in darkness.

"Goodnight, Seth," I whisper.

"Goodnight, Kylie."

16

WALK OF SHAME
WITH NO JUMPER

SETH

THE ALARM on my phone rips me from sleep, and I reach over, trying to silence it before it wakes Kylie, who stirs beside me.

"Is it time for you to leave?" she asks, her voice thick with sleep.

"Yeah. You go back to sleep though," I reply, kissing her shoulder.

"It's okay. You need to check out and I don't think housekeeping will appreciate finding a half-naked woman in the bed when they come to clean the place."

"Honestly, I think I'd be pretty pleased," I remark with a smirk, and she responds by poking out her tongue, sitting up and rubbing her eyes.

"Let me just find my clothes and use the bathroom, and I'll get out of here." She throws back the covers, but I pull her to me and kiss her softly.

"Or, you can come shower with me and we can drop you back at your hotel in our car service?"

She cocks her head to the side and places a finger on the side of her mouth, pretending to give it a lot of thought. "I suppose I could do that. Sounds far better than a walk of shame with no jumper."

I raise an eyebrow. "Walk of shame, huh?"

"Well, it kind of feels like a one night only kind of deal, so it sort of fits."

I get out of bed and lead her into the bathroom. "Believe me, if we didn't live in completely different countries, this would not be a one-night thing for me."

I can see her reflection in the mirror when I reach in and turn on the shower, and her expression looks a little sad while she studies my back. "Yeah... it wouldn't be for me either."

I turn back to face her, pushing her hair back off her shoulders and cupping her face in my hands. "Hey, let's not think about any of that right now. We can just enjoy this last hour or so together, okay?"

She nods, leaning her face into my hand and closing her eyes for a moment. "Okay."

I peel my shirt over her head, throwing it back out onto the bed before pulling her in close and kissing her again.

I could kiss her forever.

But time is pressing on, so once I've pulled my shorts off, I lead her into the massive shower before resuming kissing her, a little hungrier this time. She presses herself against my chest while raising onto her tiptoes to wrap her arms around my neck. I groan, lifting her up and pushing her back against the tiles. She gasps while bringing her legs around my waist, pulling me in so that our torsos are flush together, and the kiss grows more desperate. It's like the realisation that this is the last time we'll most likely ever see each other is hitting us both and we need to make the most of it. I lift her up higher, aligning her breasts with my mouth, and start sucking on one, then the other, until she is panting and grinding against me.

Lowering her to the ground, I drop to my knees, throwing her right leg over my shoulder and pressing my face between her legs, and she slides her hands into my hair.

"Seth," she moans when I use my tongue and finger to bring her to the edge, looking up at her when her legs tremble.

She runs her tongue over her lower lip and throws her head back when the orgasm overtakes her, a cry escaping her while I continue to work her over. But I don't let her go, instead working harder until she comes again, her body slumping a little.

I lower her leg back down and stand, pulling her against me while she gathers herself back together.

"You are very skilled at that," she murmurs against my chest.

"I do my best," I reply with a chuckle.

Once she catches her breath, she looks up at me with a glint in her eye before moving her hand to where my erection presses against her abdomen. My breath hitches while she moves her hand back and forth, slow at first, before picking up the pace. But when she lowers herself to her knees, it's my turn to moan when she takes me in her mouth.

Using a combination of her mouth and hand, she works me up and I throw my head back, forgetting about the water running down on top of my head, the water hitting my face while I moan. Looking back down, I move my hands to grasp the back of her head, gently thrusting forward. I hit the back of her throat, and my eyes widen when she appears to have almost no gag reflex. She uses her hand on my hip to guide me faster, and before I know it, I'm coming and she swallows every drop.

"Okay, that was the best blowjob of my life," I say once I've caught my breath, helping her to her feet.

"I do my best," she replies, grinning while she uses my own words on me.

After the fastest shared shower known to man, I finish packing, haphazardly throwing the last items into my suitcase. We head out into the living space where Linc is sitting on the couch, scrolling through his phone.

"Good morning. The car service is downstairs," he says, smirking.

Ignoring his amusement, I nod. "Cool. Well, we're ready to go. We'll drop Kylie at her hotel on the way."

He gets to his feet. "That sounds good to me."

The three of us head downstairs, and I check us out before joining Kylie and Linc in the car. Linc has taken the front seat, so I slide in the back next to Kylie, taking her hand in mine.

The driver navigates the early morning London streets, the mood inside the car pensive, with even Linc remaining quiet. Once we arrive at Kylie's hotel, I ask the driver to give us a minute.

I join Kylie on the sidewalk, pulling her into a hug and resting my cheek against the top of her head while she clings to me.

It had been hard enough saying goodbye to her at the end of the tour, but now, after the best day and night with her, this is a thousand times harder.

When she looks up at me, there are tears shining in her eyes, and I know I look similar.

I run my thumb lightly over her cheek before leaning down to kiss her.

"I'm going to miss you," she whispers.

I press my forehead to hers. "I'll miss you, too," I reply, my voice thick with emotion.

She grips me tight, and it's not until Linc calls out for me to get my ass moving that we finally break apart with one last quick kiss.

"Bye, Kylie."

"Bye, Seth." She places a hand to my cheek before stepping back while I climb back into the car.

I wave goodbye and then take a breath, letting my head drop back against the headrest when the driver pulls back into the traffic.

"You alright, man?" Linc asks, looking back at me with a concerned look on his face.

"Yeah. Just sucks that I met pretty much the perfect woman and there's no future for us."

He nods before turning back to face the front of the car, giving me some privacy to deal with the emotions rolling through me.

This trip has definitely had the desired effect, pulling me out of the shitty headspace I was in prior to leaving, but now, rather than getting my head back in the game, all I'm thinking about is the beautiful woman I've just had to say goodbye to.

Life really doesn't go how we want it to sometimes.

After the flight back home, the car service drops Linc at his apartment first, before dropping me at the front door of my house. I let myself in, dropping my suitcase in my bedroom before heading for the kitchen. I'd arranged for my housekeeper to get me sorted with meals yesterday so that I could get back on my nutritionist approved food plan as soon as I got back. I've got two weeks before training camp starts, and I need to hit the gym every day to make sure I'm ready. It's time to put the last three weeks behind me, no matter how perfect they were, and start getting back into my regular life.

Even if it feels like something is missing that I've never noticed before.

17
I THINK I SHOULD FIRE YOU

KYLIE

"HEY, where are you at with those invoices?" Will's voice comes through loud and clear on the speaker of my phone.

"All done and sent. What next, boss?" I listen while he rattles off a bunch of admin tasks while staring at the computer screen in front of me, trying not to sigh with boredom.

I've only been back for two weeks, and already, I have itchy feet again. Something about our little trip has awoken the travel bug in me, and the idea of doing the admin work from Will's new electrician business for the rest of my life makes me want to scream into a pillow.

Tara has fallen right back into her old routine and doesn't appear discontented at all. But she enjoys her job, for the most part. Whereas I've always found every job I've had to be beyond boring, daydreaming about doing anything else.

"Kyles? You there?" Will's voice pulls me from my doldrums.

"Yeah, sorry. What did you say?"

"Everything okay?" he asks, the concern clear in his voice.

"Yeah. Just have some return to real life blues happening."

He's quiet for a moment. "Wanna do dinner tonight?"

"Sure. What are you feeding me?"

"I can provide you with a roast chicken and salad from Woolies," he replies, and I can just picture the cheeky grin on his face.

Will has never been the best cook. Most of his culinary experience revolves around the barbecue in his backyard, and even then, he burns the meat more often than not.

I laugh. "Sounds perfect. What time?"

"I should be home by five."

"Okay cool, I'll head over around sixish then."

We hang up and I get stuck into the work he'd asked me to do, hoping to knock it all over in time to go to the gym before I head to his place. There's no question of him coming to mine. He hasn't set foot in my apartment since Annelisa disappeared, due to the fact that Tara also lives here. I really wish he'd stop being so bullheaded and just talk to her. I still haven't said a word to him about knowing where Annelisa is, and I refused to ask Tara anything about what she did with her sister while I was spending time with Seth.

As my mind wanders back to that perfect day, I stare at my phone, wondering if he's thinking about me too, or if he's just settled right back into his old life and forgotten all about me and our time together. I regret not exchanging numbers, but we'd both known there was no future for us.

Turning back to my computer, I sigh again.

Taking this as a sign that I should just go to the gym now and attempt to get back into the work once the endorphins are flowing, I close the laptop and grab my keys. The joys of working from home is that I've been in my workout clothes all day and all I need to do is throw on my runners.

I head down to the gym on the second floor of our apartment building, grateful to have the place to myself. I pop my headphones on and blast out my workout mix before hopping on the treadmill to warm up.

As I reach my first kilometre, the sound of a text message interrupts my concentration, causing me to slow to a walk in order to check who it is.

BRI

Hey you. Are you around this weekend? Jake and I will be in town and thought we'd have a catch up at the apartment.

KYLIE

Hey love. Yep, I'm around and would love to catch up. Just let me know the details and I'll be there.

I put the phone back in my pocket, trying to get back into the flow, but my mind once again wanders back to Seth.

No matter how hard I try to let the memory of him go, the heart wants what it wants... and what my heart wants is the hot Canadian who has stolen it right from my chest.

I pull up out the front of Will's place and head inside, not bothering to knock.

"Hey, I'm here," I call, walking into the kitchen.

My brother is nowhere to be seen, so I assume he's in the shower. I help myself to a soft drink from his fridge and take a seat at the bench, looking around at the clutter. It's obvious that he doesn't care about keeping the place tidy now that Annelisa is no longer around, and my heart feels heavy at the realisation.

"Hey," Will says, coming into the kitchen wearing jeans and a hoodie, his hair wet from the shower.

"Boss," I reply, saluting him.

"Yeah, about that. I think I should fire you," he says casually while he gets plates out for us.

I stare at his back while he moves around the kitchen. "Um… what?"

"Well, you're clearly miserable doing admin work. I just think you could be doing so much more than doing paperwork I could probably do myself if I could be bothered." He finally looks at me while he's ripping open the bag of pre-made salad.

"What else would I do, though? I need a job and I only have admin experience. Besides, we both know that you'd fuck up the paperwork if you went near the invoicing system. You need me."

"Okay, but I don't necessarily need you here. As in, always on hand. Why don't you look at doing more travel and work remotely on my stuff? Maybe you could go hang out in Calgary for a while? You've been saying for years you wanted to spend more time there."

I feel like I've stepped into the twilight zone. This was not how I thought this evening would go, but now the idea that I might not have to be trapped here forever is rolling around in my head.

Will continues talking while I stare at him. "I just… I know how much boredom affects you, and I don't want to be responsible for that."

This is why Will is so much more than just my brother. He has always been aware that I don't handle the mundane well and tried to find solutions for me. Being only eighteen months older than me, he's been my constant companion my whole life and always looked out for me.

"I mean, it's a good idea… But I can't just abandon my life here. I can't leave Tara with everything going on. Unless you're finally going to remove your head from your ass and start talking to her again," I say this last part with a pointed look, and Will sighs.

"I know I've been an asshole to her. I don't mean to hurt her, but every time I think about talking to her, my mind can't go past begging her to tell me where Annie is. I don't want to put her in that position." He pulls apart the chicken, looking down at his hands, so I know he can't see the conflicted look on my face.

My lack of impulse control kicks in. "It's not only Tara who knows where she is."

Will's head flies up, and he stares at me. "What do you mean?"

I take a deep breath. Tara never told me I couldn't say anything to Will, but I still feel guilty as hell for what I'm about to say. "She's in London."

The silence in the room is all-consuming while my brother remains frozen, his eyes running over my face. "You saw her?" he asks after a moment, his voice rough.

I shake my head. "No. But Tara did. I refused to see her cause I'm so fucking angry at her for just leaving without so much as a goodbye to anyone, and breaking your heart."

Will's face softens. "Kyles... There is a lot that no one knows. It wasn't all Annie's fault."

He's hinted before that stuff wasn't great for them before she left, but he's been determined to keep it to himself, saying it was between him and Annelisa. But that just makes me angrier, because he deserves closure, and her just disappearing means he will never get that.

I'm fiercely loyal to the people I love, and while once that included Annelisa, I will always have my brother's best interests at heart.

"That aside, now that you know where she is, will you please stop avoiding group catch ups and making it awkward as hell for Tara? She feels like shit when you don't show up to stuff, and you're putting everyone else in a crap position where they feel like they have to take sides in a non-existent argument." This is a well-worn discussion we've been having for months, but I refuse to let it go when two of my favourite people are hurting so much.

He is quiet for a while, continuing to pull the chicken apart like it's the most important thing in the world. Finally, when I think he's just going to ignore me once again, he gives me a considering look. "If I agree to stop avoiding Tara, will you consider my suggestion about travelling?"

"It's not just about you. I can't leave Tara while we're still in a lease. I don't want her to have to live with some random person. She'd hate that."

Will shakes his head. "You're not her mother. She's a big girl and you don't give her enough credit. She's twenty-six, has a good job and lots of friends. Just because you've been living together for the last six years doesn't mean you have to live together forever. What if one of you meets someone and wants to move in with them? It's time to put yourself first for a change, Kyles."

I ponder what he says for a while, and accept the plate of food he hands me before following him into the lounge room. It's just as much of a mess in here, and I have to sweep aside a pile of clothes to sit on the couch.

"I'll think about it, okay? Also, you really need to do something about the mess you're living in. I can't believe Mum hasn't lost her mind when she's seen how messy this place is."

He has the sense to look ashamed. "She may have tried to organise a cleaner for me the last time she was here."

"I think you should take her up on that. How do you ever expect any self respecting woman to want to hang out with you if you're living like a hobo?" I ask, knowing that the chances of him dating anyone else any time soon are pretty low. The incredulous look he gives me confirms that, and I change the subject. "Did Jake reach out to you about catching up with them this weekend?"

"Yeah. Are you going?"

"Yep. I haven't seen them in ages, and I'll never turn down a chance to hang out in that apartment." Jake won a luxury penthouse apartment eighteen months ago, and it's become the unofficial place for us all to hang out when he and Bri are in town.

"Speaking of this weekend, you up for a surf on Sunday morning?" he asks.

I nod with a smile. "God, yes, I haven't been out in months. I don't even care that it's probably going to be freezing."

We spend the rest of the evening making plans for the weekend and Will keeps pushing me to consider his idea about travelling while I work for him, which I promise to think about seriously. By the time I head home, I feel like we've made some progress regarding both our issues, and I'm looking forward to a weekend of fun with our friends.

18

STOP USING ME TO DEFLECT
THE CONVERSATION

SETH

LINC TOSSES me my water bottle from where he's taking a breather on the bench and I smoothly catch it, squirting it in my mouth while I watch the two new rookies scramble for the puck on centre ice.

"Looking good out there, Davidson." Coach Stevens stands next to Linc, studying everyone for signs that they didn't keep up with their training in the off season.

"Thanks," I reply, grateful I'd given myself that two-week window to get back on top of my nutrition and training after the trip.

"Good to see you've put last season behind you. Need your head in the game if we're going to have another shot at play-offs this year. Think we've got a good team with the new additions."

I nod in response, not sure what more to say in reply to that. Even after last season's messy end, he's kept me on as the team captain, so it's on me to keep morale up.

Coach moves down the bench to talk to one of our new defencemen, and I hand my water back to Linc.

"Dinner tonight? Mom's in town and wants to see you," he asks.

"Sounds good. Been a while since I saw Mama Claire."

Coach blows his whistle, motioning for everyone to gather in front of the bench. My team mates skate over and he gives his "good work" speech, which is much nicer than his "what the fuck was that" speech - his other favourite pastime.

Once he's done, he points to me and I hang back while the rest of the team heads back to the locker room.

"You right to host the usual dinner on Friday?" he asks.

I nod. "I've already got the events guys sorting stuff out. They have caterers coming out and will get the backyard set up for the kids."

The first Friday of training camp, the current captain is in charge of organising the welcome back party.

In the past, partners and wives of the captain have helped out, but as I don't have either of those, I've enlisted the events team to help me. Think smarter, not harder. Being antisocial means that organising a party for an entire hockey team and their families is outside of my area of expertise.

Ever since I got back from the trip, it's been nonstop with getting straight back to work. I've had media interviews where I've brushed off any comments regarding what I've now come to think of as "the unfortunate incident". My agent has also been lining me up with endorsements and events. I've barely had a chance to scratch myself, but it's been a welcome distraction from the thoughts that keep popping into my head, wondering what Kylie is up to.

"Davidson, are we going for drinks tonight?" Dean Thomas, our goalie, asks as soon as I enter the locker room.

He's been with the team even longer than I have and is a fan favourite, something he loves to use to his advantage when it comes to the ladies. Nights out drinking with him end up messy and surrounded by a sea of women who are hoping to snag them-selves a hockey player.

"Nah man, Linc's mom is in town so we're on son duties."

I don't think I've ever been more grateful to have my second mother in town than I am at this exact moment. I try to socialise with the team as much as my introverted self can manage, but the idea of a night dealing with puck bunnies just doesn't appeal to me. I'll leave that to the rookies. And Dean.

I get out of my practice gear and hit the showers, changing into my street clothes before saying goodbye to our teammates and meeting Linc at my car.

We head back to his place, where his mother greets us both with her signature warm hugs. Claire O'Malley has been my second mother since I was eight years old. She and my mother have become best friends because of Linc and I always being together since we were kids, so whenever she's in town, she checks up on me so she can report back to Mom.

"You're looking tired, Seth. Have you been getting enough sleep?" she says, holding my face in her hands after she hugs me.

"Way to make him feel good, Mom." Linc rolls his eyes while he steps in to take my place.

"What? It's true! He does look tired." Claire shrugs before wrapping her arms around her son's waist.

We both dwarf her, but she is still the boss when it comes to her boys.

"I've just had a lot going on the last few weeks. I'm fine," I reply, heading into Linc's kitchen to raid the fridge.

Unfortunately, he hasn't restocked it since the last time I was here, and it's looking pretty bare.

"I've got groceries coming. Lincoln has clearly been eating out far more than he has been at home," Claire says, giving Linc a dirty look.

"What? I've been busy with work, too. I've just been grabbing dinner with the team most nights."

"Just the team?" Claire is fishing for any news on whether Linc has met anyone, but she's wasting her time.

"Let's not go there." Linc has made it clear he has no interest in settling down anytime soon and avoids seeing anyone more than one or two times, but his mother still lives in hope.

"And what about you? Surely one of you is going to make me a grandmother soon?" She turns her pleading eyes to me.

I raise my hands in surrender. "Sorry, Mama Claire, nothing from me either."

"No one on this continent, anyway," Linc pipes up, and I glare at him while Claire's eyes widen with excitement.

"Ooohh, did you meet someone on your trip? Is it that lovely brunette in all the photos I've seen?" She all but rubs her hands with glee.

I sigh, giving up on my fruitless search for food, and grab a bottle of water from Linc's fridge. "Yes, but she lives in Australia, so there's nothing to report. It was just a holiday thing."

"Except you're still hung up on her." It's obvious that Linc is trying to keep the focus off himself, and I'm considering punching him to shut him up, but know it's not worth the effort.

The last thing I need is any of this getting back to my mother and having her nagging at me as well.

"She didn't even know the truth about what I do for a living. Because you told me to keep it to myself," I say, pointing the bottle towards Linc before taking another mouthful.

I miss beer, but this close to the beginning of the season, I'm rationing myself.

"I'm sure you could have worked it into conversation some-how," Linc replies with a shrug.

Claire is watching the entire exchange keenly, looking back and forth between us.

"This isn't something even worth discussing. She lives on the other side of the world. There's no future past the trip. Can we please change the subject?"

Linc studies me for a few moments before shrugging. "Whatever. Just don't slip back into grumpy Seth. I much preferred the Seth I saw on holiday, and I know a large part of that was because of Kylie."

"Ah ha, so she has a name!" Claire interjects, and I groan.

"Please don't say anything to Mom. I'm serious. We're never going to see each other again, so there is no point in Mom thinking there is something going on."

She pretends to zip her lips closed. "I won't breathe a word. But I would love to see at least one of you boys settling down with someone soon. Man or woman," she adds, looking pointedly at her son.

"This little bisexual is still happy being single, Mother, so you're just going to have to keep those sights set on Seth over there for the grandbabies."

"Stop using me to deflect the conversation," I grumble.

Claire shakes her head. "You boys will be the death of me."

Thankfully, that's the end of the topic and we move on to discussing Linc's older sister and her upcoming wedding. I never thought I'd be grateful to talk about a wedding, but I'm just glad the moment has passed.

I fixate on the bottle of water in my hand, unconsciously picking at the label while Linc and Claire discuss the travel arrangements for the wedding. I wonder what it would be like to attend a wedding with Kylie? Would she make it more bearable, with her bubbly personality keeping the attention on her instead of me having to try to talk to people?

Linc clears his throat and I look up to find him watching me with a grin. Claire has occupied herself in the kitchen now that the groceries have arrived and is out of earshot.

"Oh, fuck off," I mutter, straightening up.

"Whatever, buddy. You can claim its nothing all you want, but you forget how well I know you. And I've never seen you like this over a woman before. So forgive me for thinking there's more going on than you're admitting."

I shrug, deciding I'm done with this conversation and head into the kitchen to offer to help with dinner, all the while ignoring the niggling thought in the back of my mind that Linc is right.

Nothing good can ever come of Linc being right.

19

EVERYONE LEAVE KYLIE ALONE

KYLIE

ON SATURDAY MORNING, I pull up in front of my parents' house. On the first Saturday of the month, we meet for breakfast together now that all four of us kids have flown the coop.

I have come straight from the morning running club I joined a few months ago, so I brought a change of clothes to shower here and avoid stinking everyone out. The club meet every Saturday at 6 am, running five kilometres around West End near mine and Tara's apartment, and it's been a great way to channel some of my extra energy. I'm glad I'd kept up with my running with Seth and Lincoln, because I'm determined to beat my personal best now. It's my latest hyper-fixation in a long line of sport related hyper-fixations, and Tara just shakes her head when I am researching all the best gear. But she's never understood my enjoyment of exercise, not realising that it's something I need in order to keep the chaos in my mind under some form of control.

Coming from a family of early risers, I'm not surprised when my twenty-year-old sisters, Emma and Dayna, are already sitting in the kitchen, even though it's only 7:30. Dad is busy at the stove, and Mum is squeezing fresh orange juice.

I give both my parents a kiss, and Will strolls in a few moments after me, screwing up his nose when he gets near me. "Jeez Kyles, you stink."

"I was just about to shower, asshole."

"Well, get a move on. This will all be ready in the next few minutes." Dad waves his hand over all the food cooking on the stove.

I head off to the bathroom and have a quick shower before rejoining the rest of my family at the table.

"So, who was the hot guy in all your photos on your trip?" Emma asks as soon as I sit down, crunching on some maple bacon.

"His name is Seth. He's Canadian," I reply, helping myself to some orange juice before loading up my plate with a decent serving of bacon, eggs and hash browns.

"Seth... What's going on there?" Will asks through a mouthful of food, and I screw my face up in disgust.

"Gross, Will, don't talk with your mouth full. And nothing is going on there. He lives in Canada."

"Convenient. You'll have to catch up with him again when you go," he says, completely ignoring the part about not talking with his mouth full.

"You're going to Canada?" Dad pipes up, and I shoot a glare at my brother before sighing.

"Will wants me to go," I say, looking at Dad before turning back to Will. "And Canada is an enormous country, so even if I were to go, I doubt very much that I'd see him. It's like me walking up to another random Australian overseas and saying 'hey, do you know Joe?'"

"Well, he's in practically all of your photos. And he is freaking hot. You totally should have hooked up," Dayna says, deciding to add her two cents as well.

"Anyone else wanna weigh in here? Mum, how about you?" I ask, avoiding giving a response to the hooking up statement.

Emma narrows her eyes while she studies me. "Oh!" she gasps dramatically. "You did hook up!"

"Everyone leave Kylie alone," Mum interjects, and I've never been more grateful to her in my life.

I was seconds away from informing the twins they were an accident (the six-year age gap between us has always made their appearance questionable, as far as I'm concerned), and telling Will I was the favourite.

"Well, you know your grandparents would love to have you stay with them, Kylie. Grandma and Grandpa are always telling me how much they wish they got to see you kids more," Dad says, ignoring all the talk about me hooking up.

"I told her she could work for me while travelling still. As long as she has internet, it doesn't matter where she is," Will says to him, and Dad nods.

I might as well not even be here, with all these opinions on who I should sleep with and where I should travel being thrown around. Sometimes I really hate being from a big family.

"Can we please talk about something else? I told Will I'd think about Canada, and I have no intention of telling anyone who I did or did not sleep with in the presence of our parents."

"And, as your parent, I am grateful to hear that," Mum replies, giving both my sisters a stern look.

They roll their eyes in unison, something they do alarmingly often, but thankfully, the topic of conversation switches to their university studies, and I breathe a silent sigh of relief.

I'm loathe to admit it, but the idea of seeing Seth again may be something I'm taking into consideration if I follow my brother's advice and head to Canada for a while. I refuse to let my thoughts go any further, though. I only know he's from a small town in British Columbia, but maybe there aren't that many Seth James' in BC... It would seem more than a little stalkerish to just suddenly arrive in his country and ask him to make plans to see me though. And I don't want to chase after a guy. Regardless of how amazing his abs are.

I spend the rest of the day hanging out with Tara on the couch, binge watching an old sitcom on Netflix while she keeps glancing at the time on her phone. I wait for a message from Will, backing out of coming tonight, but it never comes. By the time Tara and I arrive at Jake and Bri's apartment, she's an anxious mess.

"It'll be okay, T. This is a good thing," I say, squeezing her arm while we're riding the elevator up to the penthouse apartment.

She says nothing, but gives me a very fake looking smile, her face pale. I could throttle my brother for putting Tara through this. Well, if I was going to throttle anyone, it was going to be Annelisa, but Will was the one who hurt my best friend by cutting her out of his life.

I just want to enjoy a night with my friends, but we need to get through the awkward stuff first. When Jake opens the door, Tara and I both give him a hug before going in search of Bri. We find her sitting on a sun lounger on the terrace, her legs covered by a blanket, with their little dog, Maddie, curled up beside her. They've set up three outdoor heaters to take some of the late afternoon chill out of the air.

"Hey," Bri says, getting to her feet and hugging us both, her long blond hair flowing down her back.

"Hey. The place looks great, as always," I reply, looking around at the various pot plants and garden beds that Bri has added since I was last here.

She and Jake split their time between this place and their house in Stanthorpe, but we haven't seen them as often recently. Jake has taken over his father's small electrician business, so they haven't been coming back as regularly, which saddens me. I'd become used to having Bri around again after she returned from Sydney.

"Thanks. You should see what I've done with the garden at home. I've discovered I have a green thumb and have started a veggie patch. We even got chickens," Bri says, her eyes lighting up.

I laugh. "You're turning into a real country girl now."

"She fits right in out there. She looks very cute in her gardening overalls and gumboots," Jake says, joining us outside.

"Bri looks cute no matter what she's wearing," I reply.

"Yes, she does." Jake grins, squeezing Bri's shoulders and dropping a kiss onto the top of her head. "I'm just getting dinner sorted. Do you ladies want any drinks?"

"I've got a bottle of wine out here in the fridge. I've got us covered." Bri turns over her shoulder to give Jake a quick kiss.

"No worries. Do you want something other than wine, Kyles?" Jake asks.

This is why Jake Boyd was the guy we all lusted after in high school. He notices everything and takes care of everyone all the time. While our friends know I'm no longer drinking, sometimes they forget, but Jake always makes sure I have other options.

"I'm okay with water, thanks Jake."

He nods and heads back inside. The three of us chat for a while, Tara and I filling Bri in on our trip. When we hear the intercom ring inside, Tara tenses up beside me, and Bri shoots me a questioning look.

"Will's coming," I say.

"Oh. But that's good, right?" She looks at Tara, who shrugs.

"I guess. I'm still pretty hurt by it all."

That one sentence is more than Tara has said to me about the situation in the last year. She's avoided going into too much detail and now that I think about it, it's been me ranting about Will's bullheadedness and Tara has said nothing in reply each time.

Shit... I've been such a terrible friend.

Have I done the wrong thing in insisting that they both be here tonight? I was so eager to get everyone back to normal, but maybe there was no going back from this?

Too late now though. I can hear my brother's voice inside, along with Bri's sister Morgan and her husband Chris. Within minutes, everyone is out here with us, Jake leading the way with a baking dish in his hands. The others follow behind, carrying various items, and the three of us join them over at the table. There's a moment of awkwardness. It's the first time we've all been together in over a year, and the absence of Annelisa is like an elephant in the room.

Tara and Will glance at each other before looking away, and the rest of us fidget in our seats.

I have never handled awkwardness well, so my mouth opens up and blurts out, "So, I think I'm going to move to Canada for a while."

Well, that's one way to make a decision...

20
THINGS WERE ALWAYS
BOUND TO CHANGE

KYLIE

"So, you're going to move to Canada, huh?"

These are Will's first words to me at 4:30 on Sunday morning when I climb into his ute, our surfboards loaded in the back.

"Apparently," I reply, yawning.

"You hadn't even thought about it, had you?" He knows me too well.

"Nope. Hadn't even considered it. But everyone was being weird, and the words just popped out." The follow-up questions to my little word vomit last night had flowed at lightning speed.

Tara had looked stunned, and the conversation in the car on the drive home was a little stilted. I know I need to talk to her about it today, because I dropped a bomb for both of us on a night when she was already pretty stressed. Will had pulled Tara aside before he left, but I'm not sure how it went, because Tara said nothing to me about it on the way home, and had gone to bed early.

The others all thought it was a great idea, though, and it had broken through the weirdness for the rest of dinner.

"So you're not going to go?" Will asks.

"I actually think I will. Now that I've said it out loud, it kind of seems like a great idea. You should come with me, at least for a holiday."

"I could maybe swing a week or two, but not until like December. When do you think you'll go?"

"Maybe in a few months... I need to discuss things with Tara first," I reply, trying not to think about how that conversation might go.

We spend the rest of the drive to Noosa discussing the logistics of it all, and by the time I'm pulling on my wetsuit, the excitement is hard to shake. I know I need to try not to get ahead of myself, but this is what I do. Once I decide to do something, it consumes me.

The freezing water serves as a wake up call to slow my racing thoughts down a little though.

Surfing has always been my happy place. It helps calm my mind, and I straddle my board while I wait for my first wave of the morning. There's only a few of us out here, and it's just so peaceful. The sun has just started to appear over the horizon, and a thrill runs down my spine when I see a pod of dolphins break the surface only a few metres from where I'm floating.

This was the feeling that I'd tried to explain to Seth when we were talking about the sense of peace that washes over me when I'm on the water. Sure, there are dangers to this, like sharks or injuring myself when catching a wave, but what is a life without risk?

I watch Will begin paddling, lining up with a wave about to break. Once he's moving, he pops up and rides the wave in towards the shore. I love that we have this shared passion, and that he still has something he can throw himself into after the crappy year he's had. I'm still uncertain if telling him Annelisa's whereabouts was a wise decision, but what's he going to do? Fly to London and roam the streets shouting her name? Maybe knowing where she is will finally give him the closure to know she isn't just going to walk back into his life while she's on the other side of the world.

Then again, the guy that I'm lusting over is just as far away, and that hasn't stopped me from thinking about him constantly.

I don't allow my thoughts to wander to Seth, keeping myself from daydreaming about someone I can't be with. Instead, I turn my focus to the waves, swinging my legs back behind me so that I'm lying on my belly. Spying the perfect wave, I paddle to get ahead of it, and once it breaks, I jump up, balancing with ease after over two decades of practice.

No matter how many times I do this, it never gets old. I reach my hand out to touch the water beside me as the wave fades out, the beauty of it threatening to overwhelm me. Sometimes, I find my emotions getting the better of me out here, and once I've ridden the wave to its end, I dunk my face in the water to wash away the tears that had started to flow.

After another hour, Will and I head back to shore, and I notice the cold that I'd been ignoring. Stripping out of my wetsuit, I dry myself off hastily before yanking on my tracksuit pants and hoodie over my bikini, shoving my feet back into my Ugg boots. We grab coffees from our favourite cafe and head back to Brisbane.

After Will drops me off, I enter our apartment and am surprised to find Bri sitting on the couch with Tara.

"Hey, I thought you were heading home today?" I ask, throwing myself into the arm chair facing the couch.

"Yeah, we're leaving in a couple of hours, but I thought I'd come hang out with you ladies before I go back. I've missed you both."

Tara hasn't spoken since I walked in the door, and there's something about the look on her face that has me worried.

"What's going on?" I ask.

Tara exchanges a look with Bri before turning back to me. "So... this whole moving to Canada thing?"

"Yeah... sorry about how I dumped that on you, by the way. That was really shitty, my mouth just opened, and the words fell out," I say, assuming that's why she looks upset.

"It's okay. I actually think it's a good idea."

I hadn't been expecting that. "Okay... so what's wrong, then?"

She takes a deep breath. "I've been feeling weird about everything for a while now. Obviously, we were fine on our trip, but with all the stuff with Annelisa and Will, I've been feeling the strain of being caught in the middle of it all. I'd been thinking about getting my own place for a little while, but I didn't want to say anything to you, because you're still my best friend and I don't want it to be a thing for us..." Her voice trails off.

I blink a few times, trying to work out what's happening here. "Wait, have I been making you feel bad?"

"I know that you don't mean to, but yeah, a little. You're justifiably angry with Annelisa for how much she hurt Will, and you've been mad at Will for making things uncomfortable for me. I haven't wanted to say anything to you about it, because I know your heart is in the right place, but I've just wanted to step away from it all. It's kind of why I haven't really talked to you about it, because you just get angry at the pair of them."

Bri has been watching the exchange with a sad expression, and I can tell that they've discussed this between themselves.

I try not to feel hurt, but I can feel tears start to form, and I blink again, frustrated with my body for reacting like this when it's not about me. Well, it is about me. I'm a really shit friend, apparently.

"I'm so sorry, T. I had no idea I've been making you feel so bad. You should have told me to shut up."

"I didn't want to make a big deal out of it. But last night when you said you were moving to Canada, I was taken by surprise.

Then, when I realised I felt relieved, I knew we needed to talk. I have loved living with you, and I really loved travelling with you, but I think this bit of distance will be good for us. Our lease is up in like two months, and Bri mentioned to me this morning that I could move into the apartment if I didn't want to find a new housemate cause they aren't able to come back much now... It feels like it's all happening at the right time for both of us." She picks at a thread on the cushion she's clutching to her chest, and I can tell she's having a hard time looking at me.

"I don't really know what to say... I just... Are we okay?"

"Oh hon, of course we are." She finally looks at me, and I can see tears shining in her eyes. "We've been friends for so long and lived together for six years. You'll never be able to shake me even if you tried. But I think it's time I took a step back from group gatherings and stop putting you in situations where you have to choose. From everyone having to choose."

"What the hell did Will say to you last night?" I ask, realising I hadn't asked my brother about it this morning.

"It was fine. He apologised for being a dick, but I know things will never be how they were before. As much as we are a part of the group, without my sister connecting me to them, I know I'm not as close to the others as I am to you two." She gestures towards Bri and me. "You guys are still connected to them all in a way that I'm not now."

I fight against the overwhelming urge to get on a plane, fly to London, and strangle Annelisa.

"I just wish things could go back to the way they were..." I say, and Tara gives me a sad smile.

"I know you do. But things were always bound to change, eventually."

"I guess..."

And that's how we decide that in two months' time, I'll be moving to Canada and Tara will move into Jake and Bri's apartment on her own. The three of us end up a crying mess together on the couch, but at least Tara has finally been honest with me.

I guess it's time I had a chat with my grandparents.

21

WHERE'S YOUR HEAD AT?

SETH

THE CLOCK IS TICKING DOWN on the first game of the season and the adrenaline running through my veins is a welcome feeling. We're fortunate that our first game is at home, and the crowd noise has grown from nervous to ecstatic, screaming with each goal we score.

The team is a mix of returning players and a few new ones gained in trades or graduating from the minors. It's difficult not to think's about the friends that moved on in the off-season. It was sad to see them leave, but I know management has built our roster into a strong contender with high expectations.

Linc and I are on the first line, and I flick the puck towards him while I fly down the ice, narrowly avoiding the shoulder of Denver's massive defenceman, David Elders. Elders lacks my speed but makes up for it with strength, hockey sense, and a willingness to bend the rules.

We've had beef over the years, and he's been doing his best to bash into me every time we're on the ice together, but I just flash him a cocky grin and cut around him while Linc slaps the puck into the empty net. Denver had pulled their goalie two minutes ago in a last-ditch effort to claw their way back.

The crowd goes wild and Linc throws his hands up while I barrel into him. We're now up four to two, with only thirty seconds left on the clock, so we celebrate on the bench while the second line kills the remaining time.

Once the final buzzer goes off, the crowd erupts and I grin, relieved that we were able to give the fans what they demanded.

The Denver players file off the ice with their heads bowed while we celebrate. This is exactly what we needed to start the season. A fresh start to wash away the sour ending to last season.

I grab the team flag and pass it to Jenson, our newest rookie left-winger, letting him take it for a spin around the ice. Linc had two goals and an assist, so he's named first star, and he hands a signed stick to the young kid standing on the carpet that's replaced the net.

"Way to go, buddy." I slap him on the back when he passes me on the way into the locker room, and the rest of the team lets out a cheer for him.

I'm stuck on media detail, so I have to front the cameras before I can head inside, telling the reporters how happy we are with our efforts on the ice and what a great start it is for the season.

One regular, Alana something, pipes up. "It's good to see you're not letting last season's devastating loss get to you too much. Where's your head at?"

I really hate these sorts of questions, but I've had plenty of media training, and I give the usual bland response. "We're focusing on the new season and are confident we'll be back in the playoffs this year."

I finally join the rest of the team, and after Coach gives his "well done" speech, everyone makes quick work of showering and getting dressed in their suits, each with a beer in hand.

We've got the usual family dinner afterwards, and I can't help but feel envious when I watch most of my teammates celebrate with their loved ones while we eat. I've been so busy the last few weeks that I haven't thought about Kylie as much. But she's never far from my mind, and I wonder what it would be like if she was here. Would she get along with the other partners? I know a few would be welcoming, but some of them can be pretty cliquey as well, something I notice more now that there is someone I wish was here with me.

I lean against the bar, nursing my second (and last) beer for the night, while Linc chats with Jenson beside me. I watch Dean flirting with a few of the women that have joined us and notice a couple of them looking in our direction. It's no secret that only a few of us are single, and each season we spend half of our time dodging the professional husband chasers, looking to lock down a high-paid NHL player. Dean finds it amusing and uses it to his advantage, but Linc and I both avoid these women at all costs.

Two of our newest players, Russian defenceman Pieter Volkov and Finnish right-winger Timo Hakala, saunter over to the group, and I breathe a sigh of relief when they divert the attention of the blonde who had been looking like she was about to head my way.

"I think I'm going to call it a night," I say, tapping my beer bottle to Linc's before draining the last of it.

"You don't want to come out?" he asks, looking surprised.

"Nah, I'm beat. You guys have a good night, though."

He eyes me warily before nodding slowly. I've done all the socialising I can handle and just want to go home to my book and get a good sleep.

When I hop in the car out the front and give the driver my address, I sit back and scroll through the few photos from the trip that I took, stopping on the last one. I'd snapped a photo of Kylie outside the Tower of London while she'd been smiling at some-thing I'd said. It was just after the one - and only - selfie I took with her.

It's been weeks since I last saw Kylie, yet the memory of her still hasn't faded. How is it possible to be hung up on someone I'd only known for three weeks? I guess because, for the first time in my adult life, I'd finally met someone that I didn't have to wonder if they were only interested in me because of what I do for a living.

I wish we'd exchanged numbers, something I've been cursing myself about. I miss talking to her. Even if it would have just been a brief text asking how her day was going, it would have been better than the complete silence now. Is she missing me too? She probably has a line of men vying for her attention now that she's back home. Women who are so outgoing and beautiful rarely stay single for long.

I stare out the window, watching the streets of downtown Calgary flash by. It's starting to get colder now, and we've had snow in the past week. Remembering that day in Switzerland, I allow myself to imagine Kylie sitting beside me, admiring the winter wonderland outside. Spending time with her and Tara has given me a new appreciation for the beauty of winter in Canada. As it's only fall, I'm sure I'll be over it in a few weeks once it's constantly snowing, but for now, it's a novelty once again.

The next morning, my phone rings during my workout, and I smile when I see "Dad" lighting up on the screen.

"Hey Dad," I say, pausing the treadmill and grabbing a drink from my water bottle.

"Hey bud. That was a great game last night." His voice echoes through my home gym, my phone connected to the bluetooth speaker.

"Thanks. It was definitely good to start the season with a win."

"Still can't believe I have to cheer for the Mounties," he grumbles.

I roll my eyes. "Sorry, old man. It's not likely to change anytime soon either."

Dad mutters something that sounds distinctly like "for now" before continuing to speak. "Your mother and I have got season tickets again, so we will be at the game when you play in Vancouver in a few months."

A devoted Vancouver fan, he has long lamented that he has had to cheer for Boston, then Calgary when I play. It's especially difficult for him when we play Vancouver, his loyalties torn.

It's rare for me to put my own needs first with anyone, but every time he's pushed for me to get my agent to talk to Vancouver's management, I've shut him down. The Mounties are my team, and I plan on being with them until retirement, if I can. While there's always a chance I could be traded, I'm pretty confident that I'll be staying put.

We discuss last night's game in detail while I start my weights routine.

"Your mother wants to know who the woman is in all those photos from your trip, by the way."

I pause, holding the dumbbell in my right hand to my chest. "How did Mom see photos?"

"She follows Lincoln online. He shared all the photos on his personal account."

Of course he did. He had been snapping away constantly, while I was lucky to take ten photos across the entire trip. I definitely posed for a lot, though, between him and the girls.

"Ah, okay."

"So," Dad prompts. "Who is she?"

"So what you're really saying is *you* want to know who the woman in the photos was." I shake my head, realising I better check these photos out myself.

"Correct." At least he knows he's a gossip.

"She was another person on the tour with us. She and her friend are Australian, and the four of us spent our time together on the trip."

"Well, you both looked very cosy together."

Yep, definitely need to see these photos.

"Yes, I'm sure we did. But there's nothing to report." As close as I am to my parents, I draw the line at sharing information about the women who have been in my life.

"Well, that's a shame. She is very attractive."

Refusing to take the bait that my father is dangling, I shift the conversation to less dangerous ground.

It's not until after we hang up I allow myself to think about what it would be like to introduce Kylie to my parents. And realise I've never considered that with any other women I've been with since I moved out of home.

22

GET HER SOME MOUNTIES GEAR

KYLIE

FEELING as if my eyelids have turned into sandpaper, I exit the Arrivals area of the Calgary airport, scanning the crowd for my grandparents while dragging my suitcase behind me. After my European adventure, you would think that I would have become well practiced at international long-haul flights by now. But that is not the case, and right now, all I want is to take a long, hot shower and fall into bed. I'd timed my flight from Vancouver so I'd be arriving in the evening and I'm so grateful I'd had that foresight now.

"Kylie!" I hear my name being screamed and spot my cousin, Adele, bouncing around next to our grandfather.

"Oh my god! What are you doing here?" I race over and throw my arms around her while Grandpa pats my head.

"I couldn't miss out on being part of the welcoming committee!" She rocks us from side to side, clinging tightly to me.

"Hey, where's my hug?" Grandpa demands, and Adele and I pull apart, laughing, so that I can step into his open arms.

It's been five years since I saw him, the last time he came to Australia with Grandma, and it's been far too long.

"I've missed you so much," I sob into his shoulder while he hugs me tightly.

"Now love, it's alright. You're here now. Let's get you home for some dinner and bed," he says gruffly, never one to handle big emotions well.

"Yes please, I am so tired."

He takes my bag and suitcase while Adele links her arm through mine.

"I am so glad you're here. And you're staying!"

Adele and I are very similar in our over the top personalities, something that caused issues when we were kids whenever my family visited, but we've struck up a long distance friendship since we've grown older and I'm looking forward to spending more time with her. It's turned out well to have a cousin my age who can help me get my bearings here.

When we walk outside, I yelp when the bitter, icy wind whips me in the face. I gratefully accept the jacket that Adele holds out to me, throwing it on before rushing after Grandpa to the multi-story car park.

When Grandpa drives the car out of the airport and onto the main road, I stare out the window at the snow on the ground.

"It's only October. Why is it snowing already?" I ask.

Grandpa laughs. "It can snow all year round here."

"What?" I squeak.

Adele's laughter joins Grandpas. "Ah, my sweet, Australian summer child. You have no idea what you've moved to. This is going to be fun." She sounds almost gleeful in the face of my misery.

I'm rethinking our friendship.

"You'll get used to it, Kylie, don't worry." Grandpa tries to sound reassuring, but I don't think I believe him.

Dad had warned me about the weather, but honestly, I'd

thought he was exaggerating. Who has even heard of -40 degrees, anyway?

The next morning, I stumble out of bed close to midday, cursing jet lag while I make myself a cup of coffee with Grandpa's beloved coffee machine. I'm staying in their basement suite while I'm here for the next three months, although now that Grandma has me here, she's determined to never let me go.

I'm perfectly okay with being doted over for a while.

"So, what are your plans now that you're here?" Grandma asks when I join her on the couch in their living room upstairs.

It's toasty warm, and I had almost forgotten about the weather outside until Grandpa comes stomping in from scrapping the snow off the driveway, a blast of cold air following behind him. They definitely make houses with better insulation here. If it was like this outside in Brisbane, my parents' house would be filled with ice right now.

"I'm going to keep doing Will's admin for a while, but I'll probably look at getting a job here. Just need to work out what I want to do."

"Well, your Aunt Sheryl said to call her if you want to consider working for her," Grandpa says, leaning down to undo the laces on his boots.

"At the travel agency?" My aunt and her husband run a company together, and Adele works with them while she's studying, along with her brother Jordan.

"It's not a travel agency, it's a tour company. She thought with your sunny personality, you might enjoy that more than some stuffy office job."

I consider Grandpa's words for a moment. It does sound far more interesting than admin work for Will. Maybe I could do both? It would be nice to save some money while I'm here, and it's not like I'm going to have a busy social life, at least to start with.

"I'll speak to her about it tonight at dinner. It sounds like it could be fun."

"I also think I need to take you shopping for winter clothes," Grandma says.

I nod. "Yes, please, I have nothing that is even remotely warm enough."

"I assumed as much. Your father did not prepare you at all." She tuts and I cover my smirk with my hand.

Dad isn't even here, and she's still giving him a hard time.

"Make sure you get her some Mounties gear while you're at it," Grandpa says, and I raise an eyebrow.

"That's the hockey team, right?" I ask.

He looks disgusted. "That you have to even ask that makes me very sad. I don't know where I went wrong with that son of mine."

"Aw, poor Dad. It's okay Grandpa, even though he doesn't care about hockey, he still has his Canadian accent."

I have always found it hilarious that my father avoids hockey so much, while the rest of our family are rabid fans. Grandpa has his radio constantly set to the sport channel, with hockey commentators droning on all day. And my dear, sweet Grandma has been known to scream curses at the TV when something happens she doesn't agree with. I'm not sure about my aunt, but given Adele is also a fan, I'd say she's just as into it as the others.

But Dad refused to take us to any games whenever we ventured back, claiming it gave him PTSD. I may get my dramatic nature from him...

So I get the sense that I won't get much of a choice now that I'm here alone.

Grandpa glowers. "Well, we'll get at least one of you kids to realise that hockey is in your blood."

Case in point.

"Will and I have watched a few games because of our friend Chris, so I kind of know some rules. It might be fun to go to a game sometime."

"We have season tickets. You will go to many games." His tone is final.

It's a good reminder of just how seriously this family takes the game.

Grandma takes me out a few hours later and I buy a whole new winter wardrobe, complete with super cute boots.

"We can get you some Mounties gear when we go to a game. It will add to the experience if you buy it at the stadium. So let's get you a regular toque while we're here, and then you can get one there," she says, nodding towards the table next to her.

"I don't know that I'll ever stop calling it a beanie," I say to Grandma while I sift through the pile of headwear at the big department store we've wandered into.

"We'll make a Canadian out of you yet, my child."

"How about a fancy hybrid version?" I ask, grinning.

She smiles at me. "That sounds perfect."

I've seen a few people out and about in sports jerseys, and when I spy another grandmother with her tiny granddaughter, both decked out in black and red, I turn to Grandma.

"Is there a game today? Is that why everyone is all dressed in their jerseys?"

"Yes. They're playing in Edmonton tonight, so it's the Battle of Alberta. We take it seriously here."

It blows my mind just how into hockey everyone is. None of my friends or family back home are massive sports fans, so this is all new ground for me. But it seems like it could be fun to get swept up in the city's love for the game.

"When is the next game here?" I settle on a cute red 'toque' with a bobble on top and follow Grandma to the register.

"The next home game is on Saturday night. We've bought tickets for you, Adele, and Adele's boyfriend, Ben, who's in town from Vancouver. We got a fourth ticket too, because Adele wants to bring another friend. Your seats are near ours. We wanted your first game to be memorable, so you're right beside the Mounties bench. You might even get to be on camera."

I don't know much about hockey, but I know that's impressive.

23
TELL ME AGAIN HOW IT
WAS JUST A HOLIDAY THING

SETH

THE BATTLE of Alberta is an institution, and Calgary and Edmonton fans can become pretty fired up towards each other. Any time we play Edmonton, emotions are running hot, and tonight's game is no exception. We're at the disadvantage of being on their home ice, but that just fuels our desire to win.

I can hear the crowd screaming while I skate to the bench door during a line change and take a quick moment to look up in the stands, the atmosphere adding to the adrenaline running through my veins. Currently, the game is tied with a score of two to two. But we've still got five minutes left, and now it's just a matter of which team is the hungriest for the win. I'd really like to avoid going into overtime and lean forward to holler out encouragement when Jenson flies past with the puck, ducking under the outstretched arm of Edmonton's captain, Dylan White, who slams into the boards before racing after him. Jenson flicks the puck across to Volkov before skating behind the net. Volkov sees the opening and once Jenson is in place, he shoots the puck back to him and Jenson slaps it hard, narrowly avoiding the glove of the goalie, Tatum Billings, and landing it in the net.

The crowd goes quiet save for a smattering of boos and a few cheers from our handful of fans lucky enough to get tickets in enemy territory. Those of us on the bench jump up to high-five our team mates who skate past on the ice. The third line heads to the bench while Linc and I, along with the rest of the first line, make our way out to centre ice.

I look up at the clock. Four and a half minutes left to keep the lead.

Anything could happen in four and a half minutes.

I'm determined we are leaving this game ahead. The ref skates up beside me, puck in hand, and I crouch with my stick ready, ignoring the aggravating chirping from Dylan, who faces off against me after being double shifted in a desperate attempt to tie the game.

So much about this game is about getting into each other's heads on the ice, but I've always been pretty good at blocking out the noise. Once the puck drops, I scramble for it, shoving Dylan aside and shooting the puck towards Linc. He takes off with it down the ice, streaking towards the net. Dylan races after him, and I follow suit, tracking Linc while he narrowly avoids being slammed into the boards by one of Edmonton's defencemen.

When I get near him, Linc passes me the puck and I turn to shoot it towards the net. My mind goes into slow motion when I watch the puck heading towards a gap under the blocker. I'm ready to raise my hands in celebration when the puck collides into the post with a bang and I lose sight of it.

Thankfully, Karl Lindberg, our left winger, is the first player to notice the ricochet and reaches past a defender to catch the puck with his glove, dropping it to the ice before firing it back to Linc. As I get in position to the right of the net near Tatum, who is distracted by Linc, I bang my stick down and Linc lets the puck fly.

It hits my stick and I smash it into the net before Tatum has a chance to do more than turn his head.

The majority of the crowd is silent while I throw my arms up, bracing myself when my other four teammates on the ice crash into me from all sides.

This is why I love this game. Sending rival fans to the exits early while cursing my name is almost as rewarding as hearing cheers at home.

Despite the crappy ending of last season, I don't think I could give this up. It's the only time I want the attention on myself, when our team is victorious.

I get out of media detail today, smirking when Linc gets stuck dealing with the questions while I follow the rest of the team into the locker room. Checking my phone, a name I haven't seen in a while shows up. A friend of mine and Linc's from high school, Ben, lets me know he'll be in town from Vancouver this weekend. He'll be at the game on Friday with his girlfriend and wants to know if we can catch up at some stage.

We've got a big weekend of team events ahead of us before heading on the road for several away games, but I figure I can squeeze in a catch up with him after the game and send back a quick reply suggesting a bar local to my house. Linc and I are regulars there and they usually keep away any unwanted attention when we show up, so it'll be a better way to catch up without an audience.

"Did you see the message from Ben?" Linc asks once we're back on the team bus.

"Yeah, I told him to go to Buck's Bar after the game and we'd meet them there. Did you know he was dating someone in Calgary?"

"Nah man, but I haven't heard from him in a while, not since I left Vancouver. Will be good to see him."

I go to reply, but my phone lights up, showing off my wallpaper, the photo of Kylie and I together on our final day in London. I'd changed it in a moment of weakness last week.

Linc looks down at it and snorts. "Go on, tell me again how it was just a holiday thing."

"It was. How can it possibly be anything more? This would take long distance to a ridiculous level."

"True, but you're clearly into her more than you're admitting. I've never seen you like this over a woman before. Kylie is awesome, so I think you should try to see if you can make something out of it with her." Linc points at my phone.

"What are we talking about?" Dean looks over the back of the chair in front of us.

"Seth met an awesome chick while we were away, and I think he should go for it."

"What's the problem?" Dean asks, looking at me.

"She lives in Australia," I reply, and his eyebrows shoot up.

"Jeez. Yeah, I can see why that would be a problem."

"But," Linc interrupts, "she's half Canadian and has family in Calgary. So it's not like it would be a huge leap to ask her to come here for a while."

"Even if I knew how to get in touch with her, I can't ask her to uproot her life," I say, shaking my head.

"You're never going to know if you don't ask. I'm sure if you contacted the tour company, they'd have her email address or something," Dean replies.

I let my head fall back against the headrest with a groan. "Great, now there are two of you. Look, Kylie and I agreed it was just a holiday thing. Just drop it, okay?"

"Whatever. All I know is that she got you to jump out a fucking plane, man. You wouldn't do that for just any woman."

"You jumped out of a plane?" Dean looks stunned.

"You did what, Davidson?" Coach has now joined the conversation from where he sits a few seats ahead, looking pissed.

I shoot him a wary look. "Linc did it, too."

"Oh nice, that's loyalty for you," Linc says in mock outrage.

"If I'm going down, you're going down with me."

"No more jumping out of planes, chuckleheads. You're both too expensive to replace." Coach levels us both with a glare.

"Aw, thanks Coach, I really feel the love," Linc says, placing a hand over his heart.

"Watch it, O'Malley." Coach turns back to the front of the bus.

I smack Linc up the back of the head. "Say it fucking louder next time."

While Dean and Linc continue chatting, I stare at the photo on my screen. Maybe Dean's right. Maybe I could ask the tour company for Kylie's contact details, or at least pass my details on to her. I know they'd been putting together a list of people's contact information on the last day for those who wanted to stay in touch. Linc and I hadn't bothered putting our details down, but now I'm regretting it. Why had I been so stupid and not even got her email address? Even if we weren't going to try and have a relationship, it would still have been nice to stay in touch.

Vowing to look into contacting the company once we get home, I pocket my phone and rejoin the conversation with Linc and Dean, feeling a little lighter at the idea of finding a way to have Kylie back in my life.

24

NOT ON A HOLIDAY TOGETHER

KYLIE

"So, I want to introduce you to one of my friends. I think you guys would really hit it off. He's coming to the game on Friday with us." Adele casually drops this news while we browse the racks of some store called Nordstrom, looking for a new top for me to wear.

"Hm... I don't know... I'm kind of still hung up on someone." I've never been a fan of being set up with people.

I'm also not lying. Now that I'm in Canada, Seth has been plaguing my thoughts constantly. I've even considered contacting the tour company to see if they have an email address for him. Not sure if they'd share that info, but it's worth a shot.

"The guy you met on your trip, right?" Adele holds up a very revealing top.

I eye it cautiously. "Yeah, the one in all my photos."

"I'm going to admit something that probably makes me a bad cousin, but I actually didn't really look at all the photos."

I laugh, then shake my head at the top she's still holding out.

"It's okay, I probably wouldn't have looked either. Other people's holiday photos are kind of boring."

"He's Canadian, right? Have you stayed in touch? Do you know where he lives?"

I shake my head "No. And even if we had stayed in touch, things with Seth might be completely different now that we're not on a holiday together." I'm trying to downplay my feelings, and shrug to give the impression of aloofness.

Adele doesn't buy it though. "You clearly like this guy a lot or you wouldn't still be thinking about him months later."

I sigh. "Yeah, but I'm realistic. How often do these things really work out? And besides, I didn't come here for a guy."

"Well, I, for one, won't complain if you fall madly in love and end up living here forever. Grandma and Grandpa will love it too. Oh, and Mum said to tell you to come into the office next week to chat about starting work when you're ready. We need a new tour guide for some stuff coming up and she thinks you'd be the perfect fit."

I'm interested to learn more about the tours that they run, the idea of getting to travel around for work becoming more and more appealing. But for now, I just need to focus on getting through tomorrow night and Adele's attempt to set me up with her friend.

I finally find a red top that is both warm and pretty, trying it on to applause from Adele.

"That's the one to get any man's engine racing. That's if anyone sees it, given that we will have you covered in Mounties merch for the game. I've decided I'm buying you your first jersey as soon as we get to the stadium."

"It still blows my mind how seriously you guys all take hockey here. I mean, I'm sure there are avid sports fans around in Brisbane. I just only ever saw them wearing the gear if they were on their way to or from a game. People here seem to wear the Mounties stuff as part of their daily wardrobe." I lead the way to the register, handing over the top to the smiling sales assistant.

When she tells me the price, I pause for a moment, before remembering I'm in a country that doesn't include the tax in the price listed. I suck at maths. This is going to hurt my brain every time I buy something.

"Well, we've become particularly rabid after we made the Stanley Cup final last year. Like, we were pretty full on before-hand, but this was the first time we'd made it to the playoffs in years, and we were so close to a win. But the captain, Davidson, tripped on choppy ice just as he was about to take a shot, and then New Jersey stole the puck and scored the winning goal with seconds to spare." Adele leads the way out of the store and we head for the food court.

"Wow, that sucks. Poor guy."

"Yeah, the media went pretty hard for him. Ben is actually friends with him. I've never met him before, but Ben was going to try to catch up with him while he's in town this weekend, so I might get to meet him. From what I know, he's a really nice guy but pretty reserved, so having all the negative attention probably messed with his head a bit. He seems to have come back strong this season, though." She stops at the first of many food places. "Right, what do you want to eat?"

I look at the options and feel myself becoming overwhelmed by the choices.

"Um... what's good? You guys have way more fast-food places than we do back home."

"Well, what do you feel like?"

Oh those dreaded words that have long caused me to panic. I look around, tempted just to go to McDonalds because I at least know what to expect from there. But I'm here for new experiences, so I need to expand my culinary choices as well.

"Can you just take me to one you like? Narrow down my choices?" I finally ask, and Adele nods, happy to take charge.

Next time, I'm doing more research about what my options

are. I've never been great at deciding on the fly, and other than McDonalds, I don't recognise any of the names.

Adele leads the way to a place called A&W. Staring up at the menu, she points out the different burgers to choose from, and I settle on the Mama Burger with fries and a Coke. When they hand me my order, I stare at the 'small' drink, stunned at the size of the cup. It's bigger than the large drinks back home. There's no way I'll be able to drink that much soft drink.

We might speak the same language and both be a part of the Commonwealth, but some things in this country are so different from what I'm used to. So far, it's all still a novelty, but I wonder when that novelty will wear off and I'll start missing things from back home?

25
WANT ME TO SIGN
IT FOR YOU LATER?

SETH

FRIDAY NIGHT finally arrives and we're playing our first game against Vancouver, Linc's former team and my father's one true love after my mother. Normally I'm pretty calm before a game, but for some reason, every time we play Vancouver, my stomach is in knots. Probably because I'm worried about Dad's feelings when we smash them.

I must be even quieter than normal, because Linc has been shooting me wary looks for the last half an hour while we go through the game play and get dressed before warm up.

"You gonna be able to get your head in the game tonight?" he finally asks.

"Yeah. I'm good," I reply, not wanting any unnecessary attention around my headspace.

We're finally in a good place as a team. The disaster from last year is behind us and there's been no mutterings about me keeping the captaincy.

So the last thing I need is anyone questioning if I'm in the right frame of mind for a game. One questioning remark said near the wrong person and it'll be all over the media. I've already had to deal with too many questions from that Alana lady, who keeps showing up everywhere of late.

I don't need any more fuel added to the fire.

Once everyone is ready, we file out of the locker room and head towards the tunnel, waiting for the announcer to scream our arrival before we hit the ice for warm ups.

I wonder idly how many shots of me stretching are going to end up on social media after this game. I'm slowly becoming immune to it, but it's still a little confronting finding out that some person has been filming your ass while you're stretching and making it overtly sexual. Some of the guys, like Dean, lean into it, but I'm not a fan. It's been a big issue for some other teams, especially when wives have become involved, but so far, our fan base has been respectful, for the most part. Last year, I found out that Linc and I were both featured in a post that included us in a list of the most fuckable players. Although he thought it was funny, I was not impressed, and it was the final incident that made me quit social media. I closed all my private accounts the next day, and I'm still yet to take back the official ones from the team's marketing department after the end of last season. It's made me even more wary of being photographed when I'm just trying to go about my daily life. I just wish they'd find something else to post about.

The lights in the arena go out and I shake off the maudlin thoughts, shifting my mindset to focus on the gameplay we'd discussed. Coach has been focusing on their weak spots, so I run it over and over in my mind.

"Get ready, Calgary! And raise the noise for the Mounties!" The arena erupts in screams while I lead the way onto the ice.

The lights are strobing and flashing while we circle around our end first, waving up at the crowd before we get to business. The crowd boos when the Vancouver team appears, and a bucket of pucks is dumped on the ice at both ends, while each team deliberately avoids the other. We focus on taking shots while Dean practices blocking them, before each of us eventually breaks off to focus on our own pre-game rituals.

After a few more shots at Dean and stretching out, I head for the bench to chat with Coach. As we're talking, I'm distracted by a sign being held up to the glass to my left, and I squint at it when I see my name.

Davidson, have my babies!

I snort when I realise it's Ben holding up the sign. A woman stands next to him, holding one similar, but with O'Malley instead of Davidson. I nod to Coach before skating over.

"Hey!" I yell, and Ben high fives me through the glass. Behind them are four empty seats, one piled high with bags from the merch shop.

"Hey! This is my girlfriend, Adele," Ben shouts back, pointing at the pretty brunette standing beside him.

She gives me a shy wave before turning and pointing at the back of her jersey, which has my name on it.

I laugh. "Want me to sign it for you later?" I ask, and she nods enthusiastically.

"Don't go getting any ideas, man! She bought that before we were together and I can't get her to give it up." Ben pretends to glare at her, and she blushes.

A kid appears beside them, waving another home made sign, and I smile at him, heading back to the bench to grab a puck, scribbling my signature on it before throwing it lightly over the glass to him. He squeals loudly and runs off to his parents. I've clearly started something now, and a swarm of children descend. Ben and Adele move back to allow them through, and I busily sign pucks or items they throw over to me.

Once the kids have their signed merch, they head back to their parents in various sections, but when Linc skates up beside me, there's another flurry, and he doesn't have time to do more than wave at Ben before it's time to head back down the tunnel.

"We'll catch you afterwards," I yell, and Ben raises his hand in farewell, sitting back in his seat to rest his arm behind Adele's chair.

Something about her looks vaguely familiar, but I just assume I've seen her around town and don't give it any further thought while I focus on the game ahead.

26

WHAT THE HELL?

KYLIE

FOR SOME REASON, today is the day that my grandparents are running late for the first time in my life. We were half an hour late getting out the door, and we had to park far away from the stadium, so then had to trek through the snow in -10 degrees. My hands are numb, despite the fact that I'm wearing my new gloves, and it's such a relief to get inside.

"Damn it, we've missed the warm up," Grandpa grumbles, shooting a glare at Grandma like it's her fault, when from what I could tell, it was a joint issue that kept us from getting out the door.

He hands me my ticket. "Okay, you're sitting in the front row in the same section as our seats. You should see Adele there with the boys."

I nod and follow them to their section, spying Adele in the first row. I wave goodbye to my grandparents while they file into their row before continuing on down the stairs.

"Hey! You missed the warm up!" Adele jumps up when she sees me, and waves her hands at the guy next to her to move down behind her, so that she can sit next to me. "What happened? Why were you late?" she asks, handing me a large bag with the Mounties logo on the front.

"Grandma and Grandpa were mucking around, getting ready, and bickering about something. Think they just lost track of time." I open up the bag and pull out a red and black jersey. "I didn't realise you were serious about buying me a jersey. I could have bought one. Surely this was expensive?"

"Hush. I wanted to buy it for you. I got you a Davidson one." She leans in close and lowers her voice. "Don't tell Ben, but I had the biggest crush on Davidson for years. Seriously, wait until you see this guy. He is so hot. But he's also Ben's friend, so it would be super weird for him to know I'd been lusting after this guy before we met."

"Your secret is safe with me," I say with a grin, standing up to remove my jacket and pull the jersey over my head. It's a very baggy fit, and I look down before looking back at my cousin. "This kind of negates the sexy top we went shopping for."

"Well, it's a hockey town. Who knows, maybe guys will think you look hotter in that than the top. But you don't have to wear it out later."

I sit back down and lean across Adele to talk to the attractive blonde guy beside her. "Hi, I'm the cousin."

Ben grins at me and sticks out his hand. "Hi, the cousin. I'm the boyfriend."

"The boyfriend with connections, from what I've been told. You know a couple of the guys on the team, but you're wearing Vancouver's jersey? That's cold."

He lets out a deep, booming laugh. "I like her," he says to Adele, before turning back to me. "I went to school with two of them, Davidson and O'Malley. O'Malley was with Vancouver before." He turns and points at the back of his jersey, showing his friend's name written on the back. "But he was traded to Calgary last season. Turned out pretty good for him. Got into the playoffs, and he and Davidson are pretty tight, so it was good for them to be reunited. Sad for me though, I lost my in with my team."

"Your loss is our gain, baby. Sorry." Adele gives him a quick kiss on the lips and ruffles his hair.

The other guy, a tall redhead, leans forward to give me a little wave. "Hi, I'm Matt. Welcome to Canada."

"Thanks. It's been a great first week." I wave my hand towards the ice in front of us. "I need you guys to explain the rules to me. I have no clue about this game other than they chase a small disc around and they are allowed to beat the crap out of each other."

"To be fair, that's probably the most accurate description of hockey I've ever heard," Adele says, while both guys give me mildly affronted looks.

"Just wait. Once it starts, you'll be screaming with the rest of us. It's an addictive sport." Ben points to the seating area beside me on the other side of the glass. "That area right there is where Calgary sits. These are probably some of the best seats for your first ever NHL game. We used to only get seats in the nosebleed section, like up there, when I was a kid." He points behind us, and I turn to look, seeing seats so high up that the players must be tiny specks on the ice for the people sitting there.

I turn back to reply to Ben, but as I open my mouth, the lights in the arena go out, and spotlights begin strobing around on the ice, while the music plays even louder.

"Here we go! I'm so excited for you!" Adele squeals, and I can't help but laugh.

Everyone is treating this like it's a rite of passage for me.

The announcer yells out players' names as they skate out onto the ice. The large screen hanging down from the roof above us is too hard for me to see from where we are sitting, but when the name O'Malley is called out, Ben points towards his friend, and I nod. Aside from the names on the backs of the jerseys, they all look similar in their padding and helmets, but I can tell he's tall.

When they announce Davidson, Adele elbows me in the side, and I shake my head at her. My cousin has absolutely no chill.

The players on both teams skate around in the dimly lit arena for a bit before most of them head to the glassed boxes - or the bench, as Adele informs me it's called, and the lights come back on.

"So the first line of players are the ones on the ice now, five of them, or six if you include the goalie. They'll start the game after the anthem. Then they change out in shifts every minute," Adele explains. "There's two defencemen, two wingers on the left and right, and then the centre. That's Davidson for the first line."

I nod, not entirely sure I understand what she means.

The announcer instructs us all to rise for the anthem. For the first time, it hits me how far away from home I truly am when it's the Canadian anthem being sung by some guy in a massive cowboy hat, and not the Australian one that I'm so familiar with. I hadn't felt homesick at all, but now I feel a faint stab of emotion I can't identify, and wish someone from home was with me, like Will or Tara.

But once the game starts, I get caught up in the constant flurry of motion. I don't know how anyone can track where the puck is most of the time and I wince whenever the players slam each other into the sides hard enough to make the wall wobble. It looks super painful, but I guess with the amount of padding they are all wearing, it's not too hard on them, because they just keep moving.

I spend the entire time asking constant questions, and while Adele answers them, I can see that the guys are starting to get annoyed at the distraction. After about the twentieth question, I manage to get a general idea of what's going on, although I shut up more so because I'm sensing the annoyance rather than having a proper understanding of what's going on.

Towards the end of the first period, the ref blows the whistle for a penalty, although I have no idea what it was, and Adele nods at me. "We should go for a bathroom break now, because the lines are insane during the break."

I nod and rise to my feet, just as one of the Calgary players slams against the glass in front of me, and I yelp. A Vancouver player ploughs right into him, pinning him against the glass.

I stare at his face for a moment, certain I'm seeing things. Behind the beard, I swear the face belongs to one very familiar Canadian sidekick I know well. He turns and heads back towards where the ref is standing with the puck in hand. I see the name O'Malley written on his jersey.

"You okay?" Adele asks.

I ignore her and turn to Ben, who's still watching the game intently. "Ben… What's O'Malley's first name?"

Adele squints at me while Ben looks up at me, distracted. "Lincoln. Why?"

I whip my head back towards the ice, searching for the name again. Maybe Lincoln O'Malley is a super common name in Canada? It couldn't be my Lincoln.

Davidson catches my attention when he skates past on the way to the bench. He hops through the little gate, followed closely by O'Malley. The two of them bump fists as they sit down. Davidson turns to face the ice again, and I catch a glimpse of his side profile.

It's like I'm frozen in place, unable to move my feet while I stare at the man on the other side of the glass, my mouth completely dry.

"Kylie, you gotta go. We're blocking people's view. We should have moved when the referee blew the whistle for that last penalty." Adele is trying to push me forward.

"And Davidson's first name?" I still can't get my feet to move.

"Kylie, seriously, move!" Adele's voice carries when she yells at me, and Davidson's head whips around.

I don't know how he heard her over the rest of the arena noise, but when his eyes meet mine, they widen, and we stare at each other.

"Seth," I say, my voice coming out in a hoarse whisper.

I feel like someone has knocked the wind out of me.

There's no mistaking it. It's Seth... My Seth...

My Seth with a beard.

"Yeah, his name is Seth." Adele stops beside me and follows my gaze to where Seth is staring at me, open mouthed. "What the hell?" She sounds confused, but I can't look away while my eyes remain locked with Seth's.

The buzzer sounds and the surrounding fans all leap to their feet to head out to the bathroom or for refreshments.

Every conversation I had with them both about their job runs through my head.

"We work for a sports team."

And.

"So you're like the team physiotherapist?"

Awkward pause. "Something like that."

And one that really stands out, now that I know what had happened at the end of last season.

"Work's been a bit... rough."

I feel like I exist inside of a vacuum, one where it's just Seth and I staring at each other. The rest of the players rise from the bench and start filing out. Lincoln turns to say something to Seth, and when he doesn't get his attention, he looks towards me and his mouth drops open.

I can't hear him, but I see him mouth the words "We've gotta go," to Seth, shaking his shoulder.

Seth is pulled from his own daze, looking at his friend for a second before looking back at me. I'm sure my face must show my complete shock, and he looks pretty shaken up himself.

"Kylie, what the hell is going on?" Adele sounds worried, and Seth's eyes shift from me to her, then back again.

He finally gets up and follows Lincoln, both men looking back at me constantly even as they disappear down the tunnel.

I try to sit down again, completely ignorant to the fact that the rest of the people in our row need to get past, and Adele urges me to stand, moving me into the centre of the aisle while people file past us on both sides.

"You are legitimately worrying me now. Are you okay? How did you know Davidson's name was Seth?"

Unable to process the words, I fumble for my phone in my pocket and open up my photos. I find the last one Seth and I took together, a selfie I'd snapped of the two of us in front of the museum on our day in London, and show her. Ben joins us while she stares at my phone with her eyebrows knitted together.

"How... what..." She seems to have trouble forming her questions.

"What's going on?" Ben asks, and Adele shows him the photo. "Holy shit."

I swallow hard. "Yeah. Holy shit."

27
THROW YOU OFF YOUR GAME

SETH

As soon as I get to the locker room, I grab my phone. I never go near it during a game, as it's off limits, but I've also never had the woman I'm halfway in love with show up unannounced and completely unprepared to see me on the ice.

"Don't do it, man. Just wait til after the game. She's obviously friends with Ben's girlfriend. We'll work this out." Linc tries to take my phone, but I pull my hand out of his reach, turning my back to him.

He sighs and stays there, shielding me from the eyes of the coaching staff.

I open up the text message exchange with Ben first, and I can see he's already typing. My pulse is racing from a mix of game adrenaline and having the proverbial rug yanked out from under me, so my hand shakes while I wait to see what he's got to say.

BEN

What the hell, man?

> How the hell do you know Adele's cousin, and why didn't she know you were on the team?

OK, so that's how she knows Adele, and probably why I thought she'd looked familiar. There is definitely a family resemblance there.

SETH

> We met on the trip Linc and I took. I had no idea we'd ever see each other again.

> Is she okay?

BEN

> She seems pretty shocked, but she's not crying or anything.

> She wants to change seats, though. She's worried that she's going to throw you off your game if she stays sitting there.

"Davidson! Are we holding you up?" Coach barks from across the room and I jump, dropping my phone back into my bag.

I look up to see everyone waiting for me to join in the game play discussion.

I'm torn. I want to check on Kylie, but I have a job to do, and as the captain, I need to set aside my own personal life.

Taking a seat, I try to take in what's being said, but my eyes keep drifting over to my bag, where I can see my phone lighting up against the fabric covering it.

Link taps my leg with the tip of his skate, and I straighten up. Coach is eyeing me while he's still talking, and I just know I'm going to be in for a mouthful if I don't pull my shit together.

Once Coach finishes, it's time to head back out, and I don't have time to try to sneak a look at my phone again. As soon as I hit the ice, I immediately look to where Kylie was sitting, but an older man has replaced her and is watching me closely. Adele sits next to him, her eyes narrowed.

Knowing that she comes from a family of Mounties supporters spurs me on to get out of my head and back into the game. The last thing I need is to lose focus and blow the game while we're on a winning streak, so I take a deep breath and force myself to look away. Linc nods at me when I glance over at him while we head for centre ice. Steeling myself, once the puck drops, I'm all in, determined to prove that I can lead this team, regardless of my personal life.

Vancouver is gunning for Linc tonight, and it's a relief when the ref calls yet another penalty after one of his former teammates smacks him with a high stick to the face. We'd anticipated it, and we've made good use of the three power plays this period, scoring three goals to bring the score to four to one with only three minutes left in the game. Now we're just running down the clock while I deal with the nerves swirling through me.

I'd been stuck on media detail in the second intermission, and when I'd rejoined the rest of the team, Coach was watching me like a hawk, so I still haven't had a chance to check my phone again.

When Vancouver pulls their goalie, Linc shoots the puck towards me, and I break away, taking a shot as soon as there is nothing between me and the open net. The puck sails in easily, and the siren goes off yet again for my third goal of the night. It's been a while since I've had a hat-trick, and the crowd goes crazy, hats raining down around us while my teammates jump on top of me.

When the final buzzer goes off, I breathe a sigh of relief, but it's not over yet, because I'm named first star due to my hat-trick. I wait in the tunnel, impatient, while they list off third and second, before heading to the red carpet. I give the cutest little girl with blonde pigtails a signed hockey stick, which is about three times her size, when they announce my name. Despite my churning emotions, I grin when her father runs forward to help her carry it off the rink, his smile almost as wide as hers.

This is one of the things I love the most about this job, interacting with the genuine fans. Yes, the media is noisy and there are plenty of people who are ready to rip you to shreds if you do something they don't agree with, but at the end of the day, it brings the community together, and it's worth all the other shit to see a kid happy like this.

As soon as I join everyone else in the locker room, there's more cheers, and I allow myself a few minutes to celebrate with them all before finally getting to my phone.

UNKNOWN

Why didn't you tell me the truth?

I just don't understand why you and Lincoln both kept this such a big secret. You knew Tara and I weren't even remotely into hockey.

She'd sent the messages during the first intermission and I feel my heart rate pick up. That was over an hour and a half ago.

SETH

I'm so sorry.

Please meet me with Ben tonight. I really want to talk to you and explain everything.

I head for the showers and finish in record time, getting into my suit and throwing my gear in my bag. I check my phone, but there's no response from Kylie, and I honestly feel like I might throw up.

How am I going to explain all this to her if she decides she wants nothing to do with me? I just have to hope she's going to show.

* * *

Linc drives us to Buck's , and it takes all my willpower not to leap from the car and run inside like a crazy person before he's even parked the car.

"It'll be okay. Kylie is cool. She might get angry at first, but she's not the type to freak out on you or anything. Just breathe." Linc gets out of the car, and I tap my fingers against my thigh for a few beats before following behind.

I don't know what I'm going to do if she's not here. I suppose I could plead my case with her cousin, but I'd rather talk to Kylie herself and am too old for relationship games.

As we weave our way through the busy crowd, everyone mostly ignores Linc and me, except for the occasional slap on the back and head nods from the regulars. I spy Ben sitting in a booth at the back and head straight for him. He stands when he see's us, and my heart drops when I note that he's alone.

"Where's Kylie?" I blurt out, not even bothering with pleasantries.

I can tell Ben isn't sure what to say, and Linc places a hand on my shoulder a moment later.

I look over to where he's pointing. Relief floods through me when I see Kylie standing with her back to us, waiting to be served while talking to Adele.

"Wow, dude, you've got it bad. You look like you're going to throw up," Ben says when I collapse into the chair next to him.

"I spent the whole fucking game trying not to do just that, to be honest." I keep my eyes trained on Kylie, noticing now that she's wearing a jersey with my name on it.

It shouldn't affect me the way it does, but a voice in my head immediately says, "mine," awakening the caveman brain I never knew I had. I'd heard about guys who got all riled up about their partners wearing their jerseys, but had never experienced this with anyone I've dated before, even when that was all they were wearing.

I can't let this woman walk away now, and am determined to beg on my knees for a chance at something more if it comes to it.

"So you guys met in Paris? I gotta admit, I hadn't pictured you with someone like Kylie."

I whip my head around to glare at Ben. "What the hell do you mean by that?"

Ben holds his hands up. "Whoa, steady buddy. I just meant she's so chatty. Very different to you. She about talked our ear off during that first period, asked about a thousand questions."

Linc chimes in. "Well, yeah, she has no idea about hockey. Of course she needed the rules explained to her."

"I wasn't saying it's a bad thing, guys. Chill. Adele is basically exactly the same, personality wise. I just never pictured you with someone so outgoing."

I remember how Kylie had said she often felt wary around new people, and now I'm realising why. It must be hard to tone down her natural instincts like that, worried about how it would be received by others.

If she ever speaks to me again, I vow to ensure I never make her feel like she can't be herself around me. Because a woman this amazing deserves to shine, not have her spark snuffed out by trying to meet the expectations of others.

28

WEARING MY NAME
ON YOUR BACK

KYLIE

BEN HAD PROMISED that Seth wouldn't have been playing games with me. That he wasn't that sort of guy, and I should hear him out. So, against my better judgement, I allowed them to bring me along to the bar. After spending the entire game sitting on the edge of my seat next to Grandma, watching Seth take hits, get knocked to the ground and getting smashed into the glass panels, I've been a nervous wreck for hours.

We'd told my grandparents that I couldn't see properly, so Grandpa had happily taken my seat. I'm pretty sure he'd worked out something was going on though, because Adele said he'd been eyeing Seth off for the next two periods.

I'm so close to ordering a wine, but I need to stick to my no-drinking resolution, especially when I know I'm in for a hard conversation once Seth arrives. Adele orders beers for herself and Ben, and I settle for a lemonade. A commotion behind us catches my attention, and I turn to see a group of women wearing an alarming amount of makeup and designer clothes moving towards our table. Seth and Lincoln have now arrived, and I baulk when I see one woman run a hand through Seth's hair, clearly flirting with him.

"Dammit. Just what we need, puck bunnies," Adele mutters beside me, and I wrench my eyes away from the scene behind us.

"Puck bunnies?"

"Women who chase after hockey players. NHL guys earn big money. Like, millions. And these women want in on it. Every sport has an equivalent, I'm sure, but yeah, they can be pretty ruthless in their pursuit of a life of luxury." Adele glares towards the table, and I look back over.

I'm relieved when Seth gently pushes the woman's hand away while shaking his head. His gaze meets mine, and I can see the discomfort in his expression. Lincoln appears to be trying to send the women on their way, but they don't seem to get the hint.

Adele pays for the drinks and marches towards the table, and I trail behind her.

"Ladies, don't waste your time. These guys aren't interested. If you can't tell." She slams the drinks down on the table and levels each of them with a determined look.

"I didn't realise they needed a guard dog," says the blonde who was touching Seth moments ago.

Oh, hell no.

Something inside me snaps, and I clear my throat. "What my polite cousin is trying to say is, kindly fuck right off." The woman's eyes widen, and she gasps. "I'm Australian. I have no issues with saying it like it is." And then I sit in Seth's lap, freezing when I realise what I've done.

He plays right into it, pulling me in closer to his chest. I don't miss the look of disbelief on the women's faces while they run their eyes over me.

"Seriously? Her?" Blondie says, ignoring me and looking at Seth.

"Yep, me. So, I repeat - fuck off." I have no idea when I became so bold, but something about these women is getting on my last nerve, and after the night I've had, I can't be bothered holding back.

Blondie opens her mouth again, but Lincoln speaks up finally. "Seriously, Victoria, we've asked you before to leave us alone when we're here. Don't make me get Buck." He nods towards the older man behind the bar, who is watching the scene while serving drinks to other customers.

Victoria snaps her mouth shut and glares at me. I smile while wiggling my fingers at her. She turns on her heel and storms off, closely followed by her entourage. Once they are out of sight, I stand up and move to the seat beside Seth.

He watches me for a moment, seemingly waiting to see what I'm going to do next. With the ball firmly in my court, I jump to my feet and grab his hand, dragging him outside.

Once we're away from the noise, I lean back against the wall and glare at him while I cross my arms. "Explain, Seth *Davidson*."

He visibly cringes when I emphasise his last name, but stays quiet for a beat, gripping the back of his neck with his right hand while he looks at me, his eyes scanning me from head to toe. Almost as though he can't believe I'm real.

"I'm sorry... I just... How are you here right now?" He moves to touch my face but drops his hands to his sides when I continue to glare at him.

"I'm staying with my grandparents for a while. A change of scenery... We can get into that later, though. I need you to explain why you lied to me."

He continues to stare at me, swallowing hard. Just when I think he's returned to the version of Seth that can barely speak to me, he finally starts to talk.

"When I met you, I'd just had the worst month of my life. Linc convinced me to go on the trip to get my head right. No one knew who I was, and for the first time in my adult life, I could just be me. Then I met you." He pauses, stepping closer and resting his forearm against the wall above my head, forcing me to look up into his eyes. "The more I got to know you..." He hesitates, like he's trying to find the right words. "I've never been able to trust that any of the female attention I've had wasn't because of what I did for a living. What you just witnessed in there is just the tip of the iceberg." His expression darkens a little, and he looks away for a moment. "You were like a breath of fresh air. So full of life, with no agenda. I thought about telling you so many times, but I needed to hold on to the fantasy life for a little longer. Even if there could never be a future between us, I couldn't handle the idea of you knowing about all of this and what it might do to you. Do to us."

I try to hold on to the anger and hurt I'd been feeling earlier, not quite ready to forgive him so easily, but there is a vulnerability behind his expression that I've never seen before. I place a hand on his chest, and he immediately covers it with his, rubbing his thumb over the back of my hand.

"I can understand, to a degree... But I feel like, after we spent that last night together, I deserved to know the truth. You knew me well enough by then to know that I'm not like those women. Hell, I don't care about any sport, let alone one that is barely even played in the country I'm from. You let me believe you worked behind the scenes with the team, when you're actually the captain. I didn't keep anything back from you, but it feels like now I barely knew you at all. You didn't even tell me your real last name." My voice catches, and I swallow hard to stop from tearing up - my body's automatic response to all emotions.

"I know, and I'm so fucking sorry. Professionally, I go by Seth Davidson. But my full name is Seth James-Davidson." He takes a breath, releasing it while he continues to watch me closely. When he speaks again, his voice is rough and full of emotion. "I've missed you so much these last few months, but I'd convinced myself that there was no way we could have anything more than that perfect three weeks. How could we, when we lived on two completely different continents? But everything else that you know about me is the truth. To be honest, aside from Linc, it feels like you're the one who knows me the best, which I know sounds insane after only three weeks spent together. But you brought out a side of myself I'd forgotten existed. And I like who I am when I'm with you." He has continued to rub his thumb in soothing circles over my hand throughout his whole monologue, potentially the most I've ever heard him say at one time.

His eyes search my face, and I can feel all my resolve crumbling. While I hate he lied, and how I found out the truth, I can hear the sincerity in his voice. And everything he has said about missing me echoes how I have felt about him.

"Will you please give me a chance to prove that I really am that person you met on the trip?" he asks, his voice cracking while he steps closer still. "I've been so close to contacting the tour company and trying to get your details. I can't believe you're standing right here in front of me. This is too much of a coincidence..."

I scan his face for the longest time.

He's right here. How can I just walk away now when I've been dreaming about him for months?

I wrap my arms around his neck and raise on to my toes to look him in the eye. "You are on probation. And I think we need to take things slow. I need to wrap my head around all of this. The crazy world you live in seems so far outside of anything I've ever known."

He sighs and buries his head in my neck while wrapping his arms around my waist and pulling me flush against his chest. "We'll do this however you want."

"Damn straight we will."

He chuckles softly before straightening and looking at me. "Can I please kiss you? Cause it's kind of all I've been able to think about since I realised you were wearing my name on your back."

"What, this old thing? I considered ripping it off once I

realised what was going on, but I guess you can kiss me before I do that."

He groans. "If we're taking this slow, please no talking about ripping off your clothes." He lowers his mouth to mine in the sweetest kiss while running his hand up my back and cupping the back of my head.

Tentatively, I kiss him back, and it feels like I've come home. The months apart melt away, and my libido kicks into gear, begging me to wrap myself around him and let him take me right here. I deepen the kiss, opening my mouth to him while I raise myself onto the very tips of my toes.

He pushes me back against the wall, and the kiss becomes hungrier, hands beginning to explore while we become reacquainted with each other's bodies.

When he pulls away, breathless, I let out a little whimper and he shakes his head with a smile. "Slow, remember?"

I pout, my arms still around his neck, and his eyes drop to my lips. But he's a perfect gentleman, and I know he's right to pump the brakes before I forget all about my need to take in this new reality I've found myself in and let him take me home.

"Fine. We should probably go back inside. You haven't seen your friend for a while and he's only here for the weekend. And I'm sure Adele will be out in about thirty seconds if I don't reappear."

He kisses my forehead. "Come on, I can feel you shivering. I should have made you bring your jacket outside."

I lean into his embrace, sliding my arms around his back inside his suit jacket. "Well, I was fired up, so my anger kept me warm. I approve of this whole suit thing, by the way."

"Oh you do, do you?" I can hear the humour in his voice while I burrow in closer to his chest to steal more of his warmth.

"Yep, very sexy. And the beard. Never thought I'd be into a guy with a beard."

He laughs. "I grow one during the season. It's kind of a team tradition." He guides me back towards the door, turning me so my back is flush against his chest and wrapping his arms around me to keep me warm until we get inside.

We join the other three at the table, and Seth slings his arm along the back of my chair while I lean into his side.

"So... we're all good now?" Lincoln asks, while Ben glances over at Seth, one eyebrow raised in a silent question.

Seth nods to his friend, and I narrow my eyes while I look at Lincoln. "Well, Seth and I are. But you and I are on shaky ground. You lied to me too, buddy."

He places his hand on his heart and gapes at me. "Miss Kylie, I never. I told you I worked for a sports team. It's not my fault you didn't ask questions." He flashes me a cheeky grin. I tsk, and he laughs. "I missed you, too, you know. And Tara. How is she?"

"She's okay. Maybe we can call her later. I'm sure she'd love to speak to you guys, and now that your secret identities have been revealed, she will definitely have some things to say."

Adele has been watching the entire exchange with wide eyes, her head moving between the three of us. "I still can't believe this. So you met these guys on your trip, and they just happen to be two of the best players on the Mounties, but you didn't know that when you randomly decided to move here? This is like something out of a movie." She claps her hands together.

I want to get caught up in the excitement, but I'm still reeling from tonight's revelations. And I can't shake the feeling that my life is about to change far more than I'm prepared for.

29
THOUGHT I'D BE ABLE
TO EASE INTO IT

SETH

ALTHOUGH KYLIE HAS SAID that she understands, I can sense her unease. Linc must have noticed as well, because he's been glancing over at her every few minutes with a concerned look while we chat to Ben and Adele. Kylie has been uncharacteristically quiet throughout. As the night grows later, I know I need to put her mind at ease somehow.

"What are you doing tomorrow?" I ask, and she shrugs.

"I don't really have a lot of plans in general. I don't know anyone outside of my family yet. Why?"

"We are going to the Children's Hospital tomorrow for the morning. It's something we try to do every few months to visit the kids and spend time in the community. Would you want to come along?"

She considers my words for a moment before nodding. "That sounds really sweet. Are you sure it's okay for me to come along?"

Linc pipes up. "There are usually a few partners who come along to these events. It adds to the family friendly vibe. And bonus... the professional husband chasers don't show up for those events." He nods towards Victoria's little group while they shoot dark looks over at our table.

"I like that term. Although, let's be real, they're puck bunnies," Adele says, glaring over at the women.

"Yeah. I've always avoided that term in public, though," Linc says with a shrug.

"I guess... You're more honourable than me though."

They continue discussing whether or not the term is offensive, but I focus on the troubled look on Kylie's face. "What are you thinking?"

She's quiet for a moment, and I can feel my nerves rising.

This is it. This is when she's going to say she can't handle this side of my life.

"I just find it sad that they have so little self worth that instead of trying to go out and make it on their own, they would rather find a man to support them not having a job... Cause that's what they want, right? To have rich husbands so they don't have to work?"

I breathe a sigh of relief. "I guess. I know that quite a few of the partners of our team mates have jobs though. A few of them ended up with those kinds of women. It happens, but mostly, they have families and it's quite nice when we all get together."

She still looks troubled though and I wish there was something I could say to make her feel better. I just have to hope that tomorrow goes well and she see's that there are positives to this world as well.

"So, what are your plans now that you're living here?" I ask, changing the subject.

"Well, I'm still doing admin work for Will, but I'm meeting with my aunt this week about potentially working for her." Kylie nods towards her cousin. "They have a tour company and apparently she thinks I'd be a good fit as one of their tour guides."

I nod. That seems like something she'd enjoy. I always had

trouble picturing her sitting behind a desk all day, her vibrant personality being held hostage by mind numbingly boring work.

"It will be so great. You'll love it, Kylie. I only do the occasional tour, but you're perfect for leading the groups. We get all different types of people through, and you get along with everyone," Adele says, bouncing in her seat a little.

"We'll see. It definitely won't hurt for me to give it a try, at the very least. And I'm only here for three months anyway, so it's not like it's forever."

At those words, I feel my stomach drop a little. Only three months? That doesn't feel long enough.

The next morning, I pull up outside the address that Kylie gave me and nervously wipe my hands on my jeans. I feel like a teenager taking his crush out on a first date.

Navigating the frozen path, I make it to the front door and ring the doorbell.

The man that I saw with Adele last night, who I assume is their grandfather, opens the door and does a double take, his mouth dropping open.

"Hi, sir. I'm Seth. I'm here to pick up Kylie." I put my hand out, and he takes it slowly, still staring at me.

He finally catches himself and steps aside, waving me in. "When Kylie said she had a gentleman coming to collect her, she failed to mention it was Seth Davidson." He waves at my jersey.

"I was looking forward to the look on your face, and it was worth it." Kylie skips down the stairs with a grin. "Seth, this is my grandpa, John. Grandpa, this is Seth."

"I can see that, young lady. Care to explain how you came to know the captain of the Mounties? Joy, get down here!" he hollers up the stairs, and an older woman appears, her reaction to my appearance similar to his.

"We met in Europe. He may have failed to fill me in on what

he does for a living though." Kylie is still grinning, enjoying the dramatics far too much. I am not doing great with all the attention, and she finally takes pity on me when she looks at my face. "I'm sorry, I should have told them."

"It's okay, I deserved that." I help her with her jacket while her grandparents hover nearby.

"I'll see you guys later," she says, moving towards the door.

"What time will you be home?" John asks, and Kylie squints back at him.

"Not sure. I can grab my own dinner, though."

I can see him itching to ask more questions, but Kylie shoots him a warning glance, and he keeps his mouth clamped shut.

"Don't worry sir, I'll take good care of her," I say, nodding while I guide her past me with a hand on her lower back.

"You'd better."

"Grandpa! Sorry Seth." Kylie looks horrified, but I just smile.

"It's okay. We're going to a family event at the Children's Hospital. All above board, I promise."

He still doesn't look entirely convinced, but says nothing further.

I follow Kylie to my car and open the door for her. She looks at the car for a moment before looking back at me.

"Fancy wheels," she says, her eyebrows raised.

I look back at my Porsche Cayenne, trying to see it from her point of view. I've honestly never given a lot of thought to how much money I make, but it would most likely be daunting for her.

"It has heated seats," I say, rubbing the back of my neck while I shrug.

She practically dives in while I laugh. "Thank god. Seriously, I really wasn't ready for how cold this country is."

Once I'm back in the driver's seat, I show her how to use the seat warmers, and she nestles in while I pull away from the curb.

"I thought you've been here in winter before?" I ask, navigating the snowy streets.

She reaches forward to scroll through the music options on the sound system, and I smile when she picks one of our mutual favourites. *Lightning Crashes* by Live plays quietly while she settles back into her seat.

"Yeah, winter. It's still only October! I thought I'd be able to ease into it." She's rubbing her hands together, and it's adorable seeing her all bundled up.

"Sorry, Calgary doesn't really do the easing thing. I've seen snow in pretty much every month of the year since I've lived here. It takes some adjusting. But then, I spend most of my life in cold arenas, so it's probably not as bad for me."

"No kidding. You would melt in Brisbane." She pauses for a moment. "Wait, you've been there, right? Lincoln mentioned that."

"Yeah. We had an exhibition game a few years ago, Canada vs USA." It had been a lot of fun, but I remember how warm it had been there, considering it was during their winter months.

We continue to chat about the weather and the differences between Australia and Canada for the rest of the drive, keeping the conversation on surface level, but the closer we get to the arena, the more I notice her leg jiggling. By the time I pull up in the car park, she's gone very quiet.

I reach across the centre console and take her hand in mine, squeezing gently.

"Hey. It's really fine. Nothing to be nervous about."

She squeezes back. "Sure. This is all normal for you. I've never even seen a celebrity in real life, and now I'm spending time with someone who the entire city basically worships... Nothing to be nervous about at all," she replies, swallowing hard while surveying the small crowd gathered near the team bus.

I kiss the back of her hand. "Come on. I promise, once you meet the others, you'll see there's nothing to worry about."

I get out of the car, intending to walk around to open her door, but she's already out by the time I get there. She pulls on her gloves and tugs her toque down over her ears, her nose already beginning to turn red in the icy breeze. I take her hand and lead her towards my teammates.

Our media relations manager, Sarah, nods at me when I approach. "Seth, nice of you to join us."

"I'm not late," I protest, and she tsks.

"No, but you were close. Hi, I'm Sarah," she says, putting her hand out to Kylie.

"Kylie. Nice to meet you," Kylie replies, shaking her hand.

"Is that an accent I detect?" Sarah cocks her head to the side.

"Yeah. I'm Australian. Well, Australian Canadian technically."

"Oh, an Aussie! We don't get many of you around the NHL." Sarah smiles, and I can feel Kylie relax a little at my side.

"Yeah, it's not a sport we play much. I only went to my first game last night."

"Well, what a game for your first one! Seth must have scored that hat-trick just for you," Sarah jokes, elbowing me lightly in the ribs.

"Ha. Given that he didn't know I was there until the end of the first period, I seriously doubt that."

Before the topic can wander too far into my stuff up, I jump into the conversation again. "Sarah is the wife of one of our defencemen, Oliver." I wave towards Ollie, who wanders over with Dean close behind.

"Yep, it's my job to keep these boys in line in the public eye. It's a tough gig, but someone's gotta do it." Sarah continues smiling, which seems to help Kylie relax a little more.

Once everyone arrives, we climb onto the bus, and I introduce Kylie to a few more people. By the time we reach the hospital, she seems far more comfortable, which is a huge relief.

Maybe this will all work out after all.

30
DON'T LET ME FALL

KYLIE

WATCHING Seth and the rest of the team while they joke around with the kids is doing all sorts of stupid things to my heart. I've been fighting off the butterflies in my stomach ever since I saw him standing in the doorway of my grandparents' house, dressed in his jersey and jeans, with his cap on backwards. It should be illegal how hot this man is.

While Seth has been present with each of the children while he's signed merch for them and posed for photos, his eyes have never strayed far from where I'm standing with two of the wives, Bethany, a blonde woman who could be a supermodel, from LA and Clara, a pretty, curvy redhead from Louisiana.

"So, how long have you known Seth?" Clara asks in her amazing southern accent.

"We met in Europe over the summer. We were on the same tour."

"Oh, that's right, Seth's little mental health break," Bethany says, and I detect some attitude in her tone.

I tilt my head while Clara looks at her with raised eyebrows. "Wow, that was harsh."

Bethany has the sense to look apologetic, but I've already worked out she's not someone I want to get to know too well.

Clara seems nice, though.

We're eventually joined by Sarah and Tory, the wife of one of the assistant coaches, and the women chat amongst themselves, including me enough to help me feel at ease. Other than Bethany, the rest of them seem fairly down to earth and friendly. I hadn't realised how many members of the team were from different countries, which makes me feel a little less out of place. Although Sarah is from eastern Canada, and the rest of them are from the U. S, they've told me there are a few Europeans amongst the WAGS - which I learnt stands for Wives and Girlfriends. I'm not sure how I feel about that acronym.

One thing they all have in common, however, is their love for designer labels. I feel decidedly out of place in my Target jeans, but I have never been interested in fashion, so I figure they can accept me as I am.

"How's everything going?" Lincoln has wandered over, taking a break.

"Fine. You guys are in high demand," I reply, nodding towards the long line weaving through the hospital cafeteria.

He stretches his arms above his head, exposing a hint of his rock hard abs, and I notice a couple of mothers eyeing him off appreciatively. I shake my head when he flashes me a cheeky grin, telling me he saw it too.

He slings an arm over my shoulder. "Yeah, the team does this a few times through the season. It brightens up the kids' days, and the parents love it as well."

I watch while Seth poses for a photo with a tiny girl with blonde pigtails in a wheelchair hooked up to a breathing tube, and my heart breaks. Her smile is so big it takes over her entire face, and her father looks on with tears in his eyes even while he smiles as well.

"He seems to be managing all the peopling really well," I comment, and Lincoln squeezes my shoulder.

"He's good with the kids. It's the media events he hates, but you'd never know it. And this season he's been even better. I think you might have had something to do with that. He's been more outgoing than ever since the trip. You're good for him," he says with a smile.

"I don't know that I can take that much credit. We only knew each other for three weeks."

"Three weeks on a trip like that is like one real life year, I've realised. Don't discount what you guys had together. I'm sorry for how the truth came out, but I'm glad you're giving him a chance. Just..." He pauses for a moment, searching for the right words. "Just try not to hurt him."

I search his face for a moment, admiring the loyalty he has for his friend. "I have no intention of that, Lincoln. I just hope I don't get my heart broken in the process."

"I can promise you, if you give him the chance, he will prioritise you above everything else. It's who he is. He puts the needs of others ahead of himself, sometimes to the detriment of his own happiness. However, our jobs are demanding, requiring frequent travel and dealing with people's high expectations. It's a lot for our partners to handle, which is why I prefer casual dating. But Seth is different. He hasn't dated much because he's meant for someone who will be his entire world. And I've never seen him look at anyone the way he looks at you."

He heads back towards his teammates, leaving me to ponder his words and wondering if I'm brave enough to meet the expectations behind them.

· · ·

Two hours later, the bus pulls into the arena car park. Seth has been quiet most of the bus ride back, resting his head back against the top of the chair, weariness written into every line of his face.

"Are you still okay with dropping me home?" I ask.

He rolls his head over to look at me, his eyebrows raised. "Yeah, of course. But I don't have to take you straight home, if you still want to hang out?"

I take in the hopeful glint in his eye, realising that I'd misread the situation. "I just thought you might be over hanging out with people after so much socialising this morning."

"That feeling never applies to you," he replies, and I smile, unable to ignore the butterflies in my stomach when he grins back.

"Okay. What did you have in mind?"

He thinks for a moment, then cocks his head to the side. "Can you skate?"

I shake my head. "Not really a common activity in Australia. I roller-skated a little as a kid, but most of my hobbies involved unfrozen water."

"Want a lesson from a pro?"

I grin. "An ice skating lesson from the captain of the Calgary Mounties? Lucky me."

And that's how I find myself at a local community arena with a professional hockey player strapping rented skates onto my feet. The kid at the skate hire counter had practically vibrated out of his skin when he recognised Seth, and spent ten minutes fanboying over him so hard I thought he'd die of overexertion.

"Does that happen a lot?" I ask, nodding towards where the teenager is snapping a not so covert photo of Seth while he kneels in front of me, yanking the laces tight.

He looks over his shoulder before returning to the task at hand, shrugging. "Yeah. Part of the job. Does it bother you?" He looks up at me, and I can see the apprehension on his face.

"Not if it doesn't bother you. He's just a kid. And you were great with all the kids and their parents at the hospital."

He finishes with my laces before taking a seat beside me and making quick work of getting his own skates on. "That sort of stuff is fine. But there might be some fan stuff you won't be so comfortable with. That group of women last night... There's often quite a few like them around at events that aren't quite so family friendly."

"Is that your roundabout way of warning me you have women throwing themselves at you frequently?" I ask while he helps me stand up.

"I just don't want anything to scare you off," he replies, keeping me close while he holds my gaze.

"I held my own against Victoria and her little group last night. I'm sure I can handle the rest of them."

He lets out a breath, his expression a little troubled even while he nods. "Come on, let's get this lesson started."

He leads me out onto the ice, turning to face me so that he's skating backwards while he holds my hands. I eye the other skaters, seeing kids that would be no taller than my knee skating around with ease.

I step out, suddenly feeling nervous. After all my years of surfing, balance isn't something new to me. But the slippery surface has me gripping Seth's hands tightly, and I can feel my legs shake.

"Don't let me fall," I whisper, and he squeezes my hands back.

"Never."

I let him tow me around the rink a few times while I slowly work out what to do. Bending my knees slightly, I force myself to glide rather than step, listening to the tips Seth gives me. He's a good teacher. Once he's deemed me capable enough, he moves to skate beside me, holding my hand while I stick my other one out to keep my balance.

"So, how long have you been playing hockey?" I ask, finally feeling comfortable enough to have a conversation while remaining upright.

"I actually don't remember a time when I wasn't playing

hockey. Dad was a huge Vancouver fan, and he played as a kid, so as soon as I was old enough to skate, that was it. I loved every minute of it, and he was so happy when I was drafted. He still comes to as many games as he can, even though I'm playing for the enemy."

I can hear the joy in his voice, although I'm not game enough to look at him, keeping my eyes trained on the ice in front of me.

"Have you always played for the Mounties?"

"No. My first few years I was in Boston, then I was traded here." He swings around to skate in front of me again, still only holding one hand.

"Does that happen a lot? Being traded, I mean? Ben mentioned Lincoln was traded from Vancouver last year."

"It depends, really. I was lucky to have only been traded once in my eight years, but Linc has been traded twice and some of the other guys have been traded four or five times."

I stumble a little, and he grabs my other hand, keeping me upright.

"Thank you." I'm grateful when he keeps holding on to both hands. "That must be hard for the ones with families, right? All that moving around?"

He doesn't answer straight away, and I look up to see him regarding me, his expression thoughtful. "It can be. But that's the nature of the game. A few of the guys push to be traded back to teams closer to where their partners want to live. But we are a family friendly team, and our current management team works hard to have a support network in place for everyone, including the families of the players. One of my responsibilities as captain is to organise family dinners, stuff like that."

"That seems like a lot of pressure. Especially when you don't have a family of your own."

"It's actually something I enjoy. I mean, it's a lot of socialising and I definitely need to spend some time alone afterwards, but seeing the families together... I don't know, it just makes me smile."

We let the conversation move on to other, less heavy things while continuing to do laps around the rink. Little kids zoom by, and we're stopped occasionally by Mounties fans, but overall, it's a fun hour.

Once my legs have decided they've had enough, we head back to the benches, and Seth helps me pull my skates off. The cold has seeped through my clothes, and I rub my hands together while I wait for him to return my skates.

"How do you feel about hot chocolate?" he asks when he returns to my side.

"Hot chocolate sounds amazing," I say, shivering a little.

He pulls me up and wraps his arms around me, rubbing his hand up and down my back quickly. "Come on, my little icicle."

I let him lead me into the little food area, which is far warmer than the rink, and I wait while he orders our drinks. When he returns to my side, he pushes his hands deep into his pockets and shifts his weight from one foot to the other.

"So. Have you had enough of me yet?"

I peer up at him, hiding a smile. "Depends. Will you be feeding me if I say no?"

He hums a little, pulling me into a hug. "I think I could arrange that."

I rise on to my tiptoes and wrap my arms around his neck. "Well, then, I suppose you're stuck with me."

He grins and leans down a little to kiss me. I rise higher, deepening the kiss while he runs his hand through my hair, cupping the back of my head.

"Two hot chocolates for Seth!"

We break apart when the teenager behind the counter calls out Seth's order, and he moves towards the counter while I smooth my clothes back down, suddenly conscious of our surroundings. I notice a few people looking at me before glancing at Seth, and I swallow hard.

Is this what it's going to be like every time we go somewhere together in public?

The thought fills me with apprehension.

When Seth turns back to face me with the hot chocolates in hand, I shove my concerns aside and smile, not wanting to give him any reason to worry about me. Because, other people aside, I've had a great time with him today, and I've remembered now just how easy it is to be with him.

31
I NEED A LITTLE CHAOS

SETH

ONCE WE FINISH our hot chocolates, we head back to my car. It's still early, but we skipped lunch and my stomach is growling loudly.

"How does an early dinner at my place sound? I have a fridge full of food that I need to eat before I hit the road tomorrow," I say, holding the door open for Kylie to climb into the passenger seat.

"Sure." She smiles up at me, and I grin back, tapping the roof nervously before closing the door.

Once we start heading towards home, Kylie stares out the window, her silence concerning me.

"Everything okay?" I ask, flicking my gaze towards her briefly before continuing to watch the road.

"Yeah, just looking at the massive houses here. I'm still adjusting to the differences here, compared to what I'm used to at home." She shifts in her seat, turning her body towards me.

I reach over and take her hand in mine, relieved when she squeezes it. We remain quiet for the rest of the drive, occasionally squeezing each other's hand in silent communication. It feels familiar and comforting, like we've already developed our own silent language to check in on each other. Once I reach my gated community, I tap in the code for the main gate, and Kylie gasps a little when we drive through the large estate, her eyes moving from house to house. My place is towards the back, and I can feel my nerves kicking up a notch once we get closer. I know this is more than what she's used to, and I keep waiting for something to scare her off.

When I pull into my driveway, I look over to see her reaction and find her staring at the house with wide eyes. Turning back, I try to see it from her point of view. Much like with my car, I hadn't considered how my house would look to someone new who wasn't used to the life I've started to take for granted.

"This is all one house? And you live here by yourself?"

I rub the back of my neck, sheepish. "Um... Yeah?"

"This place is massive." She sits back in her seat and shakes her head. "I don't think I've ever been in a place like this. I thought Jake and Bri's apartment was over the top fancy, but this is on a whole other level."

I'm starting to think this wasn't the best idea for our first day together. I wanted to make her feel comfortable, but it's become glaringly obvious how different our lives are.

"A few of my teammates live in this community with their families. I figured it was a good investment if I need to sell at some point. Or... I don't know... maybe have a family one day." I hit the garage door remote, trying not to show how nervous I am while I wait for the door to open fully. Once I've parked the car, I peer over at her. "Is this all too much? We can go out somewhere instead, if this is freaking you out."

She reaches over and touches my cheek. "I'm fine. This is all just a bit of a surprise, that's all. And now that I've seen the outside, there is no way in hell you're getting me out of here without showing me the inside."

I laugh a little, turning my face to kiss her palm. "Okay. Just remember, it's all just stuff. I'm still me, I promise."

"Oh, but I bet it's really cool stuff." She grins, and we both get out of the car before I step back to let her through the door ahead of me.

The garage leads right off the front hall, and we remove our shoes before I take her hand. "Okay, I'll give you a tour first, then make dinner."

Her eyes are wide when we walk into the family room, which is kitted out with an enormous sofa and matching recliners, all pointing towards the biggest TV I could fit on the wall.

"So before you freak out, I do use this for when the team is hanging out. It's not all just for me."

She turns to face me, a troubled look on her face. "You know you don't have to justify anything to me, right? I'm not judging you."

I let out my breath, my shoulders dropping slightly. I hadn't realised how concerned I was about her opinion, but hearing those words is like a weight lifting off me. I squeeze her hand again while I nod, before turning and heading for the next room.

"The kitchen is probably where I spend most of my time, aside from my bedroom," I say, stopping in front of the marble bench top in the centre of the room.

"Wow," Kylie says, her eyes running over the space that had driven me to buy this house in the first place.

The surfaces are empty, mostly, with a bench running along three of the four walls, except for a few appliances that I use regularly. The mahogany dining table and chairs sit near the floor to ceiling windows that look out over my large backyard, and Kylie stares outside at the pool area.

"A pool? In Calgary? Really?"

I laugh. "Honestly, we do get some warm weather here, I promise." I point to the building running alongside the pool. "That's the pool house and I've got a gym set up in there as well."

"Oh! Do you have a treadmill?" Her eyes have lit up, and I cock my head to the side.

"That is the strangest thing to be excited about. Yeah, I have a treadmill."

"I've missed running. I was going to look into joining a gym, because I'm honestly scared to venture too far outside on those icy sidewalks."

I nod, remembering our runs every morning on tour. "Well, you are welcome to use the gym here any time."

She claps her hands together and does a little jump. It's adorable, and before I can stop myself, I pull her towards me, bending to kiss her. "You are so easy to please," I say against her lips.

She sighs and sinks into the kiss, wrapping her arms around my neck and pressing her body close. I effortlessly lift her, and she lets out a little squeak when I put her on the bench without pulling away. She wraps her legs around my waist, and I run my hands up both her thighs before gripping her hips, holding her still while I continue to kiss her. She opens her mouth to me, and I groan when she swipes her tongue along my lower lip.

Images of our last night together have been plaguing my dreams for months, and it takes all my resolve not to recreate it right here, on my kitchen bench. But I'm determined to honour Kylie's wish to take things slow, so I pull away a little, both of us struggling to get our breath back.

"I forgot how good that feels." She presses her forehead against mine and breathes in deep, closing her eyes.

"I definitely hadn't. I think about it all the time," I admit, still holding her close.

"Yeah? What else do you think about?" She presses a kiss to the side of my neck, before gradually running her nose up to my ear and biting my earlobe gently.

An involuntary shiver runs down my spine, and I can feel the hairs on my arms lift at the sensation. "Jesus, this. I think about this." I claim her mouth again, moving a hand up to grip the back of her neck, holding her in place.

She grinds against me a little while her arms tighten around my neck.

"We should keep going with the tour," I say between kisses.

She moans against my lips, erasing all space between our bodies and pressing her chest against mine, continuing to kiss me back. "I'm good right here," she whispers back.

I step back to look her in the eye. "What happened to taking it slow?"

She sighs, reaching up to take off my cap. She puts it on backwards on her own head before running her hands through my hair. "Fine. But just know, this is taking every ounce of my self-control right now." She slides off the bench.

I pull her into my arms, kissing the top of her head. "Believe me, I completely understand."

She allows me to show her through the rest of the house until we finally reach my bedroom on the second floor.

I hesitate at the door. "Maybe we should keep the bedroom for another time."

She snorts and taps me on the chest. "Why? Are you scared I'm going to take one look at your bed and ravage you?"

I raise an eyebrow. "The thought may have crossed my mind."

She steps closer, holding my gaze. "Seth Davidson. I don't need a bed to let you have your wicked way with me. I would have let you bend me over that bench downstairs."

I swallow hard, my hand still resting on the door handle. The image of us together, her bent over the kitchen bench while I take her from behind, blazes to life in my mind.

She smirks and reaches around, pressing down on the door handle. I let it go so that the door swings open, revealing the spacious bedroom. I'd allowed the interior designer to arrange the spacious bedroom as a parents' retreat, complete with comfy chairs that provide a view of the Rocky Mountains through the large window. My California-king bed sits in the centre of the far wall, and Kylie moves towards it, running her hand over the black bedspread.

"You are very neat," she says, looking around the room.

I stay where I am, watching while she takes it all in. "Well, I have a maid service that comes in once a week, but yeah, I guess I am."

She hums a little under her breath, eventually looking back at me with a slightly concerned look on her face. "You know I'm chaotic, right? I'm messy and disorganised. Everything you're not."

I move to stand in front of her and capture her face in my hands. "And those are the things that made me fall for you. I need a little chaos. You force me to step outside my comfort zone."

She gazes up at me with wide eyes, her chest rising and falling steadily while she considers my words.

After a moment, she steps back, tossing my hat aside, and unhurriedly removing her sweater and shirt, revealing a red lace bra. "You know how I said I wanted to take things slow?"

I nod, incapable of forming words while I run my eyes over her curves. She's the most beautiful woman I've ever seen, her confidence drawing me to her like a moth to a flame.

She steps closer again. "Slow is overrated. I want you."

I allow her to pull my jersey up and over my head, my shirt following close behind. "So what you're saying is, I was right about you ravaging me after you saw my bed?"

She laughs, a deep throaty laugh that I cut off by devouring her mouth, and she clings to me while I lift her up. I turn and toss her on her back onto the bed before moving over her, holding my weight on my elbows while I kiss my way down her neck. She runs her hands through my hair while I move my mouth to cover her breast through the lace of her bra, a small gasp escaping her lips while she arches her back.

Moving my attention across to her other breast, I slide her bra strap down until she's exposed and run my tongue over her nipple, smiling when she shivers beneath me. She moans when I suck gently, her grip on my hair tightening a little before she lets go. Arching her back again, she reaches around and undoes the clip at her back, and I fling her bra aside before returning my attention to her now exposed chest.

Once she's panting, I kiss my way down her body, loving when she shivers and goosebumps appear on her skin. Once I make it to the button on her jeans, I move to kneel between her legs and gaze down at her, unable to hide the smile on my face when she looks up at me through half-closed eyes. It feels surreal to have her here, in my bed, after months of dreaming about just this moment.

"Why are you looking at me like that?" she asks, her voice husky.

"Just can't believe this is real."

She sits up, placing her hands on my hip and tilting her face up. "It's real. I'm real."

I cup her face in my hands. "Thank god for that."

32

ALL ABOUT THE BED

KYLIE

SETH KISSES ME SOFTLY, and I grip his hips, digging my fingers in, a silent request for him to kiss me harder. I don't want gentle right now. I need the commanding hockey player I watched on the ice last night.

"I want you to make me scream, Seth," I whisper against his lips.

My words seem to unleash something within him, and he deepens the kiss until I'm breathless and my lips feel swollen. He urges me to lie back, and I lean on my elbows, watching while he undoes the button at the top of my jeans and slides the zipper down. He yanks them down my legs along with my underwear, throwing them on the floor before returning to his original position, kissing down my abdomen while he swipes his thumb over my clit, causing me to moan loudly. Chuckling, he does it again, circling the spot while applying more pressure, and I fist the bed clothes in both hands. When he replaces his thumb with his mouth, I know it won't be long before I come completely undone. Releasing the bedspread, I grip his hair in both hands, moving against him while he works me up with his mouth and fingers until I'm a quivering mess.

"Seth," I scream his name when the orgasm rips through me, and he continues, working even harder while I wriggle against him, unsure if I'm trying to get closer or move away.

A second, smaller orgasm follows, and I feel like I'm floating, my body going limp while he kisses his way back up to my mouth. All the noise in my head that usually plagues me seems to go quiet when he's working his magic on me, and it's something I've never experienced in the bedroom before.

With his lips pressed to mine, he opens the drawer next to his bed, and I hear the familiar sound of a condom wrapper crinkling. I run my hand down his muscled torso and unbutton his fly, reaching inside his boxers and run my hand over him, and he groans softly against my lips when I squeeze.

"I need you, now," he whispers, and I nod.

He removes his jeans and boxers quickly before rolling the condom on while he leans back against the bedhead, before pulling me over to straddle his legs. Guiding me down, I take a sharp breath as he slides inside me. Once I've adjusted to his size, he guides me to move, and I kiss him hard while we moan together at the sensation.

"Fuck. I dreamed about this." Seth presses his mouth to my neck, nipping lightly while I pick up the pace, chasing another growing orgasm that is slowly building.

"So did I." The words tumble from my lips, closely followed by a gasp when he lifts me up, lying me back and throwing my legs over his shoulders while he thrusts into me again.

Sex with Seth is like nothing I've experienced before. Perhaps it's his stamina as a professional athlete, or the burning chemistry between us, but instead of tiring, it's like his energy has increased. At this new angle, he is hitting the spot deep inside that has my eyes rolling to the back of my head, and he reaches between us to rub my clit again, my moans spurring him on.

"Come with me," he commands, his voice hitching as he moves faster, and we both topple over the edge together.

Lowering my legs, he leans down to kiss me tenderly before rolling off and heading into the ensuite to get rid of the condom. Once we're both cleaned up, I lay with my head resting on his chest, my leg slung over his hips while he glides his fingers up and down my spine.

"I could definitely get used to this," I mutter, feeling gloriously tired and sore in all the right places.

"Yeah?"

"Yeah. Your bed is so comfy." I roll onto my back and take up the other side of the bed while he laughs.

"Oh, so it really was just all about the bed?"

"Yep. Absolutely nothing to do with you. It was all just a way for me to get onto this bed."

He moves over me quickly and nips at my neck. "Brat," he says with another laugh, before scooting off the bed and reaching a hand out to me. "Come on, let's go have that dinner."

After taking one look inside Seth's fridge and seeing all the super healthy food, I've realised I could not be a professional athlete. I like chocolate too much.

I do my best not to outright eye-fuck him while he makes us a simple dinner of chicken breast and vegetables. I thought Seth in a jersey and backwards facing cap was hot... But Seth in grey sweatpants and no shirt is way better.

"So you're going to speak to your aunt this week about that job?"

I'm pulled from my rather risqué daydreams, doing my best not to stare at his ass while he is cooking, when Seth slides my plate across the bench where I am sitting.

"Yeah. I think it could be fun. Won't know until I try, I guess."

I pick up the knife and fork he handed me earlier while he takes his seat beside me.

"It's only for three months, though, right? Didn't you say that last night?" He avoids looking my way, staring down at his plate instead.

I finish chewing and swallow slowly, peering over at him. "Is that your way of asking how long I'm staying?" He shrugs, keeping his eyes on his food. "I booked a return flight in three months, yeah. But I can always change the date if I need to."

He nods, but continues to look anywhere but at me.

"Seth, can you please look at me?" Warm brown eyes finally meet mine. "If you want me to stay longer, you can just ask."

He shakes his head. "No, I can't. I can't ask you to do anything that would upend your life... Taking it slow, remember?"

I place my hand on his arm and give it a light squeeze. "Everything with us has always been a whirlwind. And your feelings are just as important as mine."

He holds my gaze for a few moments. "How about we table this conversation for something less dramatic? I shouldn't have said anything."

I nod, not sure how to feel about the line of conversation. We both eat without speaking for a few minutes, until I finally crack, unable to handle the silence between us.

"How long will you be away for?"

"It's a five game road trip. We're headed to Florida, New York and New Jersey. So we're away just over ten days," he replies.

"Oh wow. Are all your trips that long?" I knew he had to travel a lot, but hadn't realised how long the trips were, and I feel a little disappointment growing in the pit of my belly.

"That's one of the longer ones. Sometimes it's just two or three days, but when we play further away, it usually ends up combining a few teams." He looks over at me again. "When we get back from this trip, we're around for a week, then a couple of over nighters or two-day trips. We aren't due for another longer road trip until just before Christmas, then we have the week off between Christmas and the New Year's Eve game here."

"You're going to have to give me your calendar... I can tell I'm going to have trouble keeping track of when we can see each other," I reply, looking down at my plate.

He moves to take my chin in his hand, turning my face so that I'm forced to meet his gaze. "We will make this work. It just might not look like what you're used to in other relationships. But we can pave our own way through this... If you still want to try, that is?"

I give a brief nod, keeping my eyes locked on his. "I want to be with you. Just wrapping my head around it all. If I take this job with my aunt, I may be travelling on the days you're in town, though. What if we never get to see each other?"

He moves closer and presses a soft kiss to my lips. "We will find a way. We are on the same continent, at least for a few months. That's got to count for something."

We return to our dinner, but I can't ignore the feeling that whatever is happening between us is going to be a lot harder than I first thought.

A few hours later, Seth pulls up in front of my grandparents' house and turns to face me. "I meant what I said earlier. We will make this work, okay?"

He seems so confident, but I can see the apprehension in his eyes.

I reach over and take his hand. "I know we will."

He's quiet for a few moments, then something inside him seems to snap, and he pulls me closer, pressing his mouth to mine in a bruising kiss, which I return with equal hunger.

When we finally break apart, he presses his forehead to mine and we sit in silence for a moment, our eyes closed while we both catch our breath.

"I wish I wasn't going away. I just want us to spend more time together."

"We'll find a balance. It can't all be like it was on tour if we're going to make this something more," I say, before kissing him again, gentler this time.

He threads his fingers through my hair, holding me close. The tenderness behind this kiss sets off the butterflies in my stomach again, and has me wishing that we were lying in bed together, able to explore where it takes us. But the night is growing later and Seth has an early flight to catch, so we reluctantly pull apart.

I let him walk me to the front door, and after another, all too brief kiss, I wave him off from the front door, trying to ignore the sinking feeling in my stomach.

"How did it go with Seth yesterday?" Adele curls up on the couch next to me while I work on some admin tasks for Will while waiting for him to call.

"Great. I'm a bit bummed he's not around for the next week and a half, though." I focus on my computer, attempting to seem like it doesn't worry me as much as it does.

Adele sees straight through me, though. "As someone who is in a long distance relationship, let me just say, it takes work, but it's definitely worth it. And you'll have the off season to spend time together."

"I'm only here for three months, remember? Isn't the off season in like June or something?" I may have done some Googling.

"You're not locked in to anything. You can always push your return date back. Or just not go back. I vote for not going back." She wriggles closer and gives me a one-armed hug. "I am really enjoying having you here, so I'm probably being selfish, but I want you to stay. And I can tell from how Seth was looking at you the other night that this isn't just a fling for him. I think you should stay."

"He wouldn't ask me to stay last night when I asked him." I don't know why that bugs me so much, but it has stuck with me, an annoying whisper in the back of my mind.

"Give it time. This is just as big of a deal for him as it is for you."

As I go to reply, my laptop starts making ringing noises, and Will's name pops up.

"Oh yay, my second favourite cousin," Adele says after I hit the Accept button.

"What's this second favourite nonsense? Has Kylie turned you against me?" Will's smiling face fills the screen.

"She's here. That bumped her up into first position. Sorry, not sorry." Adele shrugs, and my brother laughs.

"Where are you? That doesn't look like your place in the background," I say, squinting at the screen and trying to work out where he is.

He moves the camera closer so that all I can see is him. "Nowhere important. I have news."

Getting the distinct impression that there might be a hook-up occurring that he doesn't want me to know about, I narrow my eyes.

"Okay, you're being weird, but I'll allow it. What's your news?"

"I've booked my flights. I'm coming for three weeks over Christmas and New Year's."

Adele claps her hands and bounces in her seat next to me. "Yay! I get you both for Christmas? This is the best year ever! We're going to have such an amazing time. And you can meet Kylie's new boyfriend."

"Kylie's new what, now?" Will's eyebrows have risen so high, it's a miracle we can see them anymore.

"He's not my boyfriend," I reply, glaring at Adele.

She shrugs, not looking even slightly apologetic. "Oh boy, do we have some stories for you, William. Our Kylie here is dating an NHL superstar."

"What? How? You've only been there a week!"

I sigh before explaining everything about Seth, and by the time I'm finished, Will's expression has changed from confused to concerned.

"Well, I guess I better meet this guy."

"You are not meeting him to pass judgement on him, mister. He's a nice guy."

"I'll be the judge of that."

Why did I think my family would be cool about this?

33
IT'S ALL JUST SO EXCITING

KYLIE

AFTER I MEET with my Aunty Sheryl on Monday, I somehow end up being roped in to joining Adele the following weekend for my first tour. I'd forgotten how quickly people on this side of my family make decisions, and it's been a crazy week of trying to make sure I have everything I need, while ignoring my nerves.

"This is so exciting," Adele says, gripping my hand while we wait for the tour group to arrive outside the office.

We're heading to Banff for two nights, and the tour caters to the more mature aged (aka retirees with money to burn). I'm glad this is my first group. I've always gotten along with the older generations, so I'm hopeful they'll go easy on me when I inevitably stuff something up.

"So we've confirmed with the hotel this morning. There's been no last-minute cancellations. The bus is on time and the day tour for tomorrow is confirmed. The perfect first trip for you, Kylie." Aunty Sheryl appears at my other side, binder in hand. She hands it to me and squeezes my shoulder. "Don't worry, Adele is a pro at this, you're in good hands."

I nod, still not convinced I'm cut out to be in charge of myself, let alone a bunch of old people who will most likely expect everything to be done for them.

The first couple arrives, and when they say "hi" I immediately recognise their Australian accents. That little slice of home does something to my insides, and I shake the lady's hand with a grin.

"Diana and Philip Marshall, from Brisbane, Australia." Diana, a tiny woman with silver hair, stands back to let her very tall, white-haired husband shake my hand.

"No way! That's where I'm from." I grin, and they both laugh while shaking their heads.

"Everywhere we go, we always run into someone from back home. We Aussies sure do love to travel."

After we meet with the rest of our group, which includes several more Australians along with a few English and Irish couples, and one loud American man, we herd everyone on to the bus, and Adele introduces us over the microphone while standing at the front.

My nerves are settling now, but I still feel a little nauseous when Adele hands me the microphone to go over our itinerary for the rest of the day.

"Hi everyone, I'm Kylie. This is my first tour, so please be gentle with me." There are a few titters through the group, and several of the women give me reassuring smiles. "Our first stop today will be Lake Louise for a spot of tea at the Fairmont Château. For the more adventurous amongst us, you'll be able to wander across the lake, as it's nice and frozen right now. We'll have two hours there all up before heading into Banff, where we will drop off our bags at the hotel. Once we're all checked in, we have the optional trip up the gondola to the top of Sulphur Mountain, followed by dinner in the hotel restaurant. Then tomorrow, it's up nice and early for our walking tour around town with a local guide, and some free time in the afternoon. Then it's dinner at a brewery, and if you're interested in hockey, the Canadian national sport, we have an optional visit to a local sports bar to watch Calgary play against New Jersey." I double check the clipboard in Adele's hand to make sure I got that right.

"Oohh, we are going to a game next week and I can't wait," Diana says from where she's wedged between Philip and the window in the second row. "Those men sure like to play rough." She looks far too enthused about this for someone of her age and size.

"We happen to have some friends on the team," Adele pipes up, and I flash her a warning look.

The last thing I need is people on these trips knowing about my association with Seth. It doesn't feel professional, and I don't want strangers knowing my business, or trying to use me to get to Seth.

Once we're on our way, I pull out my phone to find a text from the man himself.

SETH

How's the tour going? I can't wait to see you on Tuesday.

I smile a little, that now familiar flip-flop sensation in my stomach still going strong.

KYLIE

So far, so good. The day is young though, so keep an eye on the news in case I'm responsible for any incidents involving senior citizens. I've missed you, too.

I'm only half joking about my fear of something happening to a person I'm responsible for. I had no idea how much could go wrong and have a newfound appreciation for what Brendan had to deal with from all us unruly children when we were travelling around Europe.

Seth sends back a laughing emoji, and we continue messaging back and forth until the bus arrives at Lake Louise.

I came out to Banff National Park when I was younger, but seeing it now is like seeing it all for the first time.

When we started driving through the Rocky Mountains, I stared at them in silent amazement, unable to believe the size of them. They certainly don't have mountain ranges like this back home. The snow-capped peaks stretch high into the clouds, and the frozen lakes and rivers give it all a magical feel. I can feel myself falling for this country with every passing moment.

Maybe there are other reasons to stay, not just for the strapping hockey player that has worked his way into my heart...

Two days later, I'm feeling more comfortable about this whole tour guide gig, and so far, no one has died or sustained a serious injury.

The biggest drama I've had to deal with was when George from Alabama was unhappy with the size of his room and moaned about it in the middle of the lobby. Thankfully, the hotel staff found him a room that was more to his liking without me having to intervene and tell him off for being so rude. He didn't seem like the type of person who cared much for being put in his place by a woman a third of his age.

He did, however, seem like the kind of man who would speak down to said woman and inform her when he thought she was wrong about something. Which was at least five times a day. He would then follow this with an explanation that made absolutely no sense while the rest of us stared at him and waited for him to run out of words.

But other than George, the rest of the group is lovely, and Diana and Philip have provided me with endless entertainment, bickering happily between themselves and exposing others to the trademark Aussie humour that I've missed.

After dinner on the second night, Adele and I lead the way along the icy foot path from the brewery to the sports bar, both of us dressed in our Mounties Jerseys, ready to introduce most of the group to hockey.

"So these are the teams that were in the grand final last year, right?" one of the Aussies, Rachel from Melbourne, asks while shivering in the cold air.

"The Stanley Cup, that's right," Adele replies over her shoulder.

"Well, this should be fun, then."

"I can't wait to go to the game later this week. It just looked so exciting on the TV," Diana says.

Philip shakes his head with a laugh. "You've been wanting to go ever since you saw those videos of them all stretching on the ice."

I turn to look at Adele with raised eyebrows. "What videos?" I whisper.

She frowns a little. "I'll show you later," she mutters.

"It's not just the stretching. It's the fights. It's all just so violent." Diana truly is a bloodthirsty little lady, her eyes shining while she no doubt pictures the game in her mind, the players beating the crap out of each other.

Once we get everyone settled at the tables in front of the TV that will play the Mounties game, I nudge Adele and nod towards the bar. She follows me while I order a round of drinks for everyone.

"What are these videos?" I ask, not entirely sure I want to know.

Adele grimaces and pulls her phone out. Opening one of the social media apps, she taps away and hands me the phone just as a reel begins to play. Someone appears to have spliced several videos, which show various NHL players stretching on the ice. The stretches could be mistaken for essentially humping the ice, and I feel slightly nauseous at the invasion of privacy for these men. And then a video of Seth pops up, and I realise with growing horror that he would despise this.

"This is sick. If this was women in these videos, there'd be a huge outcry," I mutter, scrolling through video after video of them all being objectified.

There are accounts dedicated to ranking the most attractive players (including Seth and Lincoln, naturally), with women audaciously shouting out inappropriate requests during games... There is even an account exclusively dedicated to ranking the players' wives and partners.

I swallow hard and hand the phone back to my cousin, who has been watching me with concern.

"Yeah, there are a lot of those sorts of videos in recent years, sadly." Adele's expression shows her disapproval.

"I can only imagine how Seth feels about that. One of those videos was of him."

"Didn't you say he doesn't use social media? Maybe he doesn't know?" She leads the way back to the table with the tray of drinks and begins handing them out to everyone as the game gets started.

I try to focus on the game on the screen, especially when Seth hops onto the ice. But all I can think about are the videos. Am I doing the rounds and don't even know about it? There were definitely people taking photos when we were together last week, and any of them could have easily been filming.

A lump forms in my throat while the enormity of it all threatens to overwhelm me.

Am I ready for this life?

34
SUCH A BRAT

SETH

AFTER THREE LOSSES while we were on the road, our winning streak has ended, and the trip home on Tuesday afternoon is a somber one. It had been a long stretch of wins, and we'd become complacent.

Not to mention, as soon as we lose a game, the rabid fans scream for a change in management, or demanding players are traded. It gets old, quick.

I let myself into my house and drop my gear bag in the laundry, determined to deal with it tomorrow. All I want right now is a hot shower, a beer, and to see Kylie. We have a few days before our next home game and I just want to hang out with her, without having to think about game stats and boosting team morale.

Once I'm showered, I jump in my car and drive to her grandparents' place, excitement brewing deep in my belly. It's been years since I've felt butterflies when seeing someone, and even then, it never felt this good. There's just something about Kylie that feels like coming home. I don't know what it is, but I want to cling to that feeling for as long as possible.

. . .

Pulling up out the front, her grandfather has the door open before I even make it to the sidewalk, and I can tell he's set on having a chat with me before we leave.

Steeling myself for the inevitable "what are your intentions with my granddaughter" conversation, I shake his hand and he steps aside to let me in.

"That was some bad luck on the road trip, young man." He shuts the door behind me, and I nod.

"Yes, sir. It wasn't our finest. But we're still having a stellar season so far. I'm confident we're still on track for the playoffs again this year."

He nods, then clears his throat.

Here it comes.

"So. I hear that you and Kylie met in Europe, and she didn't know who you were. I hope your intentions with my granddaughter are above board."

And there it is.

I nod again. "Yes, sir. I have no intention of doing anything that would hurt her."

"Grandpa, I hope you're not giving Seth a hard time?" Kylie appears at the top of the stairs, her jacket over her arm and a backpack hanging from one shoulder.

With her hair down and her toque pulled low over her ears, she looks adorable in her jeans and oversized sweatshirt.

"We're just chatting," I reply, while her grandfather looks chastened.

"I'm sure you are," she says, levelling her grandfather with a knowing look when she reaches the bottom of the stairs, before turning to me. "You ready?"

"Yep. Have you got everything?" I take the jacket and help her into it, slinging the backpack over my shoulder.

It's deceptively heavy.

"Sure do. Let's go. Grandpa, I'll see you later." She gives him a kiss on the cheek, and I hold the door open to let her go first.

Once the door is closed, I pull her back, threading my fingers through hers. "You look gorgeous, by the way."

She grins up at me. "Too scared to say that in front of Grandpa?"

"Definitely." I give her a quick kiss before leading her towards the car.

As I open the door, a squirrel races across the yard next to us and runs up the large tree in front of the house.

"Oh my gosh! I love squirrels! Wait a minute." Pulling her phone out, Kylie heads towards the tree, snapping photos of the little squirrel.

After she's taken several hundred, she pockets her phone and heads back over to me with a grin.

"I promised Bri I'd take photos of squirrels and send them to her at all hours of the day. Them and chipmunks."

I cock my head. "I know you guys have pretty cool creatures in Australia. I hadn't thought about it going the opposite way and you all go crazy over squirrels and chipmunks." I hold the door open for her.

"How can you not go crazy over squirrels? Have you got something against cute, furry creatures?" she asks, hands on hips.

I laugh, pulling her close and kissing her forehead. "Nope, I am completely onboard with the furry creature love."

She grins up at me. "Good, I suppose I'll come home with you then." She climbs into the car, and as soon as I get the engine started, she is fiddling with the seat warmer, shivering dramatically. "So, when we get to your place, I need to video chat with Tara. It's the only time we've been able to find that works for us both."

I laugh a little. "That's fine. You can tell her how cold you are."

She pokes her tongue out. "Whatever, it's freezing."

We chat easily on the drive back to my place, and she entertains me with stories of her first tour group, and a disastrous attempt to learn how to drive on the 'wrong' side of the road which ended in her grandfather banning her from using his car ever again and a slightly dented front bumper. Apparently, she hadn't even made it out of the alleyway before she'd hit a garbage bin on the right that she claims jumped in front of the car.

"I can take you out, if you want?"

She raises an eyebrow. "In this? Hell no, I won't be responsible for damaging a car that is worth more than I earn in a few years." She purses her lips and shakes her head quickly. "You'll just have to deal with driving me around, buddy."

I laugh and reach across to take her hand, kissing the back of it. "I can handle that." I hold her hand in my lap, driving with one hand. "So, have you spoken to Tara much since you've been here?"

She shakes her head. "No. I've not talked to anyone back home except for my brother."

"That's nice. I'm sure he's missed you." We reach my house, and I grab Kylie's bag from the backseat before following her inside.

Once she's taken off her shoes, she grabs her bag and heads for the living room while I get us a snack from the kitchen.

"How have you got food here? Didn't you just get home?" she asks when I enter the room, setting her laptop up on the coffee table.

I guess that explains why her backpack was so heavy.

"I had my housekeeping service get an order of groceries."

She looks at me, shaking her head. "We definitely live in different worlds."

I hand her a bowl of fruit salad and yoghurt and take a seat next to her. "Well, I didn't want to waste any of our time together doing grocery shopping." I sling an arm along the back of the couch behind her and twirl a lock of her hair around my finger.

She leans into my side and wraps an arm around my waist while I press a kiss to her temple. This just feels so comfortable. I wish I could come home to her every day.

Jeez Seth, slow it down. You've only been on a few dates with her. I shake off the ridiculous thought and sit quietly while she dials Tara.

After a few rings, Tara's face fills the screen, and she smiles. "Hey!" She squints. "Whoa, Seth?!"

I raise a hand. "Hey, Tara."

"Um... I have many questions."

I look down at Kylie. "Did you not tell her anything?"

"I really, really wanted to see her face when she saw you," Kylie says, giggling when her best friend stares at us both.

"You're such a brat." I kiss the side of her head again and get to my feet. "I'll let you two talk without me hanging around. I get the feeling Tara is going to want details."

"Tara most certainly does!" Tara calls out, just as a blonde woman joins her on the screen.

"Oh, babe, wait." Kylie grabs my hand and tugs me back down beside her. "I want you to meet Bri first."

I don't think she even realised she said it, but hearing her call me 'babe' gives me a little boost. "Hi, Bri. Nice to meet you." I wave again.

"Hi Seth. Nice to meet you, too." She smiles and waves back.

"Alright, you can go away now so we can grill Kylie for details." Tara makes shooing motions with her hands and I laugh, getting back up again, bending to give Kylie another quick kiss before heading to the laundry.

I figure I might as well deal with my kit while she talks to her friends.

"What the hell, Kyles? You kept that quiet." Tara's voice follows me down the hall, and I laugh a little, shaking my head.

I guess Kylie is okay with everything now, if she's having fun surprising her friends with my presence.

After a while, Kylie comes searching for me.

"Was that fun?" I ask, pulling the laundry door closed behind me so she doesn't have to deal with the smell of my sweaty gear.

"Extremely. They both had to start work. Also, Tara says she's going to smack both you and Lincoln for not telling us." She wraps her arms around my waist.

I hold her close, enjoying the feeling of her in my arms. "Probably a good thing she's on the other side of the world, then. I'll tell Linc he should call her. He can charm anyone."

"That's true." She looks up at me. "So, what are we doing?"

"Well, I wasn't sure what you felt like doing, but I thought maybe just a movie on the couch?"

She leans in to me again. "That sounds perfect."

But we don't make it past the first ten minutes of the latest Marvel movie before she's straddling my lap. Her lips press frantically to mine while she tries to tug my shirt over my head.

"Did I mention I missed you?" she asks, kissing the side of my neck, grazing my skin gently with her teeth.

I inhale sharply. "Not in the last twenty minutes."

She grinds against me, driving me crazy while I pull her sweater and shirt off. I can easily suck one nipple and then the other into my mouth without needing to bend because her breasts are perfectly positioned in front of my face, and she sighs, reaching around to undo her bra and give me better access.

We spend the rest of the evening alternating between having sex and attempting to watch the rest of the movie. By the time it finishes, I'm exhausted. It's been a long week, and all I want to do is curl up in bed with Kylie by my side.

"Stay the night?" I ask, running my hand up and down her bare back while we lay naked on the couch, her head on my chest and her leg slung over my hips, her eyes half closed while she stares at the TV.

She lifts her head to look at me. "Yeah?"

"Yeah." I run my hand right up her back and clasp the back of her neck.

She moves up to kiss me softly. "Okay."

She settles back down and is asleep within minutes. I watch her breathe, marvelling again at how we ended up here and wanting to cling to this feeling for as long as possible. Cause I'm not ready for this to be over.

The next morning, I wake to an empty bed, and for a heart stopping moment, I think Kylie has left without saying goodbye. But a quick survey of my room shows that she must still be here somewhere, her things scattered on the floor on her side of the bed.

When I can't find any trace of her anywhere in the house, I head out to the pool house, seeing the light on. Letting myself in, I find her running full tilt on the treadmill, her earphones in. She's wearing one of my Mounties shirts over the smallest running shorts imaginable, her hair piled on top of her head. Even though she's worked up a sweat, the joy on her face is clear. She'd mentioned wanting to use my treadmill, and seeing how happy she is right now, while wearing my shirt, does all sorts of crazy things to my insides.

She finally notices me and slows down. "Good morning," she says, chest heaving, while she watches me move closer.

She raises an eyebrow when I reach over and turn the treadmill off.

"I was really looking forward to waking up next to you this morning," I reply, leaning on the side of the machine.

"Oh really. And why's that?" she asks, flashing me a smile.

I reach over and pull her closer. The height of the treadmill means I don't have to bend to kiss her, and I wrap my arms around her waist while crushing my lips to hers. Something about seeing her so flushed and breathless from her run has my heart racing, and I don't hold back, showing her just how much I want her. I still have one condom left in my pocket, left over from yesterday's sexathon on the couch, and all I can think about is using it immediately.

"Someone's eager this morning," she whispers against my lips.

"You have no idea."

She reaches down to rub me over my sweatpants, grinning when I hiss. "I don't know. I think I have a pretty good idea."

I claim her lips again, kissing her hard while I slip a hand inside her tiny shorts. She gasps when I circle her clit, gripping her waist tighter to keep her upright. She moans when I slide one finger, then a second, inside her, lifting her leg to wrap around my waist and give me better access. Her breath comes in short, quick pants while I bring her to the edge. Before she comes, I pull my hand away, and she lets out a whine, which makes me chuckle.

"Not yet," I say, pulling her shorts and underwear down before kicking my sweatpants off.

Digging out the foil wrapper, I roll the condom on while watching her sway slightly in front of me, her eyes tracking the movement of my hand hungrily. Grabbing her hips again, I lift her off the treadmill, carrying her a few steps before push her back against the wall, her legs coming around to grip my waist tightly.

We both sigh together when I slide inside her, kissing her again while I begin to thrust slowly. I feel her tighten around me, the orgasm I had denied her moments before racing to overcome her, and I shift my hips to give her extra friction against her clit. She cries out, her head falling back against the wall and her eyes flutter closed. It's not long before my own release follows, and I shudder, my lips pressed to her throat as I come.

We struggle to regain our breath, and I keep her pinned against the wall, bringing my forehead to hers.

"I'll be sure to stay in bed during my next sleep over," she murmurs, biting her lip.

"I don't know. This was pretty awesome, too. But I'll take you anywhere you'll let me."

We stay like that until she shifts a little, and I let her down, sensing her discomfort.

"That was hot, not gonna lie. Definitely happy to let you take me anywhere, anytime, captain."

I groan, claiming her mouth again. "Keep calling me that, and I'll be ready to take you again, right here, right now."

She nips my lip lightly, then looks up at me with a cheeky grin.

Raising on to her tiptoes, her lips brush against my ear. "I want you to fuck me all day long, Captain."

Jesus, this woman is going to kill me.

Hours later, I return from practice to find Kylie sitting exactly where I left her on the couch. Her laptop is sitting on a pillow on her lap, and she has papers scattered all around her.

"Hey," I say, dropping a kiss on the top of her head.

"Hey. I didn't even hear you come in. How was practice?" She blinks up at me, almost as though she's trying to remember where she is, or who I even am, for that matter.

"Good..." I regard her closely. "Have you moved off this couch at all?"

She shrugs, looking a little sheepish. "Um... No?"

I raise an eyebrow. "So you haven't eaten or anything?"

She shakes her head. "I got caught up in researching for my upcoming tours. I want to have as much information as possible for any questions people might have. I'm at a distinct disadvantage, not having grown up here and all."

"I get that. But you still need to eat something." I slide the laptop off her lap and take her hand, tugging her to her feet. "Your brilliant brain needs fuel. Come on, I'll make you some lunch. Well, a late afternoon meal," I add, realising it's almost four o'clock.

I left at nine, which means she's not had anything since the cup of coffee I'd handed her before I walked out the door.

"How are you not starving right now?" I start making her an omelette while she settles on the bar stool to watch me.

"When I get caught up in a project, I tend to lose track of everything around me. I hyper fixate, basically. Once, when I was on a spiral through the depths of researching things for our trip, I almost fainted, 'cause I hadn't eaten all day." She shrugs, like it's no big deal.

"Linc gets like that. You guys are so similar it's almost scary sometimes," I reply.

"Just means you have good taste in people. We're both awesome," she says with a grin.

"Very true. Just do me a favour? Let me know when you're on a spiral so I can make sure I'm around to remind you to take care of yourself?" When she doesn't reply, I glance over to find her blinking rapidly while staring at me. "What's wrong?"

"Nothing. I'm just not used to having someone take care of me like that. Well, Will does, but he doesn't count. He's my brother. He has a vested interest in my well-being."

I abandon the omelette and round the bench to cup her face in my hands. "I have a vested interest in your well-being too, Kylie." I kiss her tenderly, and she curls her fingers to fist my shirt, pulling me closer.

"Thank you," she whispers once we pull apart.

"You're very welcome. Now stop distracting me so that I can feed you and make sure you don't faint, so that you can be the best tour guide ever." I wink at her before heading back to rescue the omelette before it burns.

She laughs. "Yes, sir."

"Hey, I said no distractions."

She tips her head back and laughs even harder. And I'll be damned if that sound doesn't slice right through my heart.

Yep, it's official. I'm gone for this woman.

35

MUCH RATHER BE
SURFING THAN SKATING

KYLIE

SETH and I settle into a routine over the next few weeks. Whenever we're both in town, I stay at his place, and I've attended a few games, though I'm still not comfortable enough to sit in the family box, preferring to sit with my own family instead.

By the time Will's plane lands a few weeks before Christmas, I'm more than a little excited to see him, along with a small mix of fear at the idea of introducing my big brother to Seth.

Seth comes with me to pick him up. I'd wanted to introduce them without the rest of our family milling around.

As soon as I see Will coming through the door at Arrivals, I run towards him and launch myself into his arms. Of all the people back home, he's the one I've missed the most. I can tell he's missed me too, with how tightly he hugs me back, lifting me so my feet are off the ground.

"Hey, Bug," he mumbles into my hair, using his favourite nickname from when we were kids.

It's been a while since I've heard him call me that, and I can feel tears well up in my eyes while I cling to him. We eventually pull apart, and he sets me back down on the ground. Seth moves to my side, having stayed back to give us space.

"Hey man, I'm Seth," he says, holding his hand out to my brother.

Will nods at him and shakes his outstretched hand. "Hey, I'm Will. Good to finally meet you."

After everything, it feels weird having the two men in my life in the same room together, and I can see Will sizing Seth up. Will is pretty tall, but Seth still has a few inches on him, and is broader. I can see a few people around us checking both men out, a few of the locals doing a double take when they recognise Seth.

"We should get moving, otherwise you're going to get swamped by fans," I say to Seth, nodding towards a group of teenagers who are talking amongst themselves and pointing towards Seth.

He looks over, wincing when he notices it too. "Good idea."

Will looks between Seth and the teenagers, a confused expression on his face. "What's happening?"

I sigh. "Seth gets attention everywhere we go in this city." We begin walking towards the exit before I pause and look at what my brother is wearing. "Um, you're going to need way more clothes on than that." I wave a hand up and down in front of him.

He looks down at his jeans and t-shirt. "What's wrong with what I'm wearing?"

"Have you forgotten everything about Canada? It's -7 degrees outside!"

Seth coughs to cover up a laugh before shrugging out of his jacket. "Here, have this until we get you back to your grandparents. I'm immune to the cold."

Will looks at the jacket that Seth holds out, before looking at me with an incredulous look. "I feel like you're exaggerating a tad."

I point towards the glass doors. "By all means, after you."

Will leads the way, stopping abruptly once we've exited the

building and turning to Seth. "On second thought, I'll take that jacket."

"One day, brother, you will learn to listen to me." I laugh while Seth hands the jacket over and puts his arm around me.

Will grumbles under his breath while he zips up the jacket, and the three of us head for the car park.

That evening, Seth, Adele, Lincoln and I take Will out for dinner, trying to keep him up until a reasonable hour before jet-lag claims him.

We end up at a local Vietnamese restaurant where the host seats us at a booth with high backs to give us the illusion of privacy. Which works well when trying to keep the identities of two over-sized Mounties players under wraps.

"So, have you got any plans while you're here?" Seth asks Will while we wait for our dinner.

"I thought we could give snowboarding a try. What do you think, Kyles?"

"Yeah, that could be fun. I haven't had a chance to get out to any of the ski resorts yet. Adele hogs those tours." I poke my tongue out at my cousin, who laughs while I turn to Seth. "Wanna come?"

He shakes his head. "I can't. Our contracts with the Mounties prohibit us from partaking in any dangerous sports during the season."

I screw up my face. "Well, that sucks."

Lincoln laughs. "You should have seen Coach's face when he found out we skydived in Europe. Best not mention to him it was your idea, Kylie."

I've met their coach a few times now, and he intimidates the crap out of me, so I shake my head quickly. "Definitely not saying a word."

"Excuse me." A small red-headed girl, who looks around eight years old, appears at our table, staring at Lincoln. "Are you Lincoln O'Malley?"

Lincoln grins. "I sure am."

Her eyes go wide and she does a cute little jump. "Oh! Can you please sign this?" She holds out a little notebook and pen.

"Sure." Lincoln takes it from her. "What's your name?"

"Evelyn," she replies with a big smile.

Lincoln gets to signing, and once she gets her notebook back, she looks at it before clasping it to her chest. "Thank you so much. Sorry to interrupt your dinner." She finally looks around at the rest of us, gasping when she sees Seth. "Oh my god, you're Seth Davidson," she blurts out.

Seth grins and gives her a little wave. It's so interesting watching him interact with the younger fans, as opposed to the adults. He makes it look effortless with the kids, while the adults make him uncomfortable.

Evelyn holds out her notebook and pen. "Can you sign it too, please?"

Seth nods and signs the same page as Lincoln before handing the book back to her.

"You're both my favourite players. I go to all the games that my parents can get tickets for."

"Remember to come see us at the glass next time. Maybe we can get you a puck or something," Lincoln says, and her eyes go even wider.

"Yes, sir." She stares at them both for a few more moments. "Okay, I'll go now. Thank you so much." She bounces off towards her family, and her father smiles at the guys before talking to his overexcited offspring.

"That was so cute," Adele says, placing her hand on her chest.

"Does that happen a lot?" Will asks.

The guys shrug at the same time. "Yeah. You get used to it after a while," Lincoln replies. "Seth gets it more than me, though."

"You're the captain, right?" Will looks at Seth, who nods.

Will's gaze turns to me. "I still think it's crazy that of all the people, you find the captain of the Mounties. Dad is still shaking his head about that."

"Yeah, what's up with your dad's dislike of hockey, anyway?" Lincoln asks, while Seth slides his arm around my shoulders.

"I think he just got tired of how much it was talked about in their house growing up. It's not like he actively has a hatred for it or anything, just has no interest, really. He'd much rather be surfing than skating," Will replies, then looks over at Seth. "We'll have to give you a surfing lesson when you come to Australia."

Lincoln laughs, although Seth and I remain quiet. Neither of us has brought up my return to Australia in a few weeks, and I feel his arm tighten around me.

"I would pay to see that." Lincoln seems oblivious to our reaction.

Adele rushes to change the subject and Will gives me a curious look before replying to her question about how his business is going.

Our food arrives, adding to the distraction, but I can feel the shift in Seth's mood, matching my own. At some point, we're going to have to talk about it, but I'm not ready for things to change yet.

Seth drops us home after dinner, and I stay in the passenger seat after Will and Adele head inside. "You sure you don't want to stay?" I ask him.

"Yeah. You should hang out with your brother," he replies, curling a lock of my hair around his finger.

"Okay. And you're also scared of Grandpa." I grin at him.

"He's slightly terrifying."

I laugh and shake my head. "The big NHL player is scared of an old man."

"No, the NHL player is scared of the deceptively spry old man who has explicitly informed said NHL player that he knows how to hide a body." That had been an entertaining conversation, which led to Grandma smacking Grandpa over the head with a newspaper.

"I'm sure he was only joking... I don't know of anyone who's gone missing yet." I smirk, and he shakes his head, leaning over to kiss me.

"You're hilarious. I'll see you tomorrow, yeah?"

"Yep. We're bringing Will for his first game, so we'll meet you at dinner afterwards."

Once I finally say goodbye to Seth, I head inside to find Will and Adele sitting on the couch, waiting for me.

"So, I've decided I like him. You may keep dating him," Will says as soon as he sees me.

"Oh, I didn't realise I needed your permission, but thank you so much." I flop down beside him, and he ruffles my hair.

"Of course you need my permission. It's my right as the older brother."

I roll my eyes but don't bother replying. I know he is all for me making my own decisions and is just trying to rile me up.

We chat for a little longer, but Will is fading fast from jet-lag, and eventually passes out on the couch while Adele and I are talking about work.

"Well, I think that all went well," Adele says, nodding towards Will, who has started snoring.

"Yeah, they seemed to get along okay."

"When are you going to cave and admit that you're in love with Seth and plan on staying here?" she asks.

I sigh. "We haven't discussed it any further since that first night. I don't know what I'm going to do. My life is in Australia." Although I've been trying to avoid it, my thoughts have often drifted to how much my life would change if I stayed, while nothing would have to change for Seth.

"Let's be honest here. You know you're going to stay. You've got a job here. It's not like you have to worry about getting a visa or anything, and you're in love with the hot hockey player, who is clearly in love with you, too." Adele gives me a pointed look.

"It's too soon to be talking about love."

She tsks. "There's no time line on love, you nutter. We can all see it. The way you both look at each other, that's not just going to go away if you decide not to stay. You admitted you missed him before you came here. It's only going to be harder if you leave after spending so much time with him."

I frown. "I'm not ready to talk about it."

"Well, you've only got a few weeks, so as much as you're not ready, you better have the conversation, or you're going to end up regretting it for the rest of your life."

I really hate it when my family meddles.

Especially when they are right.

36
THE REAL DEAL

AFTER OUR FIRST home game loss this season, the team is a little subdued when we head to dinner with everyone afterwards.

"Probably not the best game to watch for your first one," Linc says to Will, who shrugs before taking a mouthful of beer.

"It was still a good game," he replies, although I think that was more for our benefit than his.

It really was a crap game. The team felt distracted the whole way through for some reason, and it was surprising that we only lost by one goal with the way we were playing.

"It was shit," Dean grumbles beside me.

We've gotten so used to doing well that none of us is taking the loss tonight particularly well.

"You okay?" Kylie squeezes my arm.

She's been sitting beside me, watching our conversations, or lack thereof, when it comes to me. I realise I've been in my head and have barely said a word since we got here.

"Yeah, sorry." I pull her close to my side and kiss her temple, catching Will watching us.

"We tend to get a bit sad when we lose," Linc says.

"Understandable," Kylie replies, turning so that she can wrap her arms around my waist, giving me a squeeze.

Eventually, my teammates and their families start to leave, and I'm relieved. All I want to do is go home and curl up in bed with Kylie. We're reaching the part of the season where my social battery feels like it's constantly drained. But this is the first time that I've wanted someone else's company when I go home.

Before we head off, Kylie excuses herself and heads to the bathroom, leaving me standing awkwardly with Will. We haven't really chatted with no one else around yet. I've reached my word quota for the day, so I'm not sure I'm up for small talk.

Although it seems like small talk isn't on his radar either. "So, things with you and my sister seem pretty serious."

"Um, yeah." I slide my hands into my pockets.

"She surprised me when she mentioned she was seeing someone so soon after arriving here, but I can see how happy she is. Thanks for putting a smile on her face."

Well, that wasn't how I expected this conversation to go.

"It feels weird to say you're welcome to that, but not entirely sure what else would sound right," I admit, and Will laughs a little.

"She's had a bit of a rough go with guys for a few years, so it's nice to see her with someone who actually cares about her. I was worried that my relationship stuff had affected her, too." His smile drops a little, and I nod.

"She mentioned you'd had some stuff going on. Sorry."

"It is what it is, I guess. Still working my way through it all, but I'm glad Kylie is happy. Have you guys talked about what you're going to do when she comes home?"

I shake my head. "I don't think either of us wants to think about it. I can't expect her to upend her entire life for me, and it's not like I can move to Australia, at least not while I'm still playing hockey."

He cocks his head to the side and regards me closely. "So, this is just a fling for you both?" He doesn't sound thrilled.

"No. It's the real deal. At least it is for me. But Kylie needs to be the one who decides to stay. I can't let it be just for me." I rub the back of my neck, glancing towards the bathrooms.

Will presses further. "But she'd be staying for you. I mean, yeah, she likes the new job, but let's be honest, if she decides to stay, it would be for you."

To my relief, Kylie finally reappears, cutting the conversation short.

Will catches a cab to their grandparents' place, and Kylie and I head back to my place.

"Did Will give you the third degree while I was in the bathroom?" she asks from the ensuite where she's getting ready to go to sleep while I lie on the bed, still in my suit but not ready to move yet.

"Kind of. But he was mostly just happy that you're happy."

She appears at the door. "I am, you know."

I prop myself up on my elbows and run my gaze over her. She's dressed in tiny sleep shorts and an oversized, white long-sleeved shirt, her right shoulder exposed. I'm yet to see her dressed in something that she doesn't look great in, but it's this look I love the most. She has a natural beauty that takes my breath away sometimes.

"You are what?" I can't remember what we were talking about, distracted by the sight of her nipples through the thin material of her top.

She smiles while walking towards me, crawling up the bed to lie on top of me, before gently stroking my cheek. "Happy," she replies.

Her hair falls around her face like a curtain, and I push it back behind her right ear before cupping her face. "I'm happy, too."

"Oh, well, I guess you don't need me to cheer you up anymore, then." She moves to get up, and I pull her back down.

"Not so fast. How were you planning on cheering me up?"

She pretends to think for a moment. "Oh, you know, I was planning on using my womanly wiles on you, but you said you're happy now, so..." She shrugs.

"On second thought, I'm miserable." I pull a sad face and she leans down to kiss my neck.

"Really? How miserable?" She unbuttons my shirt at a leisurely pace.

"So, so miserable," I reply, my voice a little rough when she kisses down my chest while finishing undoing the last few buttons.

"Well, I guess I better kiss you all better, then." She undoes my pants, and I help her slide them down my legs.

She looks up at me through lowered lashes while she takes my semi in her hand, sliding her palm up and down until I groan.

"I think that sounds like an excellent idea," I say, the words catching in my throat when she lowers her head to take me in her mouth.

I weave my fingers through her hair, closing my eyes. She moves her head back and forth a little faster until I'm panting, determined not to blow my load just yet.

Opening my eyes, I pull her head away, and she looks up at me. "Take off your clothes," I say roughly.

She raises her eyebrows, but quickly sheds her clothes, looking at me expectantly. Waiting for instructions.

My stomach clenches, knowing she is more than happy to let me take the lead in the bedroom.

"I want your mouth again. But this time, I want my mouth on you while you do it."

Her chest rises and falls a little faster while her eyes light up. She crawls back up my body and kisses me hard. "Like this?"

I nip her lip and smack her ass. "Brat. Turn around."

She turns slowly, lowering her head again to take me in her

mouth once again. I grab her hips and position her over my face, pulling her down so I can drag my tongue over her clit, and she moans a little, the vibrations sending a shock wave through my body.

I keep going, trying to focus on her pleasure, even when I can feel myself coming apart. Determined that we come together, I work harder once I feel her legs quiver and her moans grow louder. I can feel I'm seconds away from losing control entirely when she picks up the pace. I slide my finger inside, knowing I've hit the right spot when she cries out.

My orgasm rips through me seconds after hers, and she keeps her mouth wrapped around me, swallowing it down.

We both take a minute to get our breath back, and she turns around before collapsing beside me.

"Mission accomplished," she says, raising her hand in the air.

I laugh, high-fiving her before letting my hand drop back down to my side, all energy sapped.

She slides off the bed and heads back into the bathroom. Once she returns, I remove my suit jacket and unbuttoned shirt before cleaning myself up and joining her back in bed once again.

"That was new for us," she says, her words muffled when she buries her face into my neck.

"It was."

"I liked it." She slides her arm across my stomach, and I thread my fingers through hers.

"So did I. Can't wait to do it again." I follow the words with a yawn and feel her shake with silent laughter.

"Maybe tomorrow, sleepyhead."

"Sounds like a fantastic idea."

As we drift off, I hold her tight against my chest and wish we could stay like this forever.

37
YOU'RE THE BEST BOYFRIEND

KYLIE

"How soon can you and Will be ready to go on a two-day skiing trip to Lake Louise?"

Those were not the words I was expecting to hear when I answered the phone to Adele first thing the next morning.

"Um, I mean, I don't know what we'd need to bring with us, but we could be ready in like two hours, if Seth's okay to drop me home. Why?" I ask, looking over at where Seth is sleeping beside me.

"We've had a few people cancel at the last minute on this trip, so we have some spaces available. Seth could come too, if he wants."

"It's just an overnight one?" I run my hand through my hair, trying to pull out the knots.

Seth stirs, opening one eye before raising his head to look at me curiously.

"Yeah, just for the weekend. Seth's not got any more games this weekend, right? I haven't checked the game schedule."

"No, we were just hanging out with Will this weekend. Have you called him?" I throw back the covers to get dressed.

Seth props himself up on one elbow, watching me with a raised eyebrow.

I cover the phone with my hand. "Wanna come to Lake Louise for skiing this weekend?"

"I can't ski, remember?"

Right. I'd forgotten about that rule.

I uncover the phone. "Seth can't ski because of his contract. I don't want to bail when we had plans for the weekend, but definitely check with Will."

Seth puts up his hand. "Hey, don't say no just cause of me."

"But I don't want to bail on you. We don't get to spend that much time together." I put the phone on speaker so I can pull my shirt over my head, figuring this was a three-way conversation now, anyway.

"I can just come hang out at the hotel, then. I don't want you guys to miss out on having fun while Will's here." Seth sits forward, placing his elbows on his knees awhile he watches me.

"Aw, you're the best boyfriend, Seth Davidson. Kylie, I will not accept anymore excuses. You guys are coming."

I stare at the phone. *Boyfriend...* We still hadn't used those words out loud. But Seth doesn't react, so I decide to just pretend it doesn't have any effect on me.

"Can we at least meet you at the hotel? I don't want to drag Seth on the bus, and we probably need to get our hands on some snowboarding gear."

We agree to meet Adele and her group there, and I hang up.

"Are you sure you don't mind?" I ask, and Seth gets out of bed, pulling me to him and wrapping his arms around me.

"Of course I don't mind. Will mentioned he'd wanted to go snowboarding anyway, and I can tell you really want to go. Let me just throw some stuff together and we can leave."

I watch him move around the room, throwing some clothes

into his overnight bag, and Lincoln's words from a few weeks ago run through my mind.

He will prioritise you above everything else. It's who he is. He puts the needs of others ahead of himself, sometimes to the detriment of his own happiness.

Am I just taking advantage of his easygoing nature? It's not like I'm forcing him to go, but I'm not telling him to stay either. Because I'm selfish and want him to come along, even though he'll probably be bored.

Two hours later, we hit the road, heading towards Lake Louise. Will was more than a little excited when we showed up and informed him where we were going, and we'd raced to the shops to grab some snowboarding appropriate clothes.

"So, did you ski much when you were younger? Before you were locked into contracts that banned fun?" I ask, turning in the front passenger seat so I can see both Seth and Will, who is sitting in the middle of the backseat.

Seth laughs. "I skied a bit when I was in my teens. We lived close to a ski hill in BC, so we did it for school. But hockey was pretty much my entire world."

"We've never been. I'm hoping snowboarding is just like surfing," Will says, leaning forward in his seat.

"I've never surfed, but I'm sure there are some similarities," Seth replies, keeping his eyes on the road.

We spend the rest of the drive making a rough plan for the weekend, and by the time we get to the cute little boutique hotel that the company arranged for the tour, I can feel my excitement brewing. I hadn't realised how much I'd missed surfing in the time I've been here, but now I'm eager to hit the slopes and find out if snowboarding might give me that same feeling.

"Are you sure you're cool with hanging out here by yourself? I feel bad just running off and leaving you." I watch while Seth pulls our bags from the back of his car.

He drops them near my feet and pulls me into his arms. "I'll be fine, babe. Go have fun with your brother. I'm due for some downtime, anyway. I have a book I've been wanting to start, and I can go to Banff if I get bored. But I doubt I will. And you can tell me all about how much fun it was when you get back later." He drops a kiss on the top of my head before releasing me and picking the bags up again.

I still feel bad leaving him, but the urge to slide down a mountain is strong. So I allow Will to pull me onto the bus with the rest of the tour group, telling myself I'll make it up to Seth later tonight.

It turns out, while there are some similarities in terms of balance, snowboarding is not the same as surfing. Amongst the many differences, the way snowboarders distribute their weight is different, as we discover. As surfers, we're used to focusing our weight on the back of the board, while snowboarders move to the front. Will and I had some spectacular falls when we did our first couple of runs, but by the end of the morning, we've made it down the easiest run a few times without serious injury. While it doesn't quite fill the surfing void, it is addictive, and I can't wait to get back out there after we get some lunch.

"So. When are you going to tell me you've decided to stay?" Will asks, flopping down in the seat beside me in the food hall of the lodge.

"I'm not."

"Bullshit. You love it over here. And you're clearly in love with Seth. What's stopping you from staying longer?" Will presses, and I shake my head.

"I do love it here, but I have a life back in Brisbane. Seth and I have only been seeing each other for a few months. I can't upend my life for a relationship that I don't know will last." It's the line I've been using on myself every time I consider staying.

Really, I just want Seth to ask me to stay.

Will regards me quietly, a troubled expression on his face. "Since when do you think something like that? You've always been the first to jump at new experiences and try new things. What makes you think this relationship wouldn't last?"

I shrug. "Well, look at your last relationship. We all thought you were on the marriage track, and you guys were together forever." I try to say it as delicately as possible, but there's no avoiding the truth.

If a couple as solid as Will and Annelisa were couldn't make it, I don't see a relationship with as many hurdles as Seth and mine going the distance. Even though the idea of not having him in my life makes me sick to my stomach, there's no denying how scary it is to imagine myself giving up my life in Australia for a guy. Even if that guy gets my heart racing just by looking at me.

"Kyles. Come on. Your relationship with Seth is nothing like mine was. For one thing, Seth can't just disappear on you. Probably one benefit of dating someone famous. And Annelisa and I aside, look at Morgan and Chris. You can't use my shitty experience as an excuse to run away from what I can see is real between you both."

"Morgan and Chris are not a good example. They knew from the age of twelve that they'd be together forever." I let my head fall back and stare at the ceiling, wondering how I can change the subject.

"Jake and Bri, then. Look at the shit they went through before they worked things out. And now they've got an awesome life together. Bri found a job she loved that worked in with their lives. You love the tours. I can see that from how you talk about it. You wouldn't just be staying for Seth, you have other reasons to stay."

"Can we just... I don't really want to talk about this anymore. Seth hasn't even said he wants me to stay."

My brother shakes his head. "Fine. But for the record... He wants you to stay."

We lapse into silence, and I stare out the window, watching people ski and snowboard down the mountain. The good mood I'd been in has disappeared, and now all I can think about is what I'm going to do with my future.

I'm tired of everyone assuming they know what I should do, when the one person I want to tell me what I should do has remained mute on the subject.

With the sun low on the horizon, we manage two more runs before it's time to head back to the hotel. Stripping off my jacket, I leave Will to his own devices to go in search of Seth. I find him sitting in a high-back chair in front of the fireplace in a little sitting area, resting his feet on a coffee table with his nose buried in a book.

"Hey," I say, sliding into the space beside him and draping my legs over his lap, before kissing his cheek.

"Hey you. How was it? Did you show them all up?" He puts his book down and wraps his arms around me.

I rest my head on his shoulder. "Not quite. I fell a few times to start with. I'm sure my ass is going to be covered in bruises, but it was so much fun." I stifle a yawn.

After a day of constant activity, a wave of exhaustion hits me, and I close my eyes.

"How about we get you up to the room and you can have a shower and a rest?" Seth urges me to move.

"No, I'm good here," I mumble into his chest.

He laughs. "Come on. Do you need me to carry you?" I snuggle in further, wrapping my arms around his neck, and he sighs. "Come on, sleeping beauty." He slides an arm under my knees and stands in one swift movement.

I shriek, not expecting him to lift me so easily, and cling to him tightly. "Wait! Your book!"

He nods, bending slightly so I can pluck it off the table, and I laugh while he marches off towards our room, acting like it's no big deal that he's carrying a grown woman in his arms. Somehow getting our door open with me still in his arms, he places me on the bed, a peculiar look on his face when he stands up.

"What's wrong?" I ask, swinging my legs over the side of the bed.

"Nothing. Everything's good."

He heads into the bathroom and I watch him go, confused, wondering what changed in that few seconds. When he reappears, it's like nothing happened, but I spend the rest of the evening wondering what that look meant.

38

HOW MUCH LONGER

CHRISTMAS EVE ARRIVES, and I head to the airport to collect my parents, who have decided to spend the holidays with me this year, instead of me making the trek back home. I'm pretty sure it's just a ploy so that my mother can meet Kylie, but I'm looking forward to seeing them all the same.

"Good to see you, son." Dad reaches me first, clapping me hard on the back when he hugs me.

"You too, Dad."

Mom pushes him aside and takes my face in her hands. I tower over her, but she's never let that stop her from reminding me who's the boss. "You're looking thin. Why do you look so thin?"

I shake my head and give her a hug. "I'm fine, Mom."

She tsks but lets it go. I take her suitcase and she walks along beside me while I lead them out to the car park. I feel like I've been here a lot lately.

"So, when are we going to meet this girlfriend?"

Ignoring the little flutter in my stomach at the word *girlfriend,*

I look at my watch, then back at her. "It took you two minutes to ask that? That's got to be some sort of record."

"Oh, hush you. I just want to meet the woman who makes you smile so much lately."

I shake my head with a laugh. "Kylie is spending Christmas Eve and morning with her family. I'll pick her up later tomorrow and she'll have dinner with us."

"Did you get all the food on the list I gave you?"

"Yes, ma'am. I got a turkey, the yams, brussels sprouts and all the rest of it. And we're picking up the pumpkin pie on the way home." I'd even gone to the grocery store myself to get it all, something I usually actively avoid because I hate the grocery store.

"Good boy." She pats my cheek before climbing into the back seat.

I roll my eyes at Dad, who just shakes his head and gets in the front seat. It's going to be a long forty-eight hours. I'd worry about them meeting Kylie, but after the multiple times I've endured fear-inducing conversations with her grandfather, I figure she can handle my mother for one night. I pull my phone out of my pocket and send her a quick message.

SETH

Heads up, my mother is going to be full of questions tomorrow.

KYLIE

Mothers love me, I'll have her eating out of the palm of my hand, just you watch.

I snort, pocketing my phone and sliding into the driver's seat. I have absolutely no doubt that by the time we go to bed tomorrow night, she and my mother will be the best of friends.

"So, Kylie. How long are you in Calgary for?"

My mother has known Kylie for all of five minutes and she's already going straight for the hard questions.

Kylie is sitting on one of the bar stools behind the bench in the kitchen and avoids my gaze while I get a beer from the fridge, taking a sip of her water. "Only a couple more weeks."

I hate how much it hurts every time I'm reminded that she's still planning on going back to Australia. We have continued to avoid talking about it, and now it's become the elephant in the room every time we're together. At the lodge last weekend, when I'd carried her up to our room, I'd come so close to telling her the three words that have been on the tip of my tongue for weeks. But I don't want to pressure her into staying, and a part of me is scared to be the first one to say it when I don't know where she stands.

"Oh, that's so soon." Mom pouts a little while she stirs the gravy.

Kylie shifts in her seat a little. "Yeah, it's coming up fast."

I move to stand behind her, placing my hands on her shoulders.

"Have you thought about staying longer?" Mom just keeps on pushing all the wrong buttons, and I squeeze gently when I feel Kylie's shoulders tense under my fingers.

"How much longer until dinner's ready?" I ask, hoping to derail the conversation.

Mom glances at me, and I try to convey the need for her to stop asking questions silently, widening my eyes and shaking my head slightly.

"About ten minutes. Your father just needs to carve the turkey. Why don't you kids go get washed up and I'll let you know when it's ready?"

I breathe out, very aware of the fact that Kylie practically flies out of her chair. I follow her to my room, standing back while she flops backwards onto the bed.

"Sorry," I say, watching her swallow while she stares at the ceiling.

"Nothing to be sorry for. It's not like she's the only one asking those questions."

I slide my hands into my pockets and lean against the wall.

When I don't respond, she props herself up on her elbows and looks at me. "But you still haven't asked me those questions."

I shrug. "I'm not sure I want to know the answers."

I don't want to be having this conversation today. I just want to spend Christmas with her and my parents and not think about the fact that she's getting on a plane and leaving, possibly forever.

She watches me, eerily quiet, and I force myself to hold her gaze, even though I want to look away and pretend like this isn't making me feel like crap.

She finally gets up and moves to stand in front of me, placing her hands on my chest. I cover them with my right hand, and she rises on to her tiptoes to kiss me. I lean into the kiss, allowing her to distract me with her lips so that we don't have to talk about it any further.

Dad hollers out that dinner is ready, and we break apart. I squeeze her hands gently before letting them go, following her back down to the kitchen.

We chat about meaningless stuff at dinner, and I get the sense that Dad has told Mom to ease up on the hard hitting questions, which I'm grateful for. Once we finish eating, Mom goes to their room and returns moments later with a photo album.

I groan. "Oh, no you didn't."

"I most certainly did. Kylie, here are Seth's childhood photos. It is my duty as his mother to share every awkward and adorable phase of his life." She hands the album to Kylie, who looks far too excited about this.

"Oh my god, you were so cute!" she exclaims, looking at a baby photo of me dressed in a little Vancouver onesie. "The wrong colours, though."

Dad huffs. "I'm still waiting for the day that you play for my team."

"I think you might be waiting a while. Mounties fans have claimed him." Kylie winks at me before going back to the album, defusing that slightly touchy subject with ease.

She looks at every single photo, listening to the stories my parents tell about each one while I sit beside her, watching them all.

How can I possibly watch her get on a plane when she belongs here with me? Why can't I just ask her to stay?

Because I'm worried I'm not enough for her.

That night, Kylie lies draped over me. I'm not used to her being so quiet, and I find it incredibly disconcerting. The closer we've gotten to her departure date, the more introspective she's become, and I don't know what to say or do to make the awkwardness disappear.

I know she's still awake, so it doesn't surprise me when she lifts her head to study my face in the moonlight.

"Why won't you ask me to stay?"

I run my hand up and down her back, scanning her face while I try to put into words why I can't make this decision for her. "I can't... I can't be responsible for forcing you to make that choice."

She swallows hard. "Why not?"

"Because... I just... I don't even know how to describe it... You'd be giving up so much... What if being with me makes you miserable? You've said it yourself, our worlds are so different. And you didn't sign on for having to deal with the fans and all that attention. I could never ask someone to... It's just a lot." I don't know why I can't put into words what all my fears are.

"Do you not want me to stay?"

I can't quite tell in the dark, but it almost looks like there are tears in her eyes, and I feel terrible. This is exactly why I haven't said anything before now. Because it's my own issues that have kept me from begging her to stay.

"It needs to be your choice. And I can't be the only reason you stay here."

She doesn't reply, her eyes shining in the moonlight before she nods slowly and lets out a long breath, before laying her head back on my chest.

Neither of us says anything further, but it's a long time before either of us falls asleep.

When I return from dropping Kylie home the next morning, Mom is waiting for me. I can tell something is troubling her when she hands me a cup of coffee and pats the seat beside her on the couch.

"What's up?" I ask, sitting down next to her.

"I hope I didn't cause any issues between the pair of you last night with all my questions? Your father was worried I'd upset Kylie." She bites her lip while she wrings her hands.

"It's fine. Kylie wasn't upset." I'm not sure I want to be having this conversation with my mother, as much as I love her.

"But I overstepped, didn't I? I hadn't realised it was such a touchy subject when I asked her if she was thinking of staying longer."

"We just haven't really talked about it."

"Why not? Don't you want her to stay?" She raises an eyebrow, leaning against the back of the couch.

"I do. But I would be asking her to give up everything she's ever known, and for what? To sit around and wait for me to come home for eight months of the year?" I stare at the untouched coffee in my hand.

"Seth. You have so much love to give. You are always putting everyone else's needs before your own. It's what makes you such a good captain. But Kylie doesn't strike me as the type who would just be sitting around waiting for you. She seems to really enjoy her job here, and it doesn't seem like she'd have any trouble making friends. You shouldn't be afraid to ask her to stay if it's what you really want. Does she know you want her to stay?"

"She wants me to ask her, but it needs to be up to her. I can't force her to make that choice."

Although I keep staring at my coffee, I can feel my mother's gaze burning into the side of my head.

"Asking her to stay isn't taking that choice away from her. But if you don't tell her how you really feel, you're not giving her the chance to make an informed decision. I think you need to talk to her about it properly. I know you're not great at talking about your feelings, but a woman like that doesn't come along every day."

I know she's right, but no matter how much I think about it, it just feels like I'd be asking her to give up so much with no guarantee that it wouldn't be a mistake. That she wouldn't end up resenting me for the sacrifices she had to make to be with me.

When I don't reply, Mom pats my leg and gets to her feet.

"Just don't let your own issues get in the way of what could be the best thing to ever happen to you. That's the last advice I'll give you on the subject."

She wanders off, leaving me alone to stew over her words.

39
YOU NEVER READ
THE COMMENTS

SETH

IT'S the New Year's Eve home game, a long held tradition in Calgary, and after the week off, it feels good to be back on the ice. Kylie seems to be avoiding me a little, or maybe I'm just being paranoid. We'd originally planned to spend most of the week doing things together with Will, but in the end, I only saw her a few nights and they spent three days snowboarding with Adele. I can't help but feel like she's pulling away, constantly avoiding questions from everyone about whether she's going to stay. Questions from everyone but me.

So being on the ice now is a great distraction, and a chance for me to channel my frustration into something else. We're fifteen minutes into the third period and tied with Boston two all. We are determined to give the fans what we all want - a win to see in the new year. And hopefully the end of the losing streak we are on since we lost the last home game.

Anders makes his way back to the bench along with the rest of the third line, and Linc and I jump over the boards, hitting the ice at flying speed to steal the puck back. Linc scrambles behind

Dean's net, digging the puck out of the grasp of Wilson Rogers, Boston's captain and one of our former college teammates. Coming around the net, Linc flicks the puck towards me and I take off towards the offensive zone. I duck past their beast of a defenceman to pass the puck to Linc before moving into position near the net and waiting for an opening. Linc takes a shot, and it rebounds off the goalie's pad after a quick reflex save. I manage to get the puck at the side of the net before Wilson can intercept it and I take another shot. It bounces off the skate of Popov, the Boston goalie, and I lose sight of it for a fraction of a second. Then the goal light turns red and I throw my hands in the air, cheering while Linc and Riley plough into me from both sides, closely followed by Pieter and Oliver. Skating back to the bench to celebrate with the rest of the team, I raise my stick up before pretending to sheath it like a sword, and the crowd cheers.

I search the crowd behind the bench, looking for Kylie. When I spot her sitting in her grandparents' seats with Will, I point at her, and she grins, blowing me a kiss. Will points up at the jumbotron, and I look up to see them both on the screen, before it flashes back to me.

It's the first time I've ever drawn attention to her like this, and I worry for a moment about how she feels about the extra eyes on her, but she continues to smile at me and seems to be okay with it.

We run down the clock, and once the final buzzer goes off, my teammates flood the ice to celebrate. The Boston players hit the locker room with a defeated air about them. Both teams had been hoping to end losing streaks tonight, and I'm relieved it's us who broke it.

"First round's on me!" I yell, and the others cheer.

We're heading out straight from the game to celebrate the New Year. The management team has booked out one of the cowboy bars for a night of fun, and some of the guys are looking forward to getting into the spirit and were wearing cowboy hats and boots when they arrived before the game.

Management arranged for transport to the venue, so after I've showered, I head out to meet Kylie and Will. I find them hanging out back with the other family members in the common area. Will is looking around at everyone with interest, but Kylie seems a little guarded, and I follow her gaze to see Victoria and her entourage chatting to Anders' wife, Bethany. They seem to be glancing her way while talking, and I can feel my protective instincts kicking in. I stride to her side and wrap my arms around her.

She sinks into the embrace and grips my face, smiling up at me. "Congratulations, Captain." She kisses me, and I feel some of the tension in my gut uncoil a little.

"I like it when you call me that," I say quietly against her lips.

She throws her head back and laughs. "Oh I know, Captain." She gives me a flirty wink.

Will shakes his head. "Hello, brother, standing right here."

She teases, "Oh shut up, you can handle hearing me confirm that Seth really is the captain in every aspect of his life, considering the amount of times I was subjected to your stuff over the years."

Will clamps his hands over his ears. "La la la, nope, not hearing that."

"Stop teasing your brother," I say, nipping her bottom lip before stepping back.

"Spoilsport," she replies with a grin.

We head out to the team buses that are waiting to ferry us all to the bar, and Will somehow ends up seated next to one of Victoria's entourage. I'm not even sure how they ended up included in the festivities, but once she realises he's not one of the players, she ignores him entirely. He gives me a bewildered look over the back of his seat.

I shrug. "Don't worry, it's only a short drive." I'll fill him in on the professional husband chasers later, but he's definitely dodged a bullet.

Once we arrive at the bar, Coach leads the way inside, and they have gone all out to give us the full Calgary cowboy experience. Banners hang from every available space declaring Happy New Year, and they have decked out all the tables with black and red cowboy hats featuring the team logo on the front next to each place setting.

Kylie immediately puts one on her head and strikes a pose, lifting her leg and flashing me a peace sign while blowing me a kiss.

I laugh. "You make a very cute cowgirl," I tell her, pulling her close.

She grabs the one from the next seat and plonks it onto my head. "And you're the hottest cowboy in here, partner," she drawls, putting on the worst accent.

"I'm going to grab us some drinks. Are you sticking with lemonade tonight?"

She nods. "Yes please."

After checking if Will wants a beer, I head for the bar, stopping along the way when I'm pulled into various conversations with my teammates. Once I reach the bar, I lean with my elbows on the top and wait for them to serve several others, content just to people watch for the time-being.

A woman appears beside me, placing her hand on my arm. "Hey. Buy me a drink?" she asks, flicking her long blonde hair back over her shoulder with a smile, her eyelashes fluttering.

Where's Dean when I need him?

"It's an open bar," I reply, straightening up to allow her hand to slide off.

"Oh, that's cool. We can order together."

She's persistent, I'll give her that. "I'm okay. I'm getting drinks for my girlfriend and her brother." I nod towards Kylie and Will, who are both watching the exchange.

The woman looks over her shoulder, then turns back, a confused look on her face. "That's your girlfriend? Really?"

Any thoughts about keeping the conversation polite swiftly

leave my mind. "Yeah. Is there a problem?" I don't even bother trying to hide the anger in my tone.

"Just thought you could do better, that's all. She doesn't seem like the type who knows how to handle a player."

Fuck me, this woman is awful.

"Who are you here with?" I'm ready to go off now, angry that the women I actively avoid have somehow infiltrated what is meant to be an event for the players and their families.

"Bethany." She shrugs.

I flex my hands at my sides. "Of course you are. Let me be clear. I am not a player. That is my girlfriend, and you need to step back right now." I am usually polite but firm during these uncomfortable interactions, but the way that she looked at Kylie has me seeing red.

"Everything okay?" Linc slides in beside me.

"Yep, we're good," I reply, my words clipped.

"You sure?" He raises an eyebrow.

"She was just leaving." I nod towards the blonde, who shakes her head and wanders off. "Fucking hell, I'm going to kill Bethany for letting those witches in."

"Yeah, I've already spoken to the events team. They're keeping an eye on them, so I wouldn't be surprised if they get booted after seeing that interaction. What'd she say to you? I've never seen you react like that with them before." He leans forward to rest his elbows on the bar, similar to how relaxed I'd been minutes ago.

"She was being a bitch about Kylie."

"What? How?" Linc looks surprised, glancing over to where Kylie and Will are talking, still watching us.

"She implied Kylie wasn't good enough to be with an NHL player."

Linc whistles and shakes his head. "Oh boy."

"Yep."

The bartender finally heads our way, and I order our drinks, carrying them back to the others with Linc in tow.

"What was that all about?" Kylie asks, taking her drink from my hand.

"Nothing. Just a misunderstanding," I reply, putting my arm around her while I take a mouthful of beer.

She looks up at me, and I can tell she doesn't believe me, but she doesn't push it any further.

After they serve dinner, they turn up the music and clear away the tables to make more room on the dance floor. The events team has arranged for a line dancing instructor to come in for a bit of fun, and Kylie forces me to take part, declaring she needs the full cowboy bar experience. After making absolute fools of ourselves, Linc, Will and I throw in the towel and leave her to it, watching her laugh along with Clara and Sarah while they try to keep up.

"You're heading home in a couple of days, right?" Linc asks Will, who nods in response.

"Yeah. I made the trip as long as I could, but I gotta get back to my business." He reaches into his pocket, pulling out his phone, which has lit up. He unlocks it, and after a few moments, his eyebrows raise before he looks over at Kylie, then back down at his phone. "Um... What the fuck?"

"What's wrong?" I ask, my senses on high alert when he keeps looking from his phone to Kylie.

"Look at this." He hands me the phone, and I see it's some social media app.

I look at the video that's playing, a bunch of photos of women with ratings on them and comments.

I look back at Will. "What is this?"

"Watch from the beginning."

I drag my thumb along the line at the bottom, taking it back to the beginning, and watch in horror when the words "let's rate the partners of the hottest NHL players". I can feel my heart rate pick up when photos of women going about their every day lives flash up. They have started from one star ratings, and I swallow hard when a photo of Kylie and I kissing appears, at the ice skating rink where we had our first date. A single star keeps flashing and the words "clearly he needs his eyes checked" appear, before it moves on to the next woman.

"What the fuck?!" Linc yells, watching it over my shoulder.

"Shut up." I smack him and nod towards Kylie before looking back at Will. "I don't want her to see this. How did you get this?"

"Adele sent it to me. She's pissed. So am I."

"Believe me, so am I. We can't show her this." I hand him back his phone.

Seconds later, Kylie pulls her phone out of her pocket and I suck in a breath, realising we probably should have told Adele that. I move towards Kylie, but she's already watching the video, and I can tell the second she sees herself, the smile on her face disappearing while she stares at the phone.

"Don't look at it." I reach her side, and she turns to look up at me.

"You've seen this?" she asks, her eyes looking a little glassy with unshed tears.

"Adele just sent it to Will."

"Who would do something so horrible? Look at this, it's got over a million views already! And the comments!"

I take the phone from her hand and slide it into my pocket. "Hey. You never read the comments. I may be out of loop on social media, but I know that much."

She wraps her arms around herself, turning away from the dance floor. "I'd like to go home now."

"Babe, you can't let this ruin your night," I say, trying to give her a hug, but she turns away.

Clara has joined us. "Is everything okay?"

"No." Kylie plucks her phone from my pocket and shows Clara the video.

"Oh, I've seen this account before. I've tried to report it. Kylie, this is just internet trolls. They rated me a one as well, a few months ago."

Kylie shakes her head. "It's disgusting."

"It is, but it's just someone who is jealous as hell, so they try to make everyone else miserable to make themselves feel better." She takes Kylie's hand. "Seth's right. You can't let this ruin your night. You were just having so much fun."

Kylie shakes her head. "I just need a minute." She moves off through the group.

I go to follow her, but Clara puts her hand on my arm. "I'll go. She'll be okay. It's all part of this life."

"It damn well shouldn't be. No one has the right to make anyone feel this way."

"I agree. Just like you guys don't sign up to have your butts plastered all over the internet when you're stretching, the partners didn't ask for this shit either. But unfortunately, while the internet allows these assholes to remain anonymous, there's not a lot we can do. I'll go talk to her." She heads towards the door Kylie went through, and I swallow hard, before going back to the guys.

"Is she okay?" Will asks right away.

"Not really. I wish Adele hadn't sent it to her. It blindsided her."

Will puts his beer down. "I'm gonna go check on her." He follows Clara.

I don't think I've ever felt so angry and useless in my life. This is exactly what I'd been afraid of happening. That somehow, my unwanted fame would affect her on a personal level.

Now the woman that I love, the most vibrant person I've ever met, has been hurt and I can't do anything to stop it.

40

DON'T KNOW IF I'M ENOUGH

KYLIE

I STEP OUTSIDE, angrily brushing at the tears that have rolled down my face. Even though it's freezing out here, I just need a few moments away from everyone.

How fucking dare some asshole pass judgement on mine and Seth's relationship? What gives anyone the right to rate women on social media for likes and comments? I feel violated.

I have always been pretty confident in myself, but right now, I just want to hide. The idea of going back into that room makes me feel sick, surrounded by people I barely know and a group of women who would happily step into my shoes the second Seth looked their way.

"Kylie?" Clara rounds the corner, stopping when she finds me leaning against the wall, wiping more tears away. "Oh, honey." She moves closer and pulls me in for a hug. "You can't let them win. If you give them even a little bit of an idea of how much this hurts you, the trolls win."

"I can't just ignore this and hope it goes away. This is exactly what I was afraid of. I have no business being in this world. I don't want to be judged by faceless strangers on the internet, wondering why Seth picked me when he has supermodels throwing themselves at him." I was already feeling pretty sensitive after watching that blonde woman talking to Seth, so adding the video in was more than enough to tip me over the edge.

Will rounds the corner, his expression dark. "Hey. You okay?"

I huff a laugh. "No. How can I be okay after seeing that?"

Clara steps aside while my brother moves in to hug me, and I allow myself to lean into it. He's always been an excellent hugger. I just wish this was one of those situations where a Will hug makes it all feel better.

Clara rubs her hand up and down my back. "In the years I've known Seth, this is the happiest I've ever seen him. You make him happy, Kylie. He doesn't care about the opinion of some faceless troll on the internet. Women like those inside have been throwing themselves at him for years, and I have never once seen him give any of them the time of day. He has always kept mostly to himself, and when he has dated, it was never serious. But when he looks at you... Kylie, you're it for him."

"Am I, though? He hasn't asked me to stay. He won't talk about the fact that I'm leaving in two weeks. He hates this sort of attention, so the last thing he needs is to be in a relationship with someone that everyone says isn't good enough for him." I'm so close to breaking down, but I refuse to be the crying girl outside of a bar on New Year's Eve.

Will's arms tighten around me. "Bug, I hate hearing you speak about yourself like this. This isn't you," he says close to my ear. "I told you, he wants you to stay."

"But why was he able to tell you that and not me?" I mumble into his chest.

"Because he doesn't think he has any right to ask you to stay and give up everything you know. You guys need to talk about this."

I nod, my forehead knocking against his chest.

"Kylie?" Seth's voice sounds behind me, sounding concerned.

I pull back from Will to turn and face Seth. Clara is standing behind him. I hadn't noticed her leave, but I assume she went and got him.

"We'll leave you two to talk." Will gives my shoulders a squeeze before heading back inside with Clara.

I shiver a little, finally noticing the cold, and my lack of a proper jacket. Seth moves to stand in front of me, unzipping his jacket and pulling me in close, just like the last time we were standing outside a bar in the cold having a serious conversation. I slide my arms around his back inside the jacket, stealing his warmth. At this angle, it's easy for me to avoid looking at him, and I bury my face in his chest.

"Are you okay?" he whispers, and I shake my head without looking up. "Talk to me. Please?"

I take a deep breath, turning my face so he can hear me, but I still don't have to look at him. "Why are you with me when you can have any woman you want?"

He's quiet for a moment, and I can feel apprehension creeping in. Maybe he doesn't want me after all.

"We've had this conversation before, and nothing has changed for me. I look at you and see the most beautiful woman, both inside and out, that I've ever met. You're so full of life and your confidence in who you are draws so many people to you."

I move back slightly to look at him finally. "Then why won't you ask me to stay?"

He holds my gaze, moving to wipe away the tear that has escaped my eye. "Because I don't know if I'm enough for you. You would be giving up so much to be with me, and look at what happened tonight. I couldn't even protect you from the trolls. I can't ask you to stay because it would be selfish."

Inside, I hear someone yell out that there's only five minutes to midnight.

"Why don't you think you're enough for me?" I can't comprehend how he could feel this way when he's the one with the most to offer.

"This life I lead... It's a lot to expect someone to accept. And the crap you've had to put up with in just a few months by being with me... I don't want it to dim the light in you I lo-" He cuts himself off, his eyes wide. "That drew me to you," he finishes.

I inhale sharply, hearing the word that he stopped himself from saying fully. I hold his gaze, swallowing hard.

"Maybe..." I pause, not sure either of us is ready for me to say the next sentence. "Maybe it's a good thing I'm going home... I think some time apart is what we need to work out what we both really want."

I see the moment that my words sink in, his grip on me tightening while his jaw tenses. "I..." His words trail off, anguish written into his features while his eyes search my face.

His hesitation only strengthens my resolve. "We should go inside..." I say, stepping back a little. "Don't want to miss seeing in the New Year."

I can see the pain on his face and know that mine must look the same, but he nods, taking my hand to lead me inside. When we rejoin Will and Lincoln, they both eye us warily, and I shake my head to ward off questions. I'm not sure I can talk right now anyway, the lump in my throat threatening to unleash a torrent of emotions. One word is likely to end in me bawling my eyes out.

Someone starts the countdown, getting everyone started, but I'm numb to it all. As the group counts backwards to one, Seth pulls me in close, kissing me as everyone yells, "Happy New Year!"

I can feel his emotions, the desperation and heartbreak, seeping through the kiss. I cling to him while kissing him back with equal intensity. I weave my fingers through his hair, holding him close while his grip on my right hip tightens, his fingers digging in while his other hand works its way through my hair. I can feel the prick of tears in my eyes and I squeeze them closed even tighter.

How is it possible that I can feel so much for someone in such a short amount of time? Why do we have so many obstacles to climb when everything else between us feels so right? Why did I have to fall for someone whose life is so different to my own?

We pull apart finally, and he rests his forehead against mine. "Happy New Year," he whispers for only me to hear.

I whisper it back, somehow managing not to cry. I certainly don't feel happy. Everyone around us is celebrating, but I feel like my heart is breaking.

"Should we go home?" he asks, and I nod.

Making sure Will has a way back to our grandparents' house, we say our goodbyes while the events team arranges a car to take us back to Seth's place. Seth holds my hand in his lap, running his thumb back and forth on the back of mine while he stares down at them. Neither of us says a word.

I don't know why I need him to tell me he wants me to stay. I can tell from his actions how he feels about me, but a stubborn part of me needs to hear the words.

Once we're inside, the silence in the house is broken only by the sound of our footsteps, and for once in my life, words have escaped me. Neither of us seems to know what to say or do, and I wonder if maybe I should have just gone back with Will.

"Can we... Can I hold you, please?" he asks, leaning back against the island bench in the kitchen, watching me while I stand near the door.

I nod, and he moves towards me, clearing the distance between us in two large steps, and pulling me into his arms. I lean into the embrace, finally allowing the tears to flow silently. I hate this feeling. I hate that some stupid video has pushed us into this conversation that neither of us was ready for.

I look up at him, feeling the wetness on my cheeks. "Kiss me," I whisper.

He kisses me, softly at first, but it grows into something more. We tear at each other's clothes, our shared desperation clear. Once I've pulled off his shirt, he reaches under my jersey and pulls my shirt off with it, before wasting no time in removing my bra. Dropping to his knees before me, his mouth closes over my right breast, and I moan quietly while running my fingers through his hair with one hand.

Moving to do the same to my other breast, he undoes the fly of my jeans, slipping his hand inside and working his finger over my clit through my underwear, causing me to shudder. His mouth and hand work in tandem, his tongue stroking over my sensitive nipples while he continues to apply pressure with his hand. It's not long before I'm panting and riding his hand, and he grips my hip with his free hand, urging me to move my hips back and forth without moving away from my breasts. Just as I'm about to come, he pulls back, and a whine escapes me at the sudden loss of his touch. He smirks a little while he tugs my jeans and underwear off before lifting me, and I wrap my legs around his waist while he carries me to the bench. The cold surface when he lowers me sends a shiver through me, but I allow him to push me gently back. Lowering his head, he sucks my clit between his lips, taking me right back to the edge while I gasp for breath and stare up at the ceiling, gripping his hair in my fist.

I hear him undo his fly. Raising on to my elbows, I watch him through half-closed eyes while he pulls his jeans off, barely able to keep my eyes open. While he runs his hand over himself to ease the pressure, my orgasm overtakes all my senses, and I cry out, pleasure rolling through me while my back arches off the bench top.

He slides me off the bench and turns me around, urging me to bend forward. He hesitates, his grip on my hip tightening, and I turn back to look at him over my shoulder.

"What's wrong?"

"I don't have a condom on me," he says, his voice hoarse.

While he could get one from the bedroom, I don't know that I have the patience to wait that long. "I'm on birth control," I say, holding his gaze.

He swallows, sliding his finger inside me. "Are you sure?"

I feel my eyes roll back in my head when he hits the right spot. "Yes. I just need you now."

Nodding, he moves his hand back to my hip. Lifting me on to my tip toes, he pushes inside me, hard and fast, and I cry out again.

"I've been thinking about you being bent over this bench since the first night I brought you home," he grinds out, each thrust pushing my hips bones into the cold bench.

I moan, unable to form words when he moves his hand to work my clit, urging me on as my cries grow louder.

"I'm almost there. Come with me." His words tip me over the edge again, and his moans mingle with mine when we come together.

He leans forward, pressing his lips to my neck while I struggle to get my breath back.

"I'm sorry," he whispers in my ear after a moment, and I turn to look at him over my shoulder.

"What for?"

"That wasn't how I wanted to be with you tonight. Did I hurt you?" He rubs his hands over my hips.

I shake my head, turning to face him. "No, you didn't hurt me. I wanted that, just as much as you." I touch his face. "We still have time together. I think we both needed that."

He nods, his eyes still troubled, so I kiss him softly.

"Let's go to bed. We can take our time the rest of the night."

There's no further talk about me leaving, of how we're both feeling. We spend the rest of the night seeking comfort from each other, before falling asleep as the sun rises.

41

ON MY KNEES

"I'LL MISS YOU," Kylie whispers in my ear while she wraps her arms around my neck, causing me to tighten my grip around her.

I can't seem to let her go. The day I've been dreading has arrived, and she's about to get on a plane and fly away with no return date. Why couldn't I just ask her to stay? It's one word. Possibly two if I add 'please' on to it. While I'm on my knees.

"I'll miss you," I murmur back, like the coward that I am.

I want her to choose to stay of her own free will. I want her to choose me. I want her to choose us. But I can't ask her to do that. To give up everything she knows.

People surround us, but neither of us acknowledges them, our focus entirely on one another. On how hard this goodbye is.

"You are enough, Seth. You will always be enough." Her words, whispered while we were making love on that awful night, echo in my mind.

Why can't I bring myself to believe her? To believe that I can make her happy?

. . .

"Seth! Wake up!" I jolt awake when Linc shakes my shoulder.

Blinking, I try to bring myself back to reality. Every time I've fallen asleep in the past month, I'm right back at that painful moment. To go from speaking to someone daily to exchanging a few texts a week... I've felt empty, waking up clutching a pillow like my unconscious mind was trying to conjure her up in my bed.

We'd agreed to give each other space, to work out where we both stood. But I'm over space now. If I wasn't locked into a multimillion dollar contract with teammates and fans that depended on me, I'd have been on a plane to Australia weeks ago, just for the chance to wrap my arms around her one more time.

"I'm awake," I grumble, looking around the plane, which appears to have landed and is almost completely empty.

"I was calling your name for like two minutes. Since when do you sleep so solidly?" Linc looks annoyed, but I can see the concern behind his eyes.

"Since I've been sleeping about four hours a night at most." I rub my face, trying to scrub away the dream.

"This isn't healthy, dude. I've kept my mouth shut, but you need to talk to Kylie. You're fucking miserable without her, and it's affecting everything else in your life." He hands me my backpack from the overhead locker.

"No need to sugarcoat it, thanks man," I reply, shaking my head.

"You know me, brutal honesty is my preferred method of communication."

I follow him off the plane, the rest of the team already heading towards the arrivals area in the Toronto airport. It must have taken Linc a lot longer than a few minutes to wake me.

I know he's right, that I need to talk to Kylie and finally just ask her the question she wanted me to ask. But now that she's back in Australia with her friends and family, would she even think about it? Her life is there. The idea of saying the words and having her let me down gently is something I can't even bear to consider.

No, I just need to get on with the rest of the season and hopefully the memory of her will fade with time.

Not likely, you stubborn idiot. Why didn't you just ask her when she wanted you to?

Once we've collected our gear, we get on the bus and head to our hotel. While the rest of the team is discussing tonight's activities ahead of tomorrow's game, I press my head against the window and try to get some more sleep.

Linc is right, I need to do something about how badly I've been sleeping, cause it's affecting my game, amongst other aspects of my life.

Ten minutes into the first period, and it's obvious that Toronto has brought their hunger to the game. We always tend to have rivalries amongst the Canadian teams, but Toronto is usually one of the more friendly ones.

Not today, though.

We're already up by a goal, but that felt like a fluke with how tired we all seem to be. I'm beginning to wonder if my mood is affecting the rest of the team, making them all sluggish. As the captain, it's my responsibility to lead them, and I know I've been failing in that department.

At the next line change, I hop over the boards alongside Linc and streak towards Boris Petrova, one of Toronto's centres, who currently has the puck and is making a beeline for our goal. I reach him, delivering a check that knocks him to the ice, while Linc steals the puck and heads back towards our end.

Pushing off Petrova, I follow Linc, coming alongside him so he can pass me the puck. Just as it hits my stick, one of Toronto's defencemen, Dylan Miller, slams me hard against the boards, pinning me against the glass while Petrova digs out the puck. My shoulder screams in protest, and I throw my elbow in Dylan's side to get him off me.

"You're playing like shit, Davidson. Missing your dumpy little girlfriend? I don't know why. You could do so much better," he chirps in my ear, and I turn to glare at him, finally shoving him off.

"Watch your fucking mouth." I take a swing, seeing red.

"Oh, I've hit a nerve. Guess there really is a way to get under your skin after all," he says with a smirk.

Everything else around us falls out of focus and all I can think about is punching the smug look off his face. Without thinking, I throw my gloves off and grab the front of his jersey, punching him hard.

Distantly, I hear the crowd going wild, as Miller's fist connects with the side of my helmet, causing my head to snap back.

A whistle blows, and I keep my hold on his jersey, even as the refs surround us, telling us to break it up but keeping their distance. Pulling my arm back, I punch him in the face, ignoring the way it cuts into my knuckles when my fist connects with his face shield.

Arms wrap around me from behind, while one of Miller's teammates grabs him.

"Calm the fuck down," Linc says, yanking me away from Miller.

"Yeah, listen to your little buddy," Miller taunts.

Linc tightens his grip on me when I try to push him off and launch myself at the asshole again. "Seriously, get your shit together," Linc demands.

I finally manage to push him off, skating away from Miller while trying to keep his words out of my head.

The refs give us each five minutes for fighting, and I head towards the penalty box with my head down. Once inside, Linc hands me my stick and gloves, glaring at me before heading back to the bench.

At least we're not shorthanded, but Miller is smiling smugly, knowing his team will be happy to see me off the ice.

I'm kicking myself for letting him get in my head. I've always avoided fighting, and rarely get penalties called on me, so I know that once I'm back on the bench, Coach is going to have a few harsh words for me. The feeling gets worse when Toronto ties the game just seconds before I am allowed back on the ice.

The moment between Miller and I flips a switch in the game.

Tensions ramp up over the second period with physical play taking over any attempts to score and leading to all out mayhem at the beginning of the third. I take another hard hit from Miller and slowly skate into the bench, but Linc has had enough and challenges Miller himself.

This triggers a chain reaction through everyone else on the ice, and gloves come off left, right and centre. Even Dean and the Toronto goalie decide to get in on the action, meeting at centre ice for a rather awkward fight. Not the easiest thing to do when wearing goalie gear.

Watching from the bench, I survey the mess, knowing that we've abandoned our game plan and are all going to cop it back in the dressing room.

After the chaos of the brawl, with five players kicked out from each team, it's a miracle any more goals are scored. But Toronto manages one more to eke out a 2-1 victory.

Defeated, we make our way back to the locker room with our heads down. Once Coach steps inside, everyone goes deathly quiet, waiting for the storm to break.

Looking up, I find Coach's eyes on me, his fury barely contained.

"What." His voice is barely louder than a whisper. "The. Fuck. Was. That?"

No one has an answer, and we sit with our heads bowed while Coach lets us know, in no uncertain terms, just how angry he is.

"This is not the sort of team that does that shit. Whatever the fuck is going on with you all, sort it the fuck out." He slams the locker room door as he leaves, and we stare after him.

No one says a word while we all shower and gather our belongings. I know I'm responsible for what happened and I have no words to offer anyone, so I remain silent, retreating to my thoughts and wishing I knew how to get out of this funk I've sunk into over the past month.

But I have no answers, except one. Try and work out how to get on with life without Kylie, or beg her to come back.

Neither option sounds great.

42

WHAT THE HELL DID
THAT GUY SAY TO HIM?

KYLIE

"I LOVE THIS LITTLE FRECKLE, right here," Seth whispers, kissing my nose while he hovers over me.

He works slowly down my body, kissing different points and declaring his feelings for each part. I run my hands through his hair and watch through half-closed eyes, loving the feeling of his hands on my body.

"Where did you go just now?" he asks, resting his chin on my belly, his eyes on my face.

"Was just thinking how comfortable I am here. I could stay in this bed forever," I reply, continuing to stroke his hair.

"I can arrange that, you know. I have a vested interest in keeping you in this bed forever." He runs his fingers down my side, leaving a trail of goosebumps in his wake.

"Yeah?" I whisper back.

"Yeah. I always want you here." He presses his lips to my abdomen.

"I always want to be here," I reply, arching my back.

"Stay with me."

A noise wakes me, pulling me from the latest version of the same dream I've been having for weeks. Every variation ends the same way - with Seth asking me to stay.

"Sorry, did I wake you?" Tara asks when I crawl out of my tent.

She's the first one up, from what I can see, boiling some water for a cup of tea in the food area of our campsite.

"What time is it?" I ask, my voice hoarse while I stretch.

"Just after five. The damn birds woke me up," she grumbles, and I nod, noticing the chirping for the first time.

I head towards the amenities block, breathing in the early morning air. We've been coming to Flat Rock for a week every February for years, avoiding the school holidays but still getting to enjoy the summer weather. It's so close to the beach that Will and I can surf all day if we want, wandering back for food when we feel like it. At night, the group hangs out at the campsite, just chilling out and enjoying each other's company around the little fire brazier. It was a tradition we started back in high school once Will and the older members of the group got their licences.

Sometimes new people join, but, excluding the years Bri was living in Sydney, the core group has always been here. But the last two times, including now, the absence of Annelisa has felt like a gaping hole. While we've felt it at group gatherings, it's most noticeable here.

And I get the feeling that this might be Tara's last time. While she and Will have talked in passing, the distance between them is obvious now, and Tara has avoided him for the most part. It's another change that I hate. I know that as people get older, they sometimes drift apart from the friendships they had in childhood, but I never thought it would happen to our group.

It's not only Tara who's struggling, though. For the past month, I've been distracted, as my heart has been a thousand miles away on the other side of the world, claimed by a certain hockey player. I'd been missing my friends and family here while I was away, but now that I'm back, everything feels different.

Everything feels wrong.

I miss Seth's arms around me, hearing him laugh when I do something crazy. Hell, I even miss going to the games and screaming myself hoarse while cheering for the Mounties.

But it's not just Seth that I miss. I'd really enjoyed my job working for my aunt and uncle, getting to meet new people constantly and learning about their lives while showing them a part of Canada that I had fallen madly in love with. I suppose I could get a job in the travel industry here, but it doesn't have the appeal that Canada does.

When I return to our campsite, the others are also up, and I throw myself down on the picnic blanket beside Bri, laying my head in her lap.

"Hey, you. What's wrong?" She strokes my hair and I close my eyes.

"Nothing. Everything. I don't even know anymore."

"Poor baby." She continues to play with my hair while I lie there.

Jake leans across her and pats my head as well. "Cheer up, Buttercup."

I prop myself up and look at him. "Buttercup?"

"It rhymed," he replies with a shrug.

I shake my head, sitting up. "Weirdo."

"Yep," he replies with a grin, taking a bite of his apple.

Morgan opens the door to the camper trailer that she and Chris bought last year. They are the only ones to have upgraded from tents, and look far more well rested than the rest of us. They've also been the ones to supply the generator though, so I can't be too mad about the fact that she gets to sleep on an actual mattress each night. It means that, for the first time, I've not had to ration my phone usage.

"Why is everyone up so early?" she asks, rubbing a hand over her face.

Chris appears behind her, looking like he could go for a few more hours of sleep.

"The bloody birds," Bri grumbles, yawning.

"Clearly, none of you are bird fans," Will chimes in, having just walked back from the amenities block. "Ready for a surf, Bug?"

"Yeah, I'll just get changed." I crawl back into my tent and change into my swimmers.

Maybe a surf will help clear my mind of the memories swirling around. Something's gotta give soon, surely?

Once I've pulled on my wetsuit, I meet Will at his ute and he hands me my surfboard before pulling his down.

"You okay?" he asks.

I shrug. "I guess."

"That doesn't sound particularly positive, Bug."

"What do you want me to say, Will?" I reply, frustrated.

"I guess I just want you to be honest. That's never been a problem for you in the past."

I shrug again. "I'm just trying to reconcile myself to life back here again."

"If you're feeling like that, then perhaps it's time to admit that you made the wrong choice?"

Sometimes, I really hate my brother.

I don't bother replying, striding ahead of him and stomping into the waves, craving the solitude of the water.

Hours later, Will and I return to camp to find Tara reading in her camp chair, Bri and Jake gone for a walk with Morgan, and Chris watching hockey on his iPad.

"Who's playing?" I ask, and Chris jumps, shooting me a pained look.

"Um... Toronto and Calgary."

"Ah... Okay." Pushing aside the stab of emotion his words bring to the surface, I peel my wetsuit off, trying not to show how much that bothers me. I'd just got my mind off Seth, but I can't escape him for long. "Who's winning?"

"I only just turned it on. It - holy shit." His eyes widen while he stares at the screen.

"What?" I ask, not even bothering to hide my concern while I wrap my towel around myself.

"Um... Well, Seth just took a swing at one of the Toronto players, and now they're fighting."

"What?" I move to stand behind him and squint at the screen.

Chris rewinds a little and I watch while Seth turns and punches one of the Toronto players in the face. I cover my mouth, unable to believe what I'm seeing.

Seth isn't a fighter. I've watched many games now, and he's always avoided the fights. But yet here he is, throwing his stick and gloves down before grabbing the other player by the jersey and smashing him in the face.

"Fucking hell," Will mutters, watching over my shoulder. "What the hell did that guy say to him?"

I shake my head while on the screen, Lincoln grabs Seth and pulls him away. The camera zooms in on them and I can see Lincoln yelling in Seth's ear. Seth skates away, heading for the penalty box, and I can see the moment it hits him he's just lost control. His shoulders drop when he collapses onto the bench in the box, and he takes his stick and gloves from Lincoln, not looking him in the eye.

"Is this live?" I ask Chris, and he shakes his head.

"No, it's yesterday's game." He looks up at me before returning his attention to the screen.

I bite my lip. Should I call him? I don't know his schedule anymore, but if he was in Toronto yesterday, he's probably on a plane, or even playing another game. I get my phone and stare at it, debating on what to do.

Figuring I'll just make things worse, I decide to leave it. But when Chris exclaims several more times that other fights have broken out, I end up watching the rest of the game with him.

This is the first time I've ever seen the Mounties players fight like this, and they are never usually the instigators when they do. It's unsettling. Something has set them off, and towards the end of the third period, a massive fight breaks out. I shake my head when even the goalies face off at centre ice. I can only imagine how insane Coach is going to be when the game is over, especially because the Mounties are losing.

"I think you should check in on your boyfriend," Will says, shaking his head.

"He's not my boyfriend," I say automatically.

He raises an eyebrow and shakes his head again. "Kylie, seriously. It's obvious something is up with him, and it doesn't take a genius to work out what. You've been moping for a month. I think it's time to admit that you made a mistake coming home, and he made a mistake in not asking you to stay."

I refuse to look at my brother, staring at my phone. I open up the messenger app and scroll to Lincoln's name.

KYLIE

Is he okay?

Not knowing what time zone they were currently in, I put my phone down, not expecting a reply anytime soon.

So when my phone buzzes a minute later, I jump.

LINCOLN

I take it you saw the game?

He's a mess, Kyles.

I swallow hard, trying to ignore the tear threatening to slip down my cheek. I look up at Will before looking away again when I see the knowing look in his eyes.

LINCOLN

How are you holding up?

I don't know how to respond to that loaded question. I bite my lip, contemplating my answer. Letting out a shaky breath, I type a message before deleting it and trying again. Before I can question myself a second time, I hit send.

KYLIE

Rethinking my life choices...

LINCOLN

Well, maybe we should do something about that.

Watching the sunset, I continue toying with my phone, rereading the message exchange with Lincoln over and over. It's clear he wants me to go back for Seth. And from what I saw of that game, Seth is acting out of character in a big way. We've only had a few text conversations since I've been home. I think we've both been avoiding each other because it hurts too much to think about what we had and what I walked away from.

"You okay?" Tara takes a seat in the sand beside me.

I'd been so preoccupied, I hadn't even noticed her and Bri approaching.

"Not really. Do you guys think I made a mistake? Should I have stayed, even though Seth didn't ask me to?"

They exchange a brief look before Bri responds. "Speaking as someone who never saw you in person with Seth, I can only comment based on how you've been since you've come home. You're obviously missing him, and you've also mentioned the job over there a million times as well. You've never had someone in your life that has actively chosen you, and I think that's why you were so adamant that Seth ask you to stay, but..." she trails off, looking at Tara.

"From the things that both you and Will have said, although

he may not have said the words out loud, his actions showed he wanted you to stay. The Seth that I met wasn't particularly good with the words. So I feel like expecting him to actively come out and say he wants you to leave behind everything you know and stay with him was a bit unfair to him."

I stare at Tara for a few moments, mulling over her words. Of all the people in my life, she knows Seth the best, and she's right. He was always so quick to put the wants and needs of others before himself. He would never have dreamed of asking me to make all the sacrifices, even if that's what he wanted with all his heart.

I drop my head into my hands. "I'm such an idiot."

Bri puts her arm around me. "No, you're not. Relationships are hard. Remember how much of a mess I was when I was trying to work out my feelings for Jake? We didn't have anywhere near the amount of obstacles in our way and it was still hard to work out a balance that worked for us both. I think, in your heart, you know exactly what you should do. It's just finding the courage to act on it that's the hard part."

"When did you get so wise? It's normally Tara doling out the hard facts like this," I mumble into my hands.

"I learned from the best, I guess."

Tara laughs, rubbing my back. "Yep, I have to pass on my knowledge for future camping trips if I'm not around."

I lift my head, turning to look at her. "This is your last trip, isn't it?"

She smiles, and I can see the sadness in her eyes. "I think I've been trying to force myself to keep coming to group activities, hoping that things will stay the same, but they're just not. You guys will always be my family, but... I love my sister, even though what she did was so crappy, and it's hard for me to be around when everyone is still so mad at her."

I feel my heart breaking for her. I can only imagine how it must feel. If it had been Will who had left, I would be just as torn as

Tara, wanting to keep our friendship circle the same but maintaining my loyalty to my flesh and blood.

"Nothing will change with us, though. Whether you're here or on the other side of the world, you two are my people. We'll be side by side in the old folks' home. You creating chaos, Bri taking beautiful photos, and me being the constant voice of reason."

I pull them into a hug on both sides. "I can't wait. We'll be the envy of all the oldies."

Bri gives me a squeeze. "We definitely will be."

43
CHEER THE FUCK UP

THE PAST TEN days have been a complete nightmare. Ever since the game against Toronto, it's like I'm a powder keg, waiting to explode. I can't tell if it's just my own emotions or if a secret memo has gone out telling players on the other teams to piss me off, but I've been in more fights this last week and a half than the last year combined. Did these assholes always chirp so much, or am I just overly sensitive?

Either way, Coach has had enough and now I'm sitting in his office before our first home game in two weeks.

"What's going on with you?" he asks, his tone exasperated, while he looks at me from the other side of his desk.

"Nothing," I mumble, feeling like a kid being dragged into the principal's office.

"Bullshit, Davidson, you've been distracted, picking fights and acting like a dick for weeks. Do I need to strip you of that C on your jersey? Or move you off the first line?"

"No, Coach." I shake my head, looking down at my hands.

"Well, I'd better see a change in your attitude the next few games, or we're going to be having a very serious conversation later, you hear me?"

How is it that this man, only a decade older than me, can make me feel like I'm being told off by my father?

I nod, determined to get my shit together so that I don't have to go through this again. Or, god forbid, get sent off for counselling again.

"Good. Now get out of my office and get your ass ready for the game."

I hightail it out of his office, heading for the dressing room, where Linc is waiting, leaning against the door frame with a raised brow.

"How'd that go?"

I brush past him, sliding my suit jacket off on the way to my locker. "About as well as you could expect. I'm basically on probation without being on probation."

Dean sidles over, taking a seat on the bench beside me. "That C up for grabs yet?" he asks with a smirk.

"Fuck off," I grumble, ignoring his laugh.

"So grouchy lately. Hopefully you cheer the fuck up soon." He saunters off, and I clench my jaw, glaring at his back before continuing to get ready.

Ignoring everyone around me, my mind wanders back to last night. I'd sat staring at my phone for what was probably a good hour, trying to work up the courage to call Kylie. In the end, I'd chickened out, resorting to a text that simply asked how she was. I still haven't had a reply, which has been weighing on my mind ever since. With the time difference, it would have been mid morning when she received it, and she's always been one to respond to texts quickly, so my mind has been in overdrive, spinning every scenario possible. When did I turn into the kind of person who obsessed over a simple text message?

Probably around the time that I fell head over heels in love with this woman and was stupid enough to let her walk away without telling her how I really feel.

Eventually, we're given the heads up to make our way down the tunnel ahead of warm up, and I finish getting ready before leading the way out of the locker room.

Even with everything going on in my personal life, when the announcer hypes up the crowd, the adrenaline that hits at the start of every game gives me the usual boost, and I hit the ice ahead of the rest of the team. Rock music pumps through the arena, setting the mood, and after circling our half of the rink for a few laps, we peel off, going in different directions. I head towards the bench, aiming for our equipment manager, who is holding out a bucket of pucks for me. Retrieving the bucket, I head back and empty it out, letting the pucks drop to the ice, and my teammates claim them, firing them towards Dean to get him warmed up. Linc skates over, positioning himself between me and Anders, taking a shot before turning to me.

"Have you checked out the signs yet?"

I glance over at him. "Um, no. Why?" In all our years of playing hockey together, he has never once asked me that.

It's weird.

I launch a puck at Dean, who catches it deftly in his glove and prepares for the next person.

"I just thought there might be one or two that you'd be interested in." Linc shrugs, leaning on his stick.

"Why are you being weird?" I ask, using my stick to drag another puck from the pile closer to me.

Linc sighs. "Just go and look at the signs near the bench. You exhaust me."

I hit the puck and look at Linc again. "*I* exhaust *you*? What the hell did I do?"

"For fuck's sake, Seth. Look at the signs," he replies, hitting his own puck with far more aggression than is necessary.

Dean catches it. "That was a bit hard there, buddy," he chirps at Linc.

Linc points at him. "Don't you start with me."

Having absolutely no idea what is going on, I head back towards the bench. Figuring I must have missed something, I do a quick scan of the fans who line the glass, holding up their signs. There's the usual ones saying hi from various places around the world, fans that have come from overseas and are just excited to be here.

I can't see anything that warrants Linc's little tantrum, though.

Shaking my head, I grab my water bottle from the top of the boards and lift it to squirt it into my mouth, pausing when a movement to my left catches my eye.

Turning my head, I'm met with a massive sign pressed up against the glass on the side of the bench, obscuring the person holding it from view.

Seth Davidson - Ask me to stay!

I read the sign a few times, trying to process the words. A whisper of recognition sneaks into the back of my mind, and I skate to the glass, peaking around to see if my suspicions are right.

There, standing in front of the same seat where I saw her that first game, is Kylie. She grins, those gorgeous green eyes filled with mischief, and I wonder what my face must look like to her.

How is she here right now?

Wondering if I'm dreaming, I press my hand against the glass, oblivious to the people around her, while she moves closer and raises her hand against the glass opposite mine. My heart feels like it's about to hammer right out of my chest.

"What are you doing here?" I ask, raising my voice in the hopes she'll hear me through the glass.

"Didn't you read the sign?" she replies, lifting it up again.

All I can think about is wrapping my arms around her, and it's killing me that I can't touch her.

Linc skates up beside me. "Finally," he says, his grin wide, and he leans his shoulder against the glass next to the sign. "So. Are you going to ask her the question that you should have asked her months ago?"

"You," I point at Kylie. "You better be waiting for me out the back after this game."

"Nah, I got a hot date," she replies with a smirk.

"Don't play with him too much, Kyles. He's been pretty delicate."

"You, stop talking." I point at Linc before turning back to Kylie. "You, don't be a brat."

"Shouldn't you be stretching?" she replies, waving towards the ice behind me.

"You just want to check out his ass," Linc says.

"Correct. I guess yours is okay as well." She grins.

"Do not check out his ass," I reply, and they both laugh.

Not ready to leave her, but knowing I need to finish warming up, I push off from the glass, finally seeing Ben and Adele standing nearby and giving them a wave. Slapping my hand against the glass once again before heading off towards the net, I don't even try to keep the stupid grin off my face.

"Wow, if I'd known that was what it took to get you out of your crappy mood, I'd have held a lame sign up and played hand-sies through the glass with you weeks ago," Dean says with a smirk when I come to a stop beside him.

"You can be such a douche, you know that?"

"Yep, and you love it." He claps me on the back, and I shake my head.

Maybe things will work out, after all. I've never wanted a game to be over so fast, but knowing she's watching has me ready to play the best game of my life.

44
GOOD LUCK CHARM

KYLIE

NORMALLY WHEN I watch one of Seth's games, I get caught up in the action and the time flies by.

But not tonight.

Tonight, I swear the clock has just stopped moving, and we're stuck in a time warp. The third period, in particular, feels never ending.

"This is the best he's played in weeks," Adele yells in my ear when the crowd erupts after Seth's third goal of the game.

Hats begin flying over our heads and land on the ice, celebrating Seth's hat-trick. Seth pumps his fist in the air, then points at me while Linc and Anders jump all over him. I can feel my face heat up, and I don't want to look up at the jumbotron, knowing the camera has flashed to me.

"You seem to have a pretty good effect on his game." Ben had flown in for the game when Adele told him I was coming back, not wanting to miss out on seeing Seth's reaction, and he's grinning so hard right now.

"I don't want to claim credit for anything," I reply.

"Own it, lady. There's no coincidence that as soon as he knows you're back, he has his second hat-trick of the season, and the last one was when you showed up in his life out of nowhere. Let's face it, you're his good luck charm!" Adele pulls me into a tight side hug.

She's been overly affectionate with me since I arrived yesterday, and I suspect it's because she feels bad for sending me that video. While I don't blame her for sending it, I've had to tell everyone that from now on, I don't want to know about any videos on social media that include either myself or Seth. Our relationship, if we are ever going to make this work, needs to just be between us, and I don't want the noise of others' opinions to affect how I feel ever again.

It had taken me two days to pack up my life in Australia for the last time. I think a part of me had known that my return had only been temporary, as I'd been camped out in Will's spare room and hadn't unpacked a single non-essential item. Lincoln had insisted on arranging my flights, and, being Lincoln, had put me in first class, so I had the best sleep I've ever had on a plane and arrived in Calgary well rested. He'd insisted on making my first time seeing Seth again as dramatic as possible. He'd convinced me to keep it a secret until the game, even though I would have preferred much less of an audience when I saw him again. The sign was my idea, though. Lincoln had suggested I throw my underwear at Seth on the bench, but I had vetoed that one.

Saying goodbye to my friends, knowing this time my ticket is one way only, was just as hard as I'd imagined. I'd teared up at our final dinner at Jake and Bri's apartment, where Tara now lives. We'd spent hours sitting in the spa, and I hadn't been ready for it to end. But time marches on, and I've come to realise that my future lies outside of the tight-knit group, on the other side of the world with my Canadian family and the hockey captain who owns my heart. Dad is still bemused by the whole thing. But he drove me to the airport and hugged me tightly, accepting that at least one of his four children has chosen to move back to the country he has happily left behind. If he'd had a problem with it, he probably shouldn't have arranged for all of us to have our Canadian citizenship and passports when we were kids.

My aunt happily accepted me back at work, and it all just feels right. Coming back felt like coming home, and I know this is where I'm meant to be. Now if this damn hockey game would hurry up and end, I can go tell Seth that.

The buzzer finally goes off, and the fans are screaming. It was honestly the best game of the entire season, with Calgary smashing Edmonton five to one. Of course, because of Seth's performance, they declare him the first star of the game, which means we have to wait even longer for our reunion, and I watch impatiently while he hands his stick to a cute little kid on the red carpet that they have rolled out onto the ice. As soon as he hits the tunnel, I sprint up the stairs, dodging through the crowd, and head out the back. Lincoln had given me a security pass when he'd arranged our tickets, and I flash that at the guard who waves me through. Rounding the corner, I stop short when I see Seth waiting for me. He's pulled his skates off, but still in the rest of his uniform, his hair wet with sweat.

"Hey," I say, sauntering towards him, attempting to act nonchalant.

"Hey, yourself," he replies, leaning against the wall, watching me.

Once I'm standing in front of him, the nervous energy I can feel pumping through my veins won't allow me to continue the facade, and when he reaches for me, I jump into his arms, kissing him hard. He stumbles back slightly but grips my hips while I wrap my legs around his waist (not the easiest when he's still padded up), kissing me back with the same energy.

"Fuck I missed you," he whispers against my lips.

I nod frantically, not ready to pull away yet, just getting lost in the kiss. It's even better than the ones that I dreamed about while we were apart.

Finally, we end the kiss, and I keep my arms wrapped around his neck while I press my forehead against his.

"Ask me the question, Seth Davidson," I whisper.

"Fucking stay with me. Don't leave," he replies, his voice catching.

I swallow hard, feeling my eyes well up. "Forever. Does forever work for you?"

"God, yes." He kisses me again, softer this time, and I sigh, melting into it.

"I love you," I whisper, feeling his hold on me tighten.

"I love you. So fucking much."

I could stay like this forever, but he needs to get back to the team. I slide back down, letting my feet drop to the ground, and already miss his touch.

"Wait for me in the family room. I won't be long." He squeezes my hand.

"Promise?"

"I promise."

EPILOGUE

5 MONTHS LATER

KYLIE

"I can't believe this is what you Aussies call winter." Seth squints in the July sunlight while he takes in the view of the city from Jake and Bri's apartment.

"Why do you think I spend all my time inside when it's snowing?" I reply, resting my head against his shoulder.

He puts his arm around me, holding me close while he accepts the beer that Jake hands him.

Two days after the Mounties won the Stanley Cup, we jumped on a plane and headed back to Brisbane. This is the first time Seth has met my Australian family and friends in person, and he was pretty nervous, but they've all made him feel welcome, and he's settled in nicely.

Yesterday, Will, Dad and I took Seth for his first surf, and it was hilarious. It's safe to say, his talents are best kept for frozen water, because he spent more time in the water than on top of it. But he'd enjoyed watching us, finally understanding why it's my happy place. I've been spending as much time as I can practicing snow-boarding when there's enough snow, but nothing will ever beat the feeling of catching the perfect wave. Seth has promised to bring me home in the off-season every year, and I'll do my best to come back on my own to join the others every February for the camping trip.

I moved in with Seth two months after I returned to Canada, and it's been perfect. We've managed to find a balance between his schedule and mine, and my aunt allowed me to share the tour schedule with Adele so that I'm home when Seth is in town as much as possible. Working for family definitely has its advantages, and the fact that they are all obsessive Mounties fans has meant that they are keen to help me make the relationship work.

Chris and Morgan arrive along with Will, and it feels right being surrounded by my friends while I sit with my legs slung over Seth's lap on the couch after dinner.

Tara sits beside me, chatting to Bri on her other side, and I'm relieved to see that, although she hasn't been spending time with the entire group much, she doesn't appear to be upset about everyone crashing her space today.

Will had introduced Seth and me to Kate, the woman he's been seeing for a few months, but he says it's not serious. That he didn't even consider bringing her along tonight tells me she won't be around for long. It's hard seeing my brother pine after the woman who smashed his heart apart, but I'm glad he's trying to move on.

Watching Seth talk to Chris about hockey, it's hard to believe how much can happen in a year. It's been twelve months since I met a hot, awkward Canadian at the top of the Eiffel Tower, and so much in my life has changed because of that chance meeting. When I'd started planning that holiday two years ago, I had no idea that I would find the balm that would soothe my restless heart, and I wouldn't change a thing about it.

Jake gets up and stands in front of the TV, tapping a pen against the side of his beer bottle. "So, Bri and I have some news we want to share with you all," he says, waiting for all eyes to be on him.

I grin, anticipating what he's about to say, but trying not to ruin it by blurting the words out. I've been working on my impulse control, feeling Seth's calming influence on my chaotic tendencies. Bri winks at me, no doubt sensing my nervous energy.

"You guys are engaged!" Morgan shouts, and we all laugh.

"And here I was, trying not to steal Jake's time to shine, and there you go, just blurting it all out," I say, grabbing Bri's hand while I roll my eyes at her sister.

The ring is a modest cut, a single solitaire diamond in a white gold setting, perfect for Bri. But that's no surprise, because Jake knows Bri so well that he would have had no trouble picking it out.

We all gush over Bri's ring and congratulate them both, and I feel Seth's arm tighten around me, pulling me in closer.

I try not to notice that Will has been fairly quiet through the announcement. Tara shifts uncomfortably, her smile not quite making it to her eyes. I know how hard it is on both of them, for different reasons. It's hard watching your friends' lives move forward when yours feels like it's standing still.

Sitting back down next to Seth, I turn to him with a smile while my friends all chat about the exciting news.

"Don't worry, babe. I'm perfectly content with how we are." I pat his cheek, worried that the announcement might have freaked him out.

He pulls me into his lap. "I don't know. I think I'll be ready one day soon." He kisses my nose while I stare at him, wide eyed.

"One day soon?" I repeat, taken aback.

He laughs. "Don't look so scared. I don't mean now."

I let out a sigh of relief, pretending to wipe imaginary sweat off my brow.

He shakes his head, laughing. "I love you, Kylie Anderson, you crazy woman."

I grin back, kissing him quickly. "And I love you, too, Seth Davidson." I snuggle down into his arms and close my eyes, just allowing myself to exist in this moment for a little longer.

I thought surfing was my happy place, but I realise this is it, with Seth and my friends by my side. This is the moment I will always come back to in my mind.

I smile to myself, grateful that, even with the distance that exists between us all now, we will always come back to together and celebrate each other's milestones.

What more could you ask for?

IF YOU HAVE A MOMENT

Thank you for reading! I hope you enjoyed Chasing Horizons. Next up in The Circle of Friends is Tara's story, Dance With Me, out now. Read on to check out the first chapter.

If you fell in love with Lincoln, you can read his story in On Thin Ice, the first book in the spin-off series, Calgary Mounties. This book takes place after Tara's book, but can be read separately.

Please take a moment to leave a rating or review on the platform you purchased from or Goodreads. Every review helps in an incredible way.

If you enjoyed this book and would like to stay up to date with all new releases and behind-the-scenes shenanigans, please sign up for my substack.

ACKNOWLEDGMENTS

Here we are again, my third book for 2024. Even twelve months ago, I couldn't imagine having five books to my name, especially after the hardest year of my life. Chasing Horizons was the first book written after my cancer diagnosis, and through the hell that comes with treatment. Being out the other side, this book will always have a special place in my heart, as it got me through the dark times and gave me something to smile about.

As always, so many people helped me bring these characters to life.

To my husband, Andrew, thank you for being my rock this year, and fact checking all the hockey terminology in this book. I'm glad I could help you bring your fantasy team and game plays to life. I can't wait til we can get to our next Flames game when we next head back to Calgary together.

To my daughter, Evelyn, I am so proud of you, and I love hearing that when you grow up, you want to write stories like Mummy.

To our Canadian family, whose love of hockey was the inspiration behind Kylie's family, I wish that this year hadn't come with the trials that it has for us all. The distance has felt worse now than ever before, and knowing that someone who found it so fun that I was writing a hockey romance won't be with us to read it and celebrate it with us is something that I just hadn't allowed myself to imagine. I am so glad we had that last Christmas as a family before the worst year of all of our lives commenced, and I will hold on to those moments for the rest of my life.

To my sister, Melinda, your love and support through each

book has meant so much, and I honestly don't know if I would have gotten this far without you and your honest feedback.

To Jammi-Lee, my ride-or-die and best work-wife ever, thank you for your feedback and declaring your love of Lincoln. We have you to thank for when the Mounties get their own series and he gets his own book.

To Shannon, the third member of my beta reading team and proofreading extraordinaire. Thank you for your support, chai latte deliveries and all the school drop offs when I was too sick to leave the house.

To Krystal, my amazing editor and one of my oldest friends. Without you, none of these books would exist, and I am eternally grateful for everything you do. Can't wait until we're on the same continent again.

To Lauren, for being my hockey author friend and all your feedback and ideas! And to Mel, Demi and Kaitlyn, our Writing Fridays group is one of the highlights of my week and I'm so glad I am back amongst the chaos with you all now!

To Mum and Dad, thank you for all the help this year. We couldn't have managed even half as well as we have without your support.

To all those who have supported me in the bookish community, thank you for all the messages and encouragement, cheering me on while I just kept my head above water. Having you all behind me, lifting me up and keeping my spirits soaring has meant more than you will ever know.

And finally, to my amazing street team, Maddie's Bark Brigade. Thank you so much for all your support. I can't wait for you all to read the book, and I hope you love Kylie and Seth as much as you loved Jake and Bri.

WANT A SNEAK PEEK OF DANCE WITH ME?

Read on to check out the first chapter.

1

I HATE WEDDINGS

TARA

NEW FARM PARK on a sunny Brisbane winter afternoon has long been one of my favourite places. Mind you, I'm not usually dressed quite so formally when I'm here.

"You ready, T?" My best friend Kylie grins at me, her long brown hair cascading over one shoulder in expertly styled soft waves.

My own long, red hair has been tamed into a similar style, but it doesn't have quite the same effect as it does on Kylie. Probably because Kylie is stunning. Her floor length, single shoulder emerald green dress skims her gorgeous curves, making her tanned skin and green eyes stand out even more. While I am pretty sure my fat rolls are sticking out of the back of my identical dress, and my pale skin is basically glowing, as usual. How is it possible that Kylie now lives in one of the coldest cities in Canada but can still maintain a tan, while I live in Brisbane, the capital of one of the hottest states in Australia, and I still look like a ghost? Having spent over a decade trying not to compare myself to my friends, I've always struggled with my weight and appearance, so it's near impossible not to feel like the ugly-step sister. Especially in circumstances like this one where I'm wearing the exact same clothes as two of them and don't look even half as good. Behind her, our friend Morgan smooths the skirt of her own dress, looking just as stunning, with her blonde hair styled the same as ours. She's always had the supermodel look going for her, but add in professional hair and make-up, and it's a wonder her husband can concentrate on anything else today.

You know what? I hate weddings.

As a twenty-seven-year-old woman, I know I'm not meant to say that. But when you're the perpetually single one at every wedding you've been to, the over the top displays of devoted love just serve as a constant reminder that all of your friends are happily shacking up while you're adrift in a sea of shitty tinder dates.

Growing up, I looked to my future with rose-tinted glasses. But over time, the tint darkened. Every guy I was interested in had inevitably lusted after one of my friends or my older sister, and I became like the main character in that movie *The Duff*. Relegated to friend status while they pumped me for information on whether the true objects of their affections were single and if they'd ever be interested in dating the *nice* guy. I was lucky to be surrounded by a tight knit group of friends that included my sister, Annelisa, and her boyfriend, Will, who was like an older brother to me. Then she up and left him brokenhearted, and I was once again cast aside, avoided by the one guy who had seemed like he would never treat me like the others had.

I've been single for pretty much my entire life. Except for a brief three-month relationship in my early twenties with a guy who was on the rebound and eventually realised he'd rather be single like the rest of his mates than shackled to the woman who was ready to finally be in a committed relationship. I have never had a one-night stand, so I've slept with exactly one guy... At twenty-seven... Let that sink in for a moment. My dildo gets far more action than I'm willing to admit.

So yeah, I hate weddings.

And the hardest part about this particular wedding is that the bride, Bri, is one of my best friends, which means I'm in the damn bridal party. So I have had to paste on a smile for the last several hours while we've posed for the usual pre-wedding photos, and helped Bri get into her beautiful dress. The torture is now about to continue while I walk down the aisle with Kylie, and her brother, Will. Yep, the same Will who essentially ignored me after my sister abandoned him.

He's now standing near the faux flower wall that hides us from view of the wedding guests, watching us both patiently while we gather our bouquets and do the last make-up and hair checks and wait for our turn to head down the aisle on the other side.

When the music starts, Morgan and her husband, Chris, take the first steps out past the wall, heading towards the groom - the last member of our circle of friends, Jake - who is waiting at the temporary altar next to the rose garden. Bri's Mum is a few steps behind them, holding the lead of Bri and Jake's little dog, Maddie, who is their ring bearer. Although my mood isn't particularly stellar right now, I have to admit that is freaking adorable.

Making sure my expertly crafted fake smile is firmly in place, I nod towards Kylie. "Yep, let's go."

With a final look back at Bri, who gives us a nervous smile, we take our places on either side of Will, each slipping a hand in the crook of his elbows before stepping around the wall.

Will and I have reached an understanding. We pretend there are no issues between us when we're with the group, and I completely ignore him the rest of the time. He tried to apologise for how he treated me in the wake of the break-up with Annelisa, however it was a case of too little, too late for me. But because we've been putting on such a good show of being fine, Bri and Jake hadn't thought it would be an issue to have the two of us walking down the aisle together on their big day.

At least Kylie is here to draw the attention off my tight, fake smile.

The three of us reach the altar, and Kylie and I join Morgan, while Will moves to stand with Chris and Jake. All three men are extremely attractive. Each one of them is tall with varying shades of brown hair, and the black suits definitely work for them. The nervous groom is staring intently at the flower wall, waiting for the love of his life to appear with her father. The look of anticipation on his handsome face sets off a feeling of envy that I immediately force myself to squash down. No use dreaming about something that just doesn't seem like it is going to happen for me.

Despite my anti-wedding sentiment, I have to admit that my best friend is an absolutely stunning bride, and I hold my breath while I watch Jake's face transform once Bri steps into view. I've known the two of them my entire life, and aside from Chris and Morgan, I can't imagine two people more perfect for each other. For years, I watched, mostly silent, while they danced around each other, but I'd like to think that my encouragement helped Bri to finally make the move to go from friends to lovers. And it was all worth it to see the look of pure love on both their faces right now.

Once Bri arrives in front of Jake, it's hard to imagine a more beautiful couple. Wearing a simple cream, figure-hugging lace dress, with her long blonde hair styled into a sleek bun behind her right ear, Bri is the picture-perfect bride, straight from the pages of a bridal magazine. Coupled with Jake's brown hair, tanned skin and blue eyes, the pair of them are basically Barbie and Ken brought to life.

There isn't a dry eye amongst us by the time the ceremony is over, and everyone applauds when they are declared husband and wife. Their kiss is full of emotion, which has me feeling both thrilled for them as well sad for myself that I've never had someone look at me like they are looking at each other.

. . .

Several hours later, once we make it through the photos and are finally at the reception, I can feel the cracks in my mask of happiness starting to show.

They've booked out the function room at one of the luxury hotels in the city, and it's expertly decorated with tropical plants and flowers, fitting in with Bri's love of gardens. Everything is perfect, but I'm reaching my limit.

"You okay?" Kylie asks, taking a seat next to me at the bridal table.

"Yeah, I'm good." I smile at her, but obviously something on my face gives me away.

She cocks her head to the side. "What's going on?"

"Nothing. I'm fine, I promise." I reach out and squeeze her hand.

"You two look gorgeous." Kylie's boyfriend, Seth, slides in beside her.

Kylie grins at him. "Thanks, babe. You look pretty hot yourself."

The tall Canadian definitely looks good in a suit. Well, he looks good in anything, really. Kylie and I met him and his best friend, Lincoln, on an under-thirties tour around Europe two years ago, and it was pretty much love at first sight for the two of them.

Bri and Jake had timed their wedding so that it was in the hockey off-season, which meant Seth, the captain of the Calgary Mounties NHL team, could come with Kylie, and it's great to see them both together. It's been hard, having my best friend move to the other side of the world, but seeing her so happy makes it worth it.

It also just makes me wonder if it will ever be my turn to have someone make me feel the same way.

After making it through dinner, the speeches and the first dance, once everyone has entered party mode, I finally have the chance to step away unnoticed for a little while.

Slipping into the decadent bathroom, I stand in front of the mirror, staring at my reflection for a moment, wishing that the person staring back at me looked different. Even with professional hair and makeup, it can't make me love myself like I'm supposed to. Years of being surrounded by women who may as well be super models has given me a healthy dose of low self esteem, something that I am working on. But it's not easy, and I wish I could meet someone who I wasn't worried wanted to be with one of my friends or sister instead.

One of Jake and Bri's friends from Stanthorpe stumbles drunkenly out of one of the stalls, and I turn, ready to catch her if she falls.

"Oh hey! You're one of the bridesmaids!" she declares, and I stifle a laugh while I nod. "Which one of those fucking hot groomsmen are you going to be hooking up with tonight?"

Too shocked to hold the laugh in this time, it comes out in a splutter. "Um, definitely neither of them. One is married and the other is my sister's ex."

"Oh, well, better not let all the fancy hair and makeup go to waste. Plenty of other guys at this wedding for you to get laid," she continues babbling on while she washes her hands, before touching up her lipstick.

"Yeah, I don't think that's going to be happening. Been a very long time since any guy was looking at me for a tumble between the sheets."

She pauses, the lipstick hovering over her lips while she looks at me in the mirror.

"Honey, that's all the more reason to wake those lady parts up and rip the suit off of one of the single men out there. I plan on going home very satisfied after the trip to the city, once I work out which one is coming back to my hotel room."

She shoots me a cheeky grin before heading back out to the

party, and I shake my head, wishing I had even half her level of confidence.

Sighing, I push the door open and pass the hotel bar on the way back into the ballroom. I pause at the doorway, watching my friends dancing away happily. Even Will is smiling, although I'm aware he is probably feeling just as lonely as I am amongst the many happy couples.

A lump forms in my throat, and I can't seem to make myself cross the threshold. I've had enough of playing pretend today.

Turning, I head back the way I've just come, and find myself standing at the door of the bar. I've never been much of a drinker, but after a day of too much lovey-dovey fun, I could go for a cocktail right now. The sweeter, the better.

I take a seat at the long bar, looking around for the bartender. The room is almost completely empty, aside from a couple sitting in a corner booth with their heads together, and a rather attractive guy with wavy reddish-brown hair about my age sitting at the other end of the bar, scrolling on his phone with a beer in front of him.

The bartender appears from the door leading out the back and smiles at me. "What can I get you?"

I glance at the cocktail menu before closing it. "Can I have a pina colada, please?"

She nods and gets started on putting together the fruity drink.

"They not serving cocktails in that posh wedding?" I look over to see that the guy on his own has moved closer, standing just a few stools down with his beer in hand.

Up close, it's hard not to notice how hot he is. He's wearing a blue button-up shirt with the sleeves rolled to his elbows and a pair of dark blue jeans. His short beard, cut close to his jawline, seems to be something that I find attractive, based on how dry my mouth has just become. I'm going to put my body's reaction down to the fact that it has been far too long since I've had sex. Usually I'm pretty oblivious, but right now, my lady parts have woken right up and are doing a little dance while I hold his gaze.

Clearing my throat, I shrug a little. "Maybe they are. I didn't check. Just needed a bit of a break."

"Not a fan of weddings?" He sits down on the stool beside me.

"Not so much. But when it's your best friends, you gotta put on the big smiles and be happy for them." I wave my hand over my dress.

"Ah, let me guess. Maid of honour?"

I shake my head. "No, thankfully. Her sister took that joyful job. But I got to walk down the aisle with my sister's ex-boyfriend, so that was fun." The bartender places the drink in front of me, and I wave my phone over the bank machine to pay.

He tilts his beer towards me, the universal sign to cheers him. I tap my glass to his and take a sip.

"Sounds like you've had a hell of a day." He rests both arms against the edge of the bar.

"It wasn't so bad," I concede, feeling a little guilty about how bitter I sound. "I'm glad it all went well for them. They are the sort of couple who deserve only good things. Just hard being the single one at every wedding." It must be something about him being a complete stranger that has me speaking so candidly, but it feels good not to be pretending for a change.

"I get it. I haven't really been to many weddings, but I was single at all of them. It's hard watching everyone else live their lives when yours feels like it's standing still." He's put into words what I haven't been able to say out loud for a few years now.

"Yep," I reply, the P making a popping sound, while I stare at the drink in my hand.

"Want a drinking mate?" he asks.

I turn to look at him, running my eyes over his face. He seems genuinely interested in talking to me, which sets off a swarm of butterflies in my stomach.

Attempting to appear casual, I shrug. "Sure... Why not?"